Cal watched ... you touch
everyone this much? Are you always so...
physical?"

Heat washed over her and Frankie knew her
skin flushed. "Asks the guy who knocks people
down for a living."

He held her gaze for a moment too long. Yeah,
she was upset and emotional. But also insane.
There was no other explanation for why she was
poking at Cal Stewart.

"Yeah, my job is physical, Frankie." His voice was
a low rumble in the intimacy of the office. As
he leaned forward, her heart thundered, but she
refused to back up. "And it's not always smart to
yank the dog's tail. Sometimes he'll bite."

Dear Reader,

All of us hide behind masks—some of us all the time, the rest of us part of the time. Letting another person see the real you is scary. Once someone knows who we really are, we become vulnerable. Exposed. Defenseless.

Falling in love involves stripping away the mask and baring our real selves. For someone who has protected themselves for most of their life, it's terrifying. Painful. But ultimately, it's freeing and exhilarating.

Frankie Devereux and Cal Stewart are the two most unlikely people to fall in love. They inhabit worlds at the opposite ends of the spectrum—Cal is a professional football player. Frankie runs an after-school center for at-risk teens in a dicey neighborhood. But they have something in common—both of them are hiding their true selves. When they're forced to work together, they find that deep inside, behind their masks, they're not so different after all.

I loved throwing Frankie and Cal together and watching the sparks fly. And I loved watching these two people slowly peel away the layers until they stood before each other, fully exposed. I hope you enjoy their story!

I love to hear from readers. You can contact me through my website, www.margaretwatson.com, or via email at margaret@margaretwatson.com.

Yours,

Margaret Watson

A Safe Place
Margaret Watson

TORONTO NEW YORK LONDON
AMSTERDAM PARIS SYDNEY HAMBURG
STOCKHOLM ATHENS TOKYO MILAN MADRID
PRAGUE WARSAW BUDAPEST AUCKLAND

Recycling programs
for this product may
not exist in your area.

ISBN-13: 978-0-373-71768-2

A SAFE PLACE

Copyright © 2012 by Margaret Watson

Printed in U.S.A.

ABOUT THE AUTHOR

Margaret Watson has always made up stories in her head. When she started actually writing them down, she realized she'd found exactly what she wanted to do with the rest of her life. Almost twenty years after staring at that first blank page, she's an award-winning, two time RITA® Award finalist, who was recently honored by Harlequin for her twenty-fifth book.

When she's not writing or spending time with her family, she practices veterinary medicine. Although she enjoys that job, writing is her passion. Margaret lives in a Chicago suburb with her husband and three daughters and a menagerie of pets.

Books by Margaret Watson

HARLEQUIN SUPERROMANCE

1205—TWO ON THE RUN
1258—HOMETOWN GIRL
1288—IN HER DEFENSE
1337—FAMILY FIRST
1371—SMALL-TOWN SECRETS
1420—SMALL-TOWN FAMILY
1508—A PLACE CALLED HOME*
1531—NO PLACE LIKE HOME*
1554—HOME AT LAST*
1608—AN UNLIKELY SETUP
1638—CAN'T STAND THE HEAT?
1673—LIFE REWRITTEN
1696—FOR BABY AND ME

*The McInnes Triplets

Other titles by this author available in ebook format.

For Katy.
Your passion for your job, your focus
on helping women, is inspiring and humbling.
I'm so proud of the woman you have become.

CHAPTER ONE

FRANKIE DROPPED the newspaper on her desk at FreeZone and saw the headline: Douglas Bascombe New Chief of DCFS. As she set the bag of tacos down and stowed her tote in a drawer, she wondered why she hadn't heard about the change before now. FreeZone, her after-school center for at-risk teens, had occasional contact with the Division of Children and Family Services. One of its social workers was a friend.

She probably hadn't heard because she rarely had time to actually read a newspaper. She had a free hour today only because the bakery had hired an extra worker and they'd finished early.

She unwrapped her first bean-and-corn taco and began to read as she ate. "Social worker who rose through the ranks." "Longtime employee." Yada yada. In other words, a bureaucrat.

Frankie and the previous DCFS head had worked together well, so she didn't anticipate problems with Bascombe.

She thumbed through the paper, reading the articles, relishing the luxury of a little downtime. Her kids would be here in less than an hour, and so would her new community-service person. The football player. She didn't have high expectations for him, but he could no doubt clean the place and play basketball with the boys. That would suit her fine. As long as he didn't try to take over.

The last CS person she'd had had tried to organize her office.

As Frankie turned the next page, she found the rest of the article about the new DCFS director. She didn't need to read it—she knew exactly what it would say. She glanced at the picture, though, wondering if she'd ever met the guy.

Taco filling landed on the newspaper in a smear of beans, corn and sauce. Her stomach twisted into a tight, hard knot. *Oh, my God.*

Dave.

Doug Bascombe was Dave.

One picture in the newspaper and she was right back in that room—with the terror, the fear, the revulsion. The violation.

The man who had assaulted her in juvie was now the head of DCFS.

Her stomach heaved, and she raced to the washroom just in time. After vomiting everything she'd eaten and more, she slumped on the tile floor next to the toilet. Her head ached and her hands shook.

Finally, she struggled to her feet, rinsed out her mouth and splashed cold water on her face. The kids would be arriving soon. She couldn't let them find her like this.

She wobbled back to her office, dumped the rest of her lunch in the garbage and stared at the picture. He was older, but there was no doubt Bascombe was Dave.

A social worker who molested the kids he worked with.

Now in charge of the entire agency that dealt with abused, neglected and abandoned children.

She wrapped her arms around herself. She had to do something. She had to make sure he couldn't hurt any more children.

She had to make sure everyone knew what a monster he was.

The front door opened, and she heard kids talking. Laughing as they walked in. Frankie closed her eyes and struggled to calm herself. She couldn't do anything about Bascombe right now. And she couldn't let the kids see how upset she was. She took a deep breath to regain her composure. Another. Plastered a smile on her face and stepped out of her office.

Only to see that she had another, more urgent problem. The kids stood in a circle around three boys. One was Ramon, a former member of the Insane Street Vipers gang. The others were Speedball and T-Man, two of his former associates in the gang.

Why today?

Why couldn't she have an easy day, with no problems and no drama?

She strode toward the crowd.

CAL ROLLED HIS TRUCK to a stop in front of FreeZone. The name on the building was unevenly painted in shades of green, blue and yellow, and drips of paint dotted the glass beneath the letters.

Blinds covered the windows, but it looked as if the building had started life as a supermarket. There weren't many of those in the Manor neighborhood anymore.

There wasn't much of anything here besides liquor stores, currency exchanges and bars.

It was the last place on earth he wanted to be.

He slipped on his sunglasses as he stepped out of the Escalade, and car doors slammed behind him. He waved to the reporters, waiting for them to crowd around.

"Cal, how do you feel about being sentenced to a hundred hours of community service?" one of them asked.

Pissed off was how he felt. He smiled easily. "FreeZone

is going to get every bit of my effort until I've paid my debt to society."

Another reporter shoved a microphone beneath his nose. "With all the time you have to spend here, will you be ready for training camp?"

Cal smiled at the Chicago Cougars beat reporter for the *Herald Times.* "FreeZone is open three hours every day. Other than that, I'll be at Cougars Hall, just like every day since my surgery." Until he made a deal with the woman who ran this place. Frankie Devereux would let him out of his community service if the price was right, and Cal would make sure it was. Then he'd be at Cougars Hall all day. "The doctors say I'm good to go, and I'm looking forward to getting back on the field in six weeks."

"So your knee is as good as new? You'll be the starting strong safety for the Cougars?" the first reporter asked.

"That's the plan." He waved to the journalists as he headed for the door. "Got to go. The sooner I start, the sooner I'll be back at Cougars Hall full-time."

"You got off pretty easily with just community service for that fight," a young woman called as he reached the door. "Have you heard from the commissioner? Are you going to be suspended for any games?"

"Haven't heard anything about that." He smiled, thankful for the sunglasses. "That's up to the commissioner. Take care, guys." He yanked open the door and stepped inside.

As the door clicked shut behind him, his easy camaraderie dropped away like a shrugged-off coat. Tension swirled in the air of the huge, mostly empty space. Fifteen or twenty teens of both genders milled around, the boys shuffling their feet, calling out to a group of four others who were standing off to the side.

Cal zeroed in on the four.

The three kids facing him were stocky and muscular, with identical soul patches beneath their lower lips. Two wore red baseball caps, brims turned to the side. The aggression in their faces made the back of his neck tingle and had him shifting his weight to the balls of his feet.

The fourth teenager was a lot smaller, with short dark hair, slightly baggy pants and a ragged-looking tank top. From behind, he appeared to be facing down the three bigger kids.

The place smelled like cake, disinfectant and fear.

A couple of boys in the group of spectators spotted Cal and whooped. "Look at that big dude. He can kick your ass, Ramon, and your friends, too," one called.

Without looking at them, the smallest of the four kids said, "That's enough." His low voice snapped over the others like a whip. "Everyone sit at the homework tables. Now."

Although he didn't turn his head or speak loudly, his words carried the ring of authority. The mass of youths hesitated, nervous energy flowing from one to the next. Funny that one of their peers would have so much authority, but it didn't matter how big he talked. Each of the three guys he was facing outweighed him by fifty or sixty pounds.

The mass of teens shifted, and Cal gathered himself to intervene. This was the moment when everything could go to hell.

Finally, they began drifting toward a cluster of tables in the far corner. Two boys hung back, circling behind the other four. "Hey, Ramon, what are you gonna do?" One boy danced forward and nudged the kid standing in the middle. "You staying here? You going?"

"Gotta choose, dude," the other one said as he toed a basketball off the floor and began dribbling effortlessly.

Where the hell was the woman who was supposed to be running this place? As Cal made his way toward the four teens, the smallest one said, "Ramon, did you invite these guys here?"

"No, man," the boy without the red cap said. "I don't want nothing to do with them." He glanced at the other two and his eyes flickered. The speculative expression in them disappeared so quickly Cal wondered if it had been there at all.

The short kid crossed his arms across his chest and stepped closer, somehow seeming taller. "T-Man, Speedball, you're not welcome here. Get out. Now."

"We just want to talk to Ramon," one of them said, smirking.

Short Guy took another step. "You're not going to do it here."

The two red caps stood their ground, and Ramon backed away. Cal frowned. But he wouldn't interfere unless it was absolutely necessary.

A murmur rippled through the kids clustered around the table. All of them were standing. The two closer ones glanced at the short kid uneasily. Were they afraid for him?

Every football player knew when a scene was turning ugly, and Cal's antennae were twitching.

He strode toward the group of four, flexing his hands. He wanted to grab and throw. Toss the bullies to the side. But he'd stay cool. Unless they gave him grief.

When he reached them, he grasped the cloth of the short kid's tank top and yanked him back. Cal's arm brushed the kid's side, which felt softer than a typical teenage boy's. Even worse that these three were threatening him.

Cal braced himself on splayed legs and looked from one to the other. "You boys have been asked to leave." He held their gaze. "You going on your own, or do you need help?"

One of the two red caps, reeking of sweat and stale cigarette smoke, said, "You gonna make us?"

"If I have to."

The mouthy guy nudged his buddy. "He thinks he can take us," he said, giggling.

The kid's pupils were dilated. He was high. Cal checked the other one, and found his eyes were ink-black, too.

Shit.

As Cal gathered himself, the boy behind him tried to step forward. He collided with the arm Cal instinctively stuck out. More softness bumped his forearm. Then the kid elbowed him and shoved Cal's arm aside.

"Stop this right now." The *kid* wasn't a boy. *She* was a slender young woman who vibrated with intensity. His new boss, probably. Frankie something.

Cal didn't care.

He stepped in front of her again. "Bring it on, shitheads."

The two exchanged a look, then charged. Cal held up his hands, palms out, and the teens stumbled as they ran into them. While they were off balance, he grabbed them by the backs of their shirts, lifted them off the floor and held them out to the side.

As they kicked and flailed, the kids behind him hooted. "Where you running to, Speedball?" one yelled, making the rest laugh. Speedball, on his left, punched wildly.

As Cal carried them toward the door, Frankie shouted, "Put them down. Right now."

"Gladly. As soon as they're out of here."

A whiff of citrus was his only warning before Frankie curled her fingers around his right biceps. "Let go of them."

Ignoring her, Cal pushed the door open with his hip. As he stepped into the sunlight, the reporters surged forward. He should have known they wouldn't have left yet. Cameras clicked and microphones appeared in front of his face. The sound of voices yelling his name barely registered.

The kids stumbled when Cal dropped them. Then they shoved past the throng blocking their way, and a camera hit the sidewalk with a splintering thud. Cal watched until the two disappeared around a corner.

"What was that all about, Cal?" one reporter shouted. "Who were those kids, and what did they do?"

"They just needed a little help out the door," Cal said. He waved again as he turned to go back inside. Instead of the door closing behind him, though, he felt a puff of air as it opened wider.

"No reporters or photographers are allowed in here," Frankie said as she scrambled to her feet.

Cal froze. Crap. Had he knocked her over?

He reached to help her up, but she shook off his hand. Brushing off the seat of her pants, she stood in front of the door, blocking the reporters' entry. His new boss might be small, but she was definitely tough. "I have the police on speed dial." She pulled a phone out of her pocket and held it up, staring at the group in front of her. Her finger hovered over a button.

Everyone watched Frankie and the phone. Her finger trembled, then she pressed the button.

The reporters backed out the door, grumbling. When it clicked shut, Cal's boss watched him as she held the phone to her ear. "Hey, Don," she said. "We had a little trouble with a couple of Ramon's friends and there are a bunch of reporters outside the door. I don't want things to get out of hand."

She listened for a moment, then said, "Thanks. I appreciate it." She snapped the phone closed.

Then she took a deep breath and turned to the rest of the kids. "All right, everyone. Show's over." Her voice was strained.

She pointed at Cal. "You. Stay right here."

The kids all glanced at him, pity in their eyes. As if he was supposed to be afraid of a woman less than half his size? Then chatter resumed and the tension eased. The boy with the basketball went back to dribbling. Several of the kids near the tables sat down. The rest remained standing in small groups, their voices rising and falling as they rehashed the confrontation.

Without another glance in Cal's direction, Frankie cut two sniffling girls out of the herd, draped her arms across their shoulders and steered them toward the opposite corner of the room. Three couches, two of them ugly flowery things and one dark brown, all of them shabby, were arranged in a U shape. Two worn, mismatched chairs completed a square.

The other furnishings in the place weren't any better. Cal's guess about the supermarket history of the space had been right. An old deli case stood against the back wall, now holding what looked like a bakery box. The other corners were also used for equipment, but the area in the center was wide open.

In one corner, the boy with the basketball shot with single-minded concentration. The few pieces of netting remaining on the hoop swished with every basket.

Beside that small court was a scratched and dented Ping-Pong table. A basket of balls and four paddles rested on top, and a paperback propping up one of the legs made it mostly level.

An air-hockey table and a foosball game were in the

third corner. Battered and scarred, both looked as if they'd had a hard life.

At the cluster of tables and chairs in the last corner, Ramon sat by himself. The other kids had chosen seats as far away from him as possible.

Frankie sat down on one of the couches, a girl on either side of her. She leaned close and talked to them for a minute, and the girls wiped their faces with the backs of their hands. When one of them smiled shakily, Frankie squeezed her shoulder and stood up.

And headed toward him.

"Hey, I'm sorry I knocked you down," he said as she approached.

"Don't worry about it. I assume you're Caleb Stewart, our community-service person. Let's talk in the office."

"I guess you're Frankie Devereux."

"Yes," she said evenly. She glanced at a group of kids who were clustering close.

"I thought you were one of the kids at first."

"You were wrong." Her dismissive gaze flicked over him, as if he'd just confirmed her assumptions about stupid jocks.

He clenched his teeth as he smiled. "I can see that now. I guess I was too busy trying to save your ass to take a good look earlier."

The boys watched him with shocked awe, as if no one ever spoke to her like that. The girls gave him sidelong glances and tried to talk to Frankie at the same time. One girl hung on her shoulder, and Frankie absently wrapped an arm around her and gave her a hug while listening to another.

She let the girl go and narrowed her gaze at Cal. But before he could speak, she said over her shoulder, "If you guys can't agree who plays first, find a fourth to play doubles."

What the heck was she talking about? Then Cal saw three boys standing around the Ping-Pong table hunch their shoulders and stop arguing. "Sorry, Ms. Devereux," one of them said in a soft Southern accent. They called to the boy shooting baskets, who let the ball bounce into the corner as he joined them.

She resumed talking to the girls, and her low, smoky voice was soothing. Reassuring, if you were a teenage girl. Which Cal wasn't. Why on earth had he thought that husky voice belonged to a boy?

Frankie Devereux wasn't what he'd expected.

He'd figured someone running a teen center would be older. Matronly. The last thing he'd say about Devereux's short, slender body. But her resemblance to the uptown trixies he usually spent time around ended there.

Frankie's cargo pants were frayed at the hem and a little too big for her. When she'd walked away, he'd noticed a tiny tear just below a back pocket—too small to be revealing, but big enough to catch his eye. Her black tank top was faded and one strap was held together with a safety pin. She had three piercings in one ear and two in the other. Her black hair was short and tousled-looking, as if she'd brushed it once in the morning and forgot about it.

Clearly, she hadn't dressed to attract attention. So why couldn't he drag his gaze away from her?

"Over here," she said, walking away without looking back. She headed toward the front corner of the place, and he saw a door not too far from the air-hockey game.

He followed her into a closet-size room and saw a desk covered with papers, two rickety bookshelves filled to overflowing and a chair with only one arm. He closed the door behind him.

"What the *hell* were you thinking?" She stood with her hands on her hips, practically vibrating, her bright blue eyes sharp enough to slice through him.

"I was *thinking* that things were going to explode and that someone needed to stop it. Those two punks were about to pounce."

Frankie studied him for a long moment, and he shifted his weight. "Appearances can be deceiving, Mr. Stewart. I had that situation under control." She sounded completely confident, as if those two gang members had been five-year-olds.

Oddly off balance, he said the first thing he could think of. "Are you kidding me? Those guys were twice your size."

It was as if those bright blue eyes of hers saw all the way into his soul and zeroed in on what was missing. "Is brute force the only way you know to control things?"

"I suppose you were going to *talk* them out the door."

"That's exactly what I was going to do." Frankie sank onto the edge of the desk and closed her eyes. When she opened them, she said, "I *so* do not need this today. You're probably not the right person for community service at FreeZone. Our first rule here is no violence. You broke that one before you introduced yourself."

"I was reacting to a threat," Cal said stiffly.

Before she could respond, there was a sharp knock at the office door. "Frankie? You okay?"

She sprang off the desk and opened the door. A tall, solidly built police officer stood there, his dark eyes zeroing in on Cal. Measuring. Assessing.

"I'm fine, Don. Thanks for getting here so quickly." She motioned him into the already crowded room. "This is Caleb Stewart. He's supposed to do his community service at FreeZone. Mr. Stewart, this is Officer Wilson. He's the patrol officer for our neighborhood."

The one she had on speed dial. Cal reached for his hand and shook it. "Nice to meet you."

"So, what happened here, Frankie?" the police officer asked, studying Cal.

"Two of Ramon's buddies came in and said they wanted to talk to him. I told them to get out. They were about ready to leave when Mr. Stewart showed up. He grabbed them by their collars and tossed them out the door."

"Shouldn't do that," Wilson said to him matter-of-factly. "They'll charge you with assault."

"They were threatening her," Cal said, incredulous.

"Just saying." Wilson shrugged. "You have a record. The judge wouldn't like it if you got arrested again."

"Screw the judge. I'm not going to stand by and let a couple of punks rough up a woman."

Wilson stared at him, and Cal shifted his feet wider and flexed his hands as he stared back. Suddenly, Frankie was between them.

"Don, we're okay now, but thanks for coming by. Why don't you go have a cupcake?"

Wilson held Cal's gaze for another moment, then turned to Frankie and smiled. "You know my weakness."

The police officer's vest made him appear even more imposing as he walked away. As he headed toward the kids, they crowded around him, clamoring for his attention.

"Do they always talk at the same time like that?" Cal asked, trying to ease the tension in the tiny room. "It sounds like electric drills boring into my head."

She glanced at the group of kids milling around Don. "Yes, that's what groups of teenagers do. Don't you remember?"

"I never did that," he said, his voice flat. He'd played sports as a teen, and his life had been all about discipline and obedience.

His father had made sure he didn't have free time to hang with other kids.

"I'm not sure this is going to work out," Frankie said after a long moment. "Let's see how it goes today, and we'll talk after the kids leave."

Not work out? He couldn't let that happen. "As it happens, I have a proposal for you."

"What would that be—" Heading out of the office, she stopped so abruptly that Cal almost bumped into her.

"What's wrong?"

"Those reporters are still out there." The outlines of their figures were visible through the blinds. She whirled to face him. "They came with you, didn't they?"

"They just showed up," he said.

"Get rid of them."

"How am I supposed to do that? I'm not their boss."

"And how did they know you were going to be here today?"

He shrugged one shoulder. "Maybe they read the transcript from the trial."

She folded her arms. "Cut the crap, Mr. Stewart. I know FreeZone wasn't mentioned in the transcript."

Watching him steadily, Frankie evoked memories of the nuns in grade school who'd given him the stink eye. He barely managed to keep from squirming. "Okay, maybe I told one guy."

"And now you can tell all of them to leave. I don't want to see them again."

"Not possible." Sweat pooled in the small of Cal's back. "I *need* them. I need to keep my face in the news. I'm going to be… I'll have competition at training camp in six weeks. I have to shape my publicity."

"You can shape it into a pretzel for all I care. But you're not doing it here."

Okay, different tactics. He forced himself to smile. "This can be good for you, too, Ms. Devereux. We can work something out. I'll make sure they talk about Free-Zone and all the good sh…things you're doing." No swearing was probably one of the rules, too. He glanced around at the bare-bones furnishings. "It looks like you could use some donors. I'll talk you up a few times, they'll get some shots of you, maybe with some of the kids, and the money will flow in."

Frankie recoiled as though he'd struck her. "That's it. You're not doing your community service here. Get out, Mr. Stewart."

CHAPTER TWO

FUMING, FRANKIE STARED at the man who was trying so hard to charm her. Caleb Stewart wanted photos of the vulnerable kids at FreeZone, *her* kids, in the paper. To promote himself. Pictures of her, too.

Fear overwhelmed her anger.

Bascombe would see her.

She couldn't let that happen. Not until she was ready to confront him.

"Take your reporters and get out of FreeZone. Now."

"Relax, Ms. Devereux," he said with a smile that didn't reach his eyes. "I just got here."

Frankie squeezed the bridge of her nose, trying to stave off the building headache. "I don't care. Get out."

His smile slipped. "You need to calm down. Think about this. I'm already here. Give me something to do."

"I just did. Get rid of the reporters."

"You haven't thought about the possibilities," he said.

"Oh, yes, I have." Another wave of anxiety rolled over her. "I want those reporters gone."

"You sure?"

The guy was good-looking, if you liked tall, muscled and blond. Even in jeans and a dress shirt with rolled-up sleeves, he was imposing. An impossible-to-ignore presence.

But Frankie didn't trust charmers. And Cal Stewart was as slick as a politician looking for votes.

Sarah, the judge who'd sentenced Stewart to CS here, would yank this guy out of FreeZone and send someone else. Someone who wouldn't be a problem. Cal Stewart had trouble written all over his lean, dimpled face.

"FYI, relentless pushing doesn't work with me. Charm doesn't, either," she added when he tried to speak. "The reporters are nonnegotiable. Get rid of them now."

His eyes narrowed a little, he opened his mouth, then shut it again. He shrugged, and she read his expression easily. He'd figure out a way to get around her. "I'll be right back."

She waited near the office as he spoke to the reporters. One of them tried to get into the center. Stewart glanced over his shoulder at Frankie, then blocked the woman.

"Sorry, guys, but I have to get to work." He flashed them a smile and stepped inside. "Happy now?" he said to Frankie.

"Not until you're out of my life."

"We got off on the wrong foot, Ms. Devereux. Give me another job."

Any other day, Frankie would have refused. But she was too upset, too frazzled to concentrate today. "Fine. Help the kids with their homework while I deal with Ramon."

Ramon sat at a table, slouched in a chair, his legs spread wide. A thick gold chain hung around his neck, and his white T-shirt with the sleeves torn off exposed his heavily muscled and tattooed upper arms. He was watching the kids playing Ping-Pong. Frankie sighed to herself and began to walk toward him.

"You're letting him stay?" Cal asked incredulously, stopping her with a hand on her arm. He let go when she narrowed her eyes at him.

"Of course I'm letting him stay."

"After he brought gang members in here?"

It wasn't hard to see that Ramon had been in a gang, as well. The boy didn't try to hide the crude tats on his arms and hands. "He's a former gang member. He's trying to leave, and the two guys you threw out are enforcers, trying to change his mind."

Cal stared at Ramon for a moment. Then he turned back to her. "Watch him," he said abruptly. "And don't trust him."

"Ramon has never given me any reason not to believe him," she said, her hackles rising. What did this stranger know about her kids? "He wants out."

"And you took him completely at his word?" Cal gave her a disbelieving look. "A banger? It didn't occur to you that he might have another agenda?"

She could lie and tell him no, that she trusted all her kids. But that would make her stupid. She grabbed Cal's wrist and dragged him toward her office again, where no one would hear them.

"Yes," she said, letting him go. Even his wrists were muscular. "I wondered at first. But he's been here for two months and he hasn't slipped. I can't be suspicious of every kid who walks in here. I want them to trust me. I have to trust them back."

"Don't trust Ramon. That's all I'm saying."

"And you know him so well after being here for a half hour?" Scorn for this rich football player's casual dismissal of Ramon made her stand straighter. "Because he made a mistake, he's irredeemable? Not worth trying to save?"

"God, you do-gooders are all the same. You think you can save the world. But some people don't want to be saved." Cal shoved his hand through his shaggy blond hair. "I saw something when his two buddies were here. Something in his expression."

He glanced over his shoulder, and she followed his gaze to where Ramon sat. He wore earbuds and he was nodding his head in time with the music on his iPod. Right now, he looked like any other teenager.

Cal Stewart thought she was a dewy-eyed idealist, determined to rescue the misunderstood bad boys. He had no idea how wrong he was. Every ounce of naivete had been crushed out of her a long time ago.

She knew exactly what Ramon was.

"Everyone deserves a second chance." She shoved her fists into her pockets. "Even bangers and street kids."

Cal stilled as he studied her, but she kept her gaze on the kids. "Look, Ms. Devereux, I'm not an expert on adolescents or how to treat them," he finally said. "I'm just a football player. But I—"

She interrupted. "That's right. You're a football player and *I'm* the one who runs FreeZone. I've been doing this for two years, so you can shove your opinions of Ramon."

A smart man would have backed down. But Cal continued to stare at her. "Football players know violence. And that's what I saw in Ramon and his buddies. Hostility. Aggression."

She glanced at Ramon again. He'd retrieved his backpack and was reaching inside. When he pulled out a schoolbook and a pad of paper, she said to Cal, "Looks pretty dangerous, doesn't he? He's doing his homework, which is exactly what he's supposed to do. But I appreciate your perspective. Thank you for sharing it with me."

"Which means I can stick my perspective up my ass, right?"

Exasperated, she said, "Mr. Stewart, we have a few rules here at FreeZone. The first one is no violence, which you broke when you manhandled me and threw Ramon's former buddies out the door. The second one is no swearing. I hope you're not going for the trifecta, because if you're carrying any drugs or weapons, I'll call Don back to arrest you."

"Nope. No drugs. No weapons." He held his arms out to the side. "You want to frisk me?"

She let her gaze drift down his body, then up again. "Not particularly," she said, knowing she'd kept her voice cool and uninterested when his mouth tightened.

"Fine. I'm here, you trust that gangster, and I've already broken most of your rules. What's next?"

Why me, Sarah? I don't have time to babysit a spoiled jock.

"You can leave or you can help. Do you know anything about math? Algebra, specifically?"

"Some," he said cautiously, rolling his shoulders and glancing at the kids and their textbooks.

Did he think it would hurt his tough image to admit he was good at math? "Great. Math isn't my strong suit. Go on over to the homework tables and find out who needs help. Someone always does."

"I guess I can do that."

"Good." With any luck, he'd stay there until the kids left and she could get rid of him permanently. "One other thing. The kids call adults by their last names here. If someone calls you Caleb, you don't react."

"It's Cal."

"Don't answer to that, either. You're Mr. Stewart to them. They need to respect adults."

"Respect. Right." He straightened his shoulders and sauntered toward the kids bent over their books.

Twenty minutes later, Frankie was helping Harley Michaels with her English assignment when she heard whispering at the other end of the tables. Cal was leaning against the wall, texting.

She hadn't told him about the no-cell-phone rule.

She wanted to ignore him. He'd be gone after today, and she wouldn't see him again. But with the kids all watching, she had to take a stand.

"Work on your last paragraph, Harley, and I'll be right back," she said quietly. But instead of bending over her assignment, Harley joined the rest of the group, waiting to see what would happen.

Cal's thumbs flew over the keyboard as she approached. "Mr. Stewart, we don't use cell phones at FreeZone," she said in a low voice.

He looked up, his fingers poised above his iPhone. "What?"

"No texting," she said.

He nodded as his thumbs began moving again. After what felt like an eternity, he hit the send button and slipped the phone into his pocket.

Was he being irritating on purpose? Or did he just not care? "Maybe we should talk about this in my office."

"Sure." He strolled toward the corner of the room as if he owned the place, and her chest began to burn as she followed him.

She closed the door and held on to the handle. "I don't allow phones for a reason," she said. "I want the kids to focus on their homework, or actually talk to other people. They're on their phones constantly otherwise. I ask the adults who help out here not to use them, either, because I need their attention on the kids."

He shrugged. "Fine. I'll have to do a couple more tweets today, but I'll come in here next time."

Remembering the reporters outside, Frankie frowned. "What were you tweeting about?"

"What I'm doing, of course." His fingers tapped the phone in his pocket. "My agent's orders. I need to do six updates a day."

"Part of your publicity shaping?" She tried to keep the contempt out of her voice, but realized she'd failed when he glared at her.

"Yep. Training camp starts in a month and a half. I need to…" He swallowed. "I need to be visible. Get the fans behind me." His foot tapped a staccato rhythm on the floor.

She knew what training camp was. After the judge told her who she'd be getting as a CS placement, she'd studied up on the subject. Why was he nervous about training camp? She nodded. "Fine. Do your tweeting in here. Just don't tweet about where you are."

It was impossible to misinterpret his expression.

"You already did, didn't you?" She grabbed his arm, not bothering to hide her irritation. A star athlete like him would have thousands and thousands of followers on Twitter.

"Of course I did. That's the point. People want to know what I'm doing." He glanced at her hand on his forearm.

She let him go, his short, blond arm hairs tickling her fingers. "Oh, my God."

"What's the problem? It's publicity for you."

"That's very considerate of you, but I don't want my kids used that way. Did you not get that message when I told you to get rid of the reporters?" If there were throngs of people here, the reporters would come back, too.

"Fine. I'll keep the kids out of it. But look at this place. You *need* the publicity. You need money."

"Yes, I do, but I'll get it my own way. A way that won't make the kids run a gauntlet of people when they come and go." A way that would let her deal with Bascombe on her own terms. "Besides, I doubt your groupies are going to be making contributions to FreeZone when they show up to fawn over you."

"They're not groupies. They're fans."

"Same difference. They're not part of my donor profile."

He leaned against the desk as if it was his. "You have a lot of rules, don't you?"

"Yes. In this neighborhood, rules are all that stand between civility and chaos. These kids need to have at least one stable thing in their lives, and for a lot of them, this is it. The kids who come here *need* rules."

So did Frankie.

She gestured at his phone. "Tweet again and tell them you've left."

"You want me to lie?"

"Like a rug."

He shook his head slowly. "I'm not one of your kids, *Frankie*. And you're not my coach. I'm not going to ask how high when you tell me to jump." He gestured toward the pocket he'd put his phone in. "If you want that tweet to go out, you'll have to send it yourself."

So it was going to be a pissing contest. It wouldn't be the first time with a community-service volunteer. Holding his gaze, Frankie slid her fingers into the snug denim, releasing the subtle scent of fabric softener. The muscles of his thigh were rock hard and coiled like a spring, ready to explode.

All that muscle generated a lot of heat. She tried to ignore it as the tip of her finger touched plastic, and she plucked out the phone with a shudder of relief.

She palmed the phone, warm from his body, and touched the Twitter icon. When his screen popped up, she typed a few words, then hit the send button.

She slipped the phone back into his pocket and tapped it into place. "Don't call my bluff."

He watched her hand retreat. "Do you touch everyone this much?" he asked. "Are you always so…physical?"

Heat washed over her and she knew her skin flushed, but she managed to raise her eyebrows. "Asks the guy who knocks people down for a living."

He held her gaze for a moment too long, and sweat trickled down her sides. Yeah, she was upset and emotional. But also insane. There was no other explanation for why she was poking at Cal Stewart.

"Yeah, I'm a physical guy, Frankie." His voice was a low, pissed-off rumble in the intimacy of the office. As he leaned forward, her heart thundered, but she refused to back up. "And it's not always smart to yank the dog's tail. Sometimes he'll bite."

"Thanks for the life lesson." His chin was inches from hers, close enough to smell spearmint on his breath and see the flecks of gold in his green eyes. She stepped away from him and her heart slowed. "I need to get back to the kids."

He nodded. "Fine. Don't yank my chain again."

CAL WATCHED FRANKIE walk out of the office and sit down beside a redheaded girl as if nothing had happened. Adrenaline churned in his veins, making him edgy and revved up. She should know better than to bait a guy like him.

She should know better than to touch him, too. He could still feel those small fingers, burrowing through his pocket. She'd been quick and had barely brushed the denim of his jeans, but the memory burned.

After the fight, the team psychologist had explained that Cal needed to learn control. Which had told him everything he needed to know about that pompous ass. Cal maintained control every minute of his life. The only time he let it go was on Sunday afternoons.

And on one ugly Saturday night at a club, after a guy had been needling him for hours. Even then, Cal had managed to hold back until the guy started shoving a woman around.

Loser was lucky he'd escaped with only a broken jaw.

One moment of lost control, and he'd ended up at this place, with a bunch of punk losers and an irritating woman.

And now he had to convince the irritating woman to let him stay. The judge had said he had one chance or he would go to jail. So he'd better look busy.

The front door opened and a slender African-American boy walked in. He carried a backpack that seemed as if it weighed about as much as the kid. As Cal watched, he hurried over to the tables, greeted a couple of kids and pulled out a book. A math book. *Count to ten. Focus.* Cal headed toward him.

"Hey," he said as he reached the table. "You need some help with that?"

The boy glanced up at him, pushing his glasses up his nose almost absently. "No, I'm okay. But thank you for offering." He paused, staring at Cal for a moment. "You're Cal Stewart."

"Yeah," he said, studying the kid more carefully. "I am."

"Are you going to be playing for the Cougars this year? Bummer about your knee, but my dad and I read in the paper that you're doing good with your rehab."

"It's going well." He hesitated. "What's your name?"

"Sean. Sean Green."

"Thanks for asking, Sean. I expect to be out there when training camp starts. After that? It's up to the coaches."

Sean looked down at his paper and wrote out an equation. Calculus. "I've heard you say that on the news."

It was Cal's standard response to the question half the city of Chicago had been asking him. So why did the kid look disappointed? Had he expected Cal to reveal a secret? To tell him what the doctors had said and Cal refused to believe?

"It's tough coming back from an injury like this," he heard himself say to Sean.

God, now he was spilling his guts to a teenager. This place was messing with his head. He had to get out of here. He'd started to rise when Sean nodded.

"If it was just your ACL, you'd be okay," Sean said matter-of-factly. "But tearing the lateral collateral ligament at the same time isn't so good."

Who *was* this kid? Cal sank back onto the chair. "God, you sound like my doctor."

Sean's eyes brightened. "That's what I'm going to be. An orthopedic surgeon."

"Yeah?" Cal tapped his left knee. "You going to figure out a way to make this as good as new?"

"I'll do my best, Mr. Stewart."

"Hey, you can call me Cal," he said without thinking.

Sean glanced at Frankie out of the corner of his eye. "Not here, I can't."

Another broken rule. "Right. Sorry. I'm going to get in trouble, aren't I?"

Sean grinned. "I won't tell on you."

"Thanks, dude." Cal held out his fist, and Sean bumped it. "If I need help with math, I'll come and talk to you."

Sean stared at him for a moment, then went back to his equations. "I don't think you'll need help from me, Mr. Stewart. You got a degree in math from UCLA."

Cal froze, then struggled to smile. "Hey, I needed to know how to count my money," he said.

He'd never hidden his degree, but he hadn't flaunted it, either. He didn't want to be the geek freak on the team. He just wanted to be one of the guys.

"I think it's chilling," Sean said.

"Yeah. Thanks." He shoved away from the table. This wasn't going to work. He'd come close to a fight with a couple of punks, he'd had an uncomfortably intimate conversation with a too-perceptive kid, and he'd butted heads with a woman with a major attitude problem. A woman who was supposed to be his boss for the next six weeks.

And he'd been here for only a couple of hours.

Maybe she would sign off on his community service if he gave her a chunk of money, enough to pay someone else to do the work. He'd be able to concentrate on football; she wouldn't have to deal with him.

With an extra four hours of rehab every day, he'd make the team with no problems. He'd have plenty of time to take those last few steps to complete recovery.

Win-win for both of them.

CHAPTER THREE

CAL LEVERED HIMSELF OUT OF the chair, hating that he needed to push off the table. It was the last step in his rehab, his therapist had told him. Being able to get up from a chair without help. She'd warned him it would be hard.

Yeah, it was tough. But it was a breeze compared to the prospect of never playing football again.

He glanced at Sean to see if the kid had noticed, but he was doing his calculus. Good thing. Cal had let his guard down for a minute with the kid, and that probably made him think they were best friends now. Even so, if he saw Cal struggling, he would probably post it on Facebook.

Cal helped two kids with their math, getting more irritated and antsy as the time crawled by. He was stuck here talking about equations when he should have been working on his knee or studying his playbook. And on top of that, he'd probably have to grovel to get Frankie Devereux to let him stay. Unless he could convince her to take his money.

He had a bad feeling about that. She was probably way too righteous to take a bribe.

He'd just have to make sure it was big enough to trump her principles.

Suddenly he heard chairs scraping against the floor, and the kids all rushed over to the deli case. Two girls—the ones who'd been crying earlier—were setting cupcakes on a cloth-covered table. A plastic container of cut-up carrots, celery and cucumbers sat next to the treats. Two of the boys carried milk jugs and paper cups over.

Frankie was leaning against one of the homework tables, watching them. Her shoulders drooped, but she was smiling. Now that she wasn't bristling at him, he noticed the lines of weariness around her eyes.

This place was a lot to run and organize. And she seemed to do it by herself, since there were no other adults here. She needed help. Maybe she *would* be receptive to his offer of money.

At the very least, he should be able to convince her to let him stay.

"Hey," he said as he got closer to her. "I helped three kids with their math."

Her shoulders straightened as she faced him, and the vulnerability he'd seen a moment ago disappeared. "I noticed. Thanks," she said, her voice cool.

He nodded toward the kids, who were discussing the cupcakes. "Cupcakes for a snack? I figured you'd be all about healthy food."

To his surprise, her cheeks got pink. "There are healthy things there, too, and they know they have to eat the vegetables if they take the cupcakes. But the cupcakes make them smile."

"Kind of a pricey snack, aren't they?"

"A local bakery donates the day-old ones that don't sell by noon." She rolled her shoulders, as if she was uncomfortable, and continued to watch the kids.

"Ooh, they're pretty today, Ms. Devereux," one of the girls said.

Cal stepped closer and saw cupcakes decorated with elaborate long flowers. One featured a lion looking over his shoulder and winking. Another held a frog, amazingly lifelike. There were dancing cows and laughing horses. All of them were whimsical. Fanciful. Made by someone who knew exactly what would catch a child's eye.

As Cal watched, one of the girls rushed over, clutching a pastry as if it was a prize. "Ms. Devereux! Did you make this for me?" She held the cupcake with a frog.

Frankie smiled. "I might have had you in mind."

"Thank you!" Holding her cupcake carefully to the side, the girl threw her other arm around Frankie's neck for a fierce hug, then scampered back to the group.

"You made those cupcakes?" Cal asked.

"I did," she replied without looking at him.

Tough, take-no-prisoners Frankie Devereux had a whimsical side? He studied her more carefully, trying to see past her prickly exterior. "They're amazing."

"Thank you."

He frowned. "But you said they were leftovers from a bakery."

"Yes."

"So you work there? I thought this was your full-time job."

"Donations to FreeZone barely cover the insurance and rent on this building." She shrugged, but a shadow crossed her face. "I don't take a salary. We need every penny we get."

"So you work two jobs."

"A lot of people work two jobs." Her voice was cool again. "I work at a neighborhood bakery so I can spend my afternoons at FreeZone." She shifted on the chair and ended up a little farther away from him.

"Those things are works of art. They look like they should be sold at one of those upscale cupcake joints."

She lifted one shoulder. "Thanks. But they're only a means to an end."

He spotted the girl with the frog cupcake nibbling around the edges, as if saving the frog for last. "But a frog? On a cupcake?"

FRANKIE SHRUGGED AGAIN as she watched Lissy. She tried to give the girl extra attention. Her mother worked long hours, and she'd recently remarried. From what Lissy said, her stepfather was no prize.

"I knew Lissy would like it. She has a thing for frogs." If making her a frog cupcake made the girl smile like that, Frankie would do it more often. "She has a stuffed frog she carries around in her backpack. Her father got it for her when she was a baby. Just before he was killed in a drive-by shooting."

"Poor kid."

Lissy bit off the frog's head with a giggle.

"A lot of the kids who come here have similar stories," Frankie replied, standing abruptly. He sounded sympathetic. Understanding. It made him seem like a normal man.

Which he most definitely was not. She didn't want anything to do with Cal, especially not have a personal conversation. She wouldn't see him again after today.

"When they finish eating, they play games or just hang out for an hour," she said briskly. "Then they go home, and you're done."

"About that, Frankie." He jerked his head toward the kids cleaning the area around the deli case. "You obviously need help here. I think I should stay."

She desperately needed help. But not from him. "Judge Kelly will send me someone else."

"But…"

"For the next hour, your job is to interact with the kids," she said, ignoring his attempt to change her mind. He was a self-centered jerk, and dealing with him would take too much of her attention away from the kids.

"Some of them will want to talk to you," she told him. "They like their sports heroes." She tried to let go of the tightness in her chest and the tension in her shoulders. She'd tried not to think about Bascombe, but it was impossible. Having to deal with Cal as well was too much. But tomorrow, things would be better. Cal would be gone, and in a few days she'd have someone else to help her. Someone more appropriate. "If you don't want to talk football, you can play games with them. The only thing you can't do is stand around and watch."

"That's not a problem," he said coolly. "I don't watch. I *do*."

"Have at it, then," she answered, equally coolly. But he was already strolling away.

She waited for him to head into the office, phone clutched in his hand, but he had morphed into the perfect volunteer. He answered every question from the starstruck boys, laying it on thick. And they fell for his charm, laughing and joking with him as if they'd known him forever.

Julio walked over to the group, the ever-present basketball tucked beneath his arm, and a few moments later, all the boys surged toward the hoop. Cal held back for a moment, then followed them.

The girls plopped onto the couches and began chattering. Lissy and Harley headed toward the foosball table. Frankie waited a few minutes, but when it became clear that no one needed her, she grabbed a stack of paperwork from the office and sat down at a homework table. And stared at the donor requests she needed to write.

No way could she concentrate on this. All she saw was Bascombe's face, staring at her from the newspaper. She thumbed through the stack and found one intended for

DCFS. God! Had Bascombe ever handled grants? Had she submitted a request to him at some point?

She pretended to work, but her hands were shaking again. So she set her pen on the stack of papers and watched the basketball game. The boys on Cal's team shouted and gave him high fives. He'd apparently done something good.

Julio and the boys on the other team huddled together. When they started playing again, Julio cut in and out between players, took a pass and laid it in the basket. Now his team was the one celebrating.

Frankie stood abruptly and went into her office. She needed to be calm, focused when she called the judge. Sarah knew her well enough to hear the tension in her voice. Frankie had to be rational about asking for a different volunteer.

Finally the clock hit six, and she stepped out of the office. "Okay, everyone. Time to pack up."

Cal bumped fists with most of the boys, clapped Sean on the back and put the basketball into the cabinet as the kids hurried over to get their bags. He smiled at the girls, then watched with his hands in his pockets as they straggled out the door.

"You want me to lock it?" he called to her after the door finally closed.

"Yes. Thank you." She gathered her papers and headed for the office. "I'll call Sarah, then you're free to leave."

"Hold on, Frankie."

Cal headed toward her, and it almost looked as if he was limping.

"Did you hurt yourself playing basketball?" she asked.

"I'm fine." He slowed down, and the limp disappeared. "You're really going to call her?"

"That's what you want, isn't it?"

"I have another idea that would work for both of us. Why don't I give you some money to hire someone who actually knows how to work with kids? That leaves me free to concentrate on football and gets you competent help. We'd both get what we need and Judge Kelly wouldn't have to be involved."

Frankie narrowed her eyes. "Let me make sure I understand you. You're offering me a bribe to sign off on your CS hours."

"'Bribe' sounds so harsh. Think of it as a creative use of my money and your skills."

Frankie counted to ten before speaking again. "What makes you think I'd be amenable to a bribe?"

"This place needs money. You don't want me working with your kids. Seems logical to me."

"It seems exactly like something you'd think of. And the answer is no."

"Then let me stay." He stopped in front of her and glanced toward the basketball hoop. "I had a good time with the kids. I'd like to come back."

"Sorry, Cal." Her conscience pricked at her. The boys did seem to enjoy having him here. But she didn't want anyone this…corrupt in her center. And she was the boss. "You're not the right fit."

"We got off to a bad start. Let me try again."

Two red flags stained his cheeks. He probably never had to ask twice for anything. She turned and headed toward her office. "They'll find you another place that will work better with your skill set." She closed the door before he could answer.

It took several minutes for Sarah's clerk to track her down. Frankie heard Cal moving around in the other room and wondered what he was doing, but she didn't open the door to look. It didn't matter.

"Hey, Frankie," Sarah finally said. "How did it go today with Cal Stewart?"

"That's why I'm calling." She swiveled away from the door. "It didn't work out. You need to take him back and send me someone else."

Silence stretched out uncomfortably long. Finally Sarah said, "Sorry, Frankie. That's not going to happen. You're stuck with him."

"Why? I know you assign community service to a lot of people. Put Cal somewhere else and send me the next one." Someone not so aggressive. So in her face. So disruptive.

"Do you have any idea how many CS people you've sent back?" When Frankie didn't answer, Sarah continued. "Way too many. There's always something wrong with them. I'm beginning to think the problem is you, Frankie. Not the volunteers."

"I haven't sent that many back," she protested. "The last guy was making the girls uncomfortable. He needed to go."

"You're right, and I didn't have a problem with that. But what about the librarian? She was perfect for FreeZone."

"She wanted to reorganize everything," Frankie muttered. "Do things her own way."

"She wanted to help you," Sarah retorted. "Take some of the load off your shoulders." The judge sighed. "I've gone out of my way to assign people to you. I put you at the top of the list, but you always find something wrong. You're not asking them to do brain surgery, for God's sake. They're playing basketball and helping with homework. How tough can that be?"

"There were specific problems with Cal today," Frankie said stiffly. "He broke almost all the rules, for one thing."

"You and your damn rules. Give the guy a break. It was his first day." She lowered her voice. "Bottom line, Frankie. If you send Stewart back, Kenny will be your enemy for life."

Frankie tossed her pen onto the desk. "What does your clerk have to do with anything?"

"He's in charge of the placement list. He keeps you on top because I ask him to, but he won't forget this. He's a huge Cougars fan, and if you reject Cal, his hero goes to jail. Kenny will never forgive you for making one of the team's stars miss the season. It will be a cold day in hell before you get anyone else."

"What do you mean, Cal goes to jail? He was assigned CS."

"I gave him one shot at CS. If it doesn't work out, he doesn't get a second chance. He gets four months in County Jail. I'm sick of athletes and their entitled attitudes. If Stewart doesn't work out, I'll make him an example."

"Damn it." Frankie spun the chair around and stared at the door, but didn't hear a thing. Had Cal already left? "So I'm stuck with him?"

"Pretty much. Or you can send him back and turn Kenny and every other Cougars fan against you. And never get help again."

"So I have to keep him."

"That's up to you."

Every nasty word she knew, and she knew a lot of them, rolled through her head. "Fine. I'll keep him." She closed her phone without letting Sarah respond.

There were still no sounds from the other side of the door. If Cal had left, she'd have to chase him and ask him to stay.

She'd never liked the taste of crow.

She wrenched open the door. That character fault had gotten her into trouble too many times in the past. She hoped to God he was still here.

CHAPTER FOUR

FreeZone was empty.

Cal wasn't here.

A dab of pink icing flattened on the floor sent up the sweet smell of vanilla as Frankie headed toward the front of the center. As she passed the basketball net, the sharp scent of teenage-boy sweat mingled with the cloying mix of the girls' perfume. The place needed to be aired out, but she'd do that tomorrow.

Tonight, she had to find Cal and ask him to stay.

Maybe he'd already left.

She sprinted for the front door, then relaxed when she saw the white Escalade. In this neighborhood, a car like that could only belong to Cal.

"Looking for me?"

Frankie spun around. He stood in the doorway that led to the storage room and the back exit.

"Thought I'd check on your car." She closed the front door, ignoring the flood of relief she felt. "It's not the kind we usually see around here."

"Worried about me?" He sauntered toward her.

"Worried about your car. It's temptation on four wheels."

"Not a problem. The alarm on that sucker can wake the dead." He leaned against the wall a few feet away from her. "Were you afraid I'd left without saying goodbye?"

Her fingers itched to wipe the smirk off his face. "My

luck hasn't been that good today." Damn it. She was supposed to be asking him to stay, not goading him into leaving.

He grinned. "Admit it, Frankie. Since money is off the table…?" He raised his eyebrows, and she scowled. "You want me to stay." He nodded toward the basketball hoop. "The boys had a great time."

"Yeah, you put on quite a show—the stunt with Ramon and the bangers, ducking in and out of my office to tweet, encouraging the reporters to hang around. The kids were on pins and needles, wondering what you'd do next."

"Maybe a little excitement would be good for the place."

"These kids get all the excitement they need." She wrenched open the closet, took out the broom and began to sweep. "Peace and calm is what I offer here."

He plucked the broom out of her hand and began to sweep the floor, nudging the glob of icing until it came loose. "The thing is, I can do things you can't do with them."

"Such as…?"

"Basketball. They liked playing with me."

She reached into the closet for the disinfectant spray and started spritzing the tables, pulling the trigger so hard the solution spattered the chairs. "I can play basketball with them. Usually do, as a matter of fact. And *I'm* not a ball hog."

He looked over his shoulder. "Ball hog?" His voice dropped to a low growl, and a chill rippled over her skin. "You think you can take me, Frankie? Get the ball. I'm ready."

His eyes glittered, and she realized she'd poked a little too hard. He was a professional athlete. He lived to compete. "Nah, I'll give you a break. I saw you limping. I don't want to hurt you."

His face lost all expression as he stared at her. The air was hot and close, and the walls pressed in on her. Then he grinned and began sweeping again. "I like you, Frankie. I'm going to enjoy working here."

"I didn't say you could stay."

"But you want me to."

She needed him to. She opened her mouth to tell him so, but the crow feathers stuck in her throat. "I'll give you another day and we'll see how it goes," she finally said. "Since you asked to stay."

"And since *you* asked so nicely, I'll give you another day."

"Fine."

"Good."

They worked in silence as he swept the floor in straight, even lines. He knew how to clean, she'd give him that.

Finally, when the room was ready for the next day, she replaced all the cleaning supplies in the closet. "I'll see you tomorrow. I arrive at three to open up. Please be here then."

He shoved his hands into his pockets and watched her. "I'll do that."

He didn't move.

Neither did she.

Finally, she said, "Was there something else?"

"I'm trying to be a gentleman. Waiting for you to leave first."

"I'm not leaving yet. Go ahead so I can lock up."

Instead of hurrying out, as she'd expected, he glanced around the empty space. "You're not leaving?"

"I have some things to do."

"Like what?"

"Not that it's any of your business, but I have letters to write. Bills to pay. Some phone calls to make."

His expression sharpened. "Hold on."

"What?"

His dimples flashed. "I have a proposition for you."

She didn't want to see those dimples. They tempted her to overlook what a jerk he was. "Not interested. Because if it's anything like your last one, I'll regret my offer to give you another day."

"Since you're going to be here, anyway, let me stay and work longer. I need to fulfill my community-service obligation quickly. My football team starts practicing in six weeks, and I need to be there. I can't be late for camp."

"We've already cleaned. There's nothing else to do."

"I could help do the books. Or write letters for you."

Her surprise must have shown on her face, because his expression hardened. "I'm a football player, but I'm not illiterate. I know how to write a business letter. I know basic bookkeeping." His face became cool and impossible to read. "How do you think I keep track of my own finances?"

"Based on what you offered me, I assume you pay someone to do that for you."

Instead of snapping back, he drawled, "Of course I do. But that doesn't mean I can't do it myself."

"I've always taken care of the bookkeeping and letters."

"So now you have some help. You'll get home earlier to whoever is waiting for you." He raised one eyebrow, as if waiting for her to tell him all about her life. Which was *so* not happening.

He didn't need to know that the only one waiting for her was the stray cat she fed in the evenings. And Frankie would *not* ask who was waiting for him.

"Fine. If you want to write thank-you notes, be my guest." She turned the lock, then headed for her office.

He waited in the doorway, and she was intensely aware

of how cramped her office was. With him so big and so close, it felt even smaller than usual. She picked up the ancient laptop she used, and a manila folder, then headed to the main room. Darkness had fallen outside, and beneath the glare of the fluorescent lights, the linoleum was a sickly green. Gouges and graffiti carved into the tables were harshly illuminated.

Frankie pried open the laptop and booted it up, then opened the file containing her letters. "This is the letter I use for thank-yous. The computer file named Donors has addresses. The manila folder has a list of recent donations. Include the amount of the donation in the letter. The printer is in my office, and it's wireless."

He glanced at the laptop. "This POS actually works with a wireless printer?"

"As long as the hamsters are running fast enough on their wheels."

He grinned. "I like a woman with attitude."

"Is that right? I figured your taste ran more to trixies, frat boy."

Instead of bristling as she'd expected, he laughed. She moved abruptly toward her office. She had too much to do to waste time with Cal Stewart.

"How many of these letters do you want written?" he called.

"As many as you want to do," she said without looking back. "I'll be here awhile."

She'd intended to write a grant to DCFS. But no way would she do that now. She thought about Bascombe and shuddered.

She'd call Emma Sloane instead. Emma was a DCFS social worker who stopped by sometimes to see Harley, and she and Frankie had become friends. Emma would be straight with her, and she wouldn't run to the new boss and tell him Frankie had been asking questions.

The sound of a chair being dragged across the floor made her turn and look. Cal was lowering himself into one of the flimsy plastic folding chairs the kids used. His long body made it look like a kindergarten chair.

She paused in the door of her office and watched. His hands dwarfed the keyboard, but he typed quickly. She'd expected he would use the hunt-and-peck method.

After a moment, she turned away and opened the newspaper again. Bascombe's picture stared back at her, all smug bureaucrat. She remembered the tail of the lanyard hanging out of his pocket that day so many years ago. She clearly wasn't the first girl he'd molested. He'd been smart enough to take off his ID badge and give her a false name.

As she studied the picture and figured out what she would say to Emma, the rhythmic clatter of the keyboard in the other room distracted her. Finally, Frankie reached out and pushed the door closed.

"Hey, Emma," she said into the phone a few moments later. "How are you doing?"

"I'm good, Frankie. You want to catch dinner one of these nights?"

"Love to, but do you have time now to answer a few questions?"

"Sure." Emma's voice sharpened. "What's up?"

"I just saw that Doug Bascombe has been appointed head of DCFS. Do you know anything about him?"

"Like what?" her friend asked cautiously.

"Do you know him?"

"We've met. He started as a social worker, so he takes an interest in the kids—who they are, how they're doing. He's asked me about a few of them."

Frankie's stomach churned. She'd been clinging to the

very faint hope that he'd changed. "Really? He's that high up and he still works with kids?"

"Less than he used to. He's mostly an administrator now."

"So what do you think of him?"

"Why do you ask?" Emma said after a pause.

"Just wondering how to get along with him."

Frankie could hear the sound of Emma's door closing. "Stay away from him, Frankie. He's the kind of guy who will drive you nuts. He's pretty impressed with himself, and he lives for opportunities to be in the spotlight."

"Sounds like a gem," Frankie answered, forcing herself to laugh. "Thanks, Emma. I'll steer clear. Appreciate your candor."

"Take care, Frankie."

Frankie stared at the phone in her hand for a long time before she slid it into her pocket. There was no way she could steer clear of Bascombe. She *had* to confront him. Especially if he still had contact with kids.

SEATED AT A HOMEWORK TABLE, Cal finally let out a long breath and released the tension that had been building. She'd promised him only another day, but she would let him stay. He'd make sure of it. He should have just asked, explained why he needed to stay, but he couldn't do it.

Show No Weakness had been his mantra since his days in peewee-league football. He'd learned early that his old man would jump on any sign of hesitation or uncertainty.

Cal's ploy had been risky, but any successful athlete was a gambler. Which way was the ball going to be thrown? How was the other guy going to break? He could usually read his opponent's moves. Sometimes, though, he had to roll the dice and take his chances.

And this time, he'd rolled a winning number. He'd take

care of his community service and get to training camp on time. There were worse places he could spend six weeks.

Cal's mouth curled into a bitter smile. His old man had always warned him that if he didn't concentrate on football, he'd end up in the county public-works department, picking up roadkill.

Compared to that, FreeZone was a cushy assignment. Playing basketball with a bunch of kids versus scraping flattened carcasses off the asphalt? It didn't take a genius to choose.

The sun was hidden behind tall buildings, and dark shadows crept across the floor. Without sunlight to brighten it up, the empty space looked even shabbier. The sliver of light from beneath Frankie's office door sliced across the linoleum, and he studied it for a moment. Then he stood up and dragged the table to her doorway.

She nudged the door open. "Is something wrong?"

Her blue eyes seemed sad, and he wondered why. "I thought I should work over here. In case I have any questions."

Sadness changed to annoyance. "It's not rocket science. You just copy the letter. You don't need my help for that."

"It's cozier over here in the corner."

"You want cozy?" She made a noise that sounded suspiciously like a snort. "Did you bring your knitting?"

The coldness that had settled in his stomach when he'd thought about his father began to dissipate. "No, but thanks for reminding me. I'll bring it tomorrow. I'm working on a darling little hat."

Her mouth twitched for a moment, then she scowled. "I'm immune to charm, so don't bother."

"Good to know," he said as he settled into the uncomfortable chair. He glanced over his shoulder, but her head was bent over her desk. The light caught the fine hairs at the nape of her neck, making them gleam. In the stark light, she looked small and delicate. Fragile. Nothing like her tough, in-control persona.

A neck is what holds the head up. That's all. Focus on your job and getting out of here ASAP.

He finished typing the first letter, then noticed her name at the bottom of the page. Francesca Devereux.

He swiveled in his chair. "Is your name really Francesca?"

Her back stiffened, then she looked over her shoulder, her expression wary. "Yes. Why?"

"I figured you called yourself Frankie because you didn't like your real name. But Francesca…that's a beautiful name."

"I've been Frankie since I was a kid." She tapped a pencil on her desk. "I don't answer to Francesca."

"I bet your mom doesn't call you Frankie."

The pencil stopped bouncing, and she turned in her chair so all he saw was the rigid line of her spine. "Just write the letters, *Caleb*. I'm not giving you CS hours for psychoanalyzing me."

Her pencil scraped across paper, but he would bet his next paycheck she wasn't writing anything legible. Her spiky black hair bristled. The three metal hoops in her right ear glittered beneath the harsh fluorescent lights. Right now, there was nothing soft about Frankie Devereux.

Francesca was a soft name. Feminine. Gentle.

Which was the real woman?

It didn't matter. He was here for one hundred hours. He didn't have time to unravel the secrets of his annoying, controlling boss.

With the single-minded focus he'd learned years ago, he forced himself to concentrate on the letter. It was well written. Professional. But he could see a couple places

where he could tweak it a bit. Play on the donors' compassion. Or their vanity. Whatever would nudge them to
contribute a little more money.

FreeZone clearly needed it. And it sounded as if Frankie
was always scrambling for funding.

Too bad she wouldn't take his money, but he wasn't
surprised. She was a do-gooder. A save-the-world idealist. She was determined to save these kids—even the ones
like Ramon, who didn't want to be saved.

Cal was lucky she hadn't booted him out when he'd offered the bribe.

But she still could. And if she did, the judge would
throw his ass in jail.

That would be the end of his football career.

The doctor's words echoed in his head, but he ignored
them. He was ready to play. Or he would be, in six weeks.

He sent the letters to the printer, suddenly anxious to
get out of here.

As he pulled the table back where it belonged, he heard
the printer clanking as it slowly spit out the pages.

When he got back to the office, Frankie was frowning
as she read the top one.

"This isn't the letter I gave you."

"Yeah, I made a few improvements," he said easily.
"You want to get repeat donations. I thought the changes
in the second paragraph would persuade some of your
donors to fork over more money."

"This doesn't sound like me." She slapped it onto the
desk. "I didn't ask you to rework the letter. I asked you to
make copies."

"I thought this might be more effective."

"Not your job, Stewart." Her movements were jerky as
she squared the papers on her desk. "I give my CS volunteers specific jobs for a reason."

"Fine. Don't use it," he said coolly. His letter was better than hers. Why wouldn't she admit it?

"Good night, Cal. I'll see you tomorrow." Her shoulders were tight and she didn't turn around. Her hand were trembling.

"You okay?" he asked. All this tension couldn't be because of a stupid letter.

"I'm fine. Good night."

CHAPTER FIVE

As Frankie approached Doug Bascombe's assistant two
weeks later, she smoothed her damp palms down the skirt
of her black business suit. She was an adult, she reminded
herself. Not a powerless child. She was doing the right
thing.

She smiled at the young woman sitting at the desk. "I'd
like to speak to Mr. Bascombe, please."

The woman looked up. "I'm afraid he's on a conference
call at the moment. Do you have an appointment?"

"No, I don't. But I think he'll see me."

The assistant—Miranda, according to her nameplate—
didn't seem convinced. "What's your name? I'll ask him
when he's finished the call."

"Frankie Devereux."

Miranda wrote it down, and Frankie seated herself in
one of the plush chairs lining the wall. She pulled a book
out of her bag and opened it, but none of the words made
sense. She continued to stare at it, though, turning pages
occasionally. She wanted to appear calm. Cool. Confident.

After a while, Miranda disappeared into the office
behind her. When she emerged, she sat back down, shaking her head apologetically at Frankie.

After another ten minutes, her phone buzzed and she
stood up. "Mr. Bascombe will see you now."

As if he were a king, granting her an audience. It made

Frankie straighten her shoulders and hold up her head as she marched into the office.

His desk was massive and made out of cherry. Artwork hung on the walls, and all of it looked expensive. A leather couch stood along one end of the room, and two chairs were positioned in front of the desk.

"Ms. Devereux. To what do I owe the pleasure?" He smiled impersonally, as if he didn't remember her.

Maybe he didn't. It had been a long time.

His suit was expensive and tailored, his hair carefully styled. But his eyes were the same—cold. Predatory.

Her hands began to tremble, and she gripped the strap of her purse.

"We need to talk. *Dave.*" Her heart pounded so hard she could feel it against her ribs.

His smile faltered. "My name is Doug."

"Not always." She held his gaze until he looked away, then she sat down.

"What is this about?"

"I think you know." When he simply stared at her, she gripped the strap of her handbag even tighter. "I'm your past, come back to haunt you."

When his eyes flickered, Frankie relaxed her hands. "So you do remember. Juvie. Twelve years ago. A small conference room." Her stomach threatened to rebel the way it had two weeks ago, and she struggled to ignore it.

"I helped a lot of kids back then."

She held his gaze. "I'll bet you did, Dave."

His mouth thinned. "Let's cut to the chase, Ms. Devereux. What do you want from me?"

"I want you to resign as DCFS director. Immediately."

A muscle in his jaw jumped. "You're out of your mind."

"No, I'm not. I'm offering you a choice. Resign or I go public."

He dropped all pretense of politeness. "Go public with what? Baseless accusations? You have no proof of anything, and no one is going to believe the word of a street punk. Which is what you were."

"Really, Dave? You want to risk that? You want me to go to the newspapers? The news stations' investigative reporters?"

He leaned toward her, his eyes narrowed. "The head of DCFS has a lot of power, Ms. Devereux. You start making accusations, and I'll shut down your little teen center so fast that you'll be on the street before you have time to take a breath. Is that what you want?"

"Threaten me all you like. It doesn't change what you are. Or what I have to do." She stood up, her legs shaking. "I'll give you a week or two to come up with a face-saving explanation. If you don't resign, you'll leave me no choice."

"I'm not resigning, Ms. Devereux." He leaned back in his expensive chair. "So bring it on. I'll be waiting for you."

She walked out of the office and down the hall. When she was out of sight, she slumped against the wall.

Had she really expected him to agree? To resign? From everything she'd learned about Doug Bascombe over the past two weeks, he was too power hungry, too egotistical to do that. But maybe she'd shaken his confidence a little. Maybe he'd think twice before he harmed any more children.

Until she could figure out a way to get him out of power, it was the best she could do.

HE'D BEEN AT FREEZONE for two weeks, and his knee hurt like hell.

Cal let the weights drop for the final time, then grabbed

his towel from the floor and wiped down his face. He had four more weeks. He needed to improve faster than this.

"Hey, Cal."

His agent, Jonas Grant, strolled up, wearing a suit and tie. Cal had never seen the guy without his armor, even here in the Cougars' weight room.

"Jonas. What are you doing here?" Cal swung his leg over the machine and managed to stand up without bracing himself.

Jonas glanced at his knee and quirked one eyebrow. "You're favoring that leg."

"Of course I am. I just finished lifting."

"How's it doing?"

"The knee is great."

Jonas glanced at it again and then looked quickly away, as if the thing had a contagious disease he didn't want to catch.

Like end-of-career-itis.

"You're good to go, then?"

"Absolutely. I'm here every morning, working with the trainers." Cal slung the towel over his shoulders and headed toward the lockers. "Four, five hours a day."

"Cal." Jonas put a hand on his arm, stopping him. "You can be honest with me. You're limping."

"Jeez, keep your voice down. It's a minor setback. Temporary."

"What was this setback?"

"I was playing basketball with the kids at CS yesterday." He played every day, and it had finally caught up with him.

"Are you out of your frigging mind? *Basketball?*" Jonas spoke in an incredulous whisper. "Do you *want* them to cut you?"

"It was mostly catch and throw," Cal muttered.

"Don't do it again, you dumb-ass. Do you have any idea how many hours I've spent on the phone massaging the coach's ego, trying to make sure you have a shot at a roster spot? And you're playing basketball with a bunch of loser kids?"

Those loser kids were keeping him at FreeZone. If they liked him, Frankie wouldn't be able to fire him and send him to jail. "Did you drive all the way here to harass me, Jonas? Or was there another reason?"

"Your father called me the other day. He wanted to know how your knee was doing. If you'd be ready for the season." The agent paused. "You should call him, Cal."

"What, now you're my mother?" He threw his towel in the hamper with a little more force than necessary. "He wants his season tickets. Get him a set, send them to him and keep him off my back."

"Whoa." Jonas held up his hands. "He's concerned about you."

"He's concerned about losing the perks that come with having a son in the NFL."

"That's harsh."

"It's the truth." His father had pushed him relentlessly for as long as he could remember. Cal's life had been about nothing but football since the first time he'd strapped on the pads. It had always been about what his father wanted. Not what he wanted. "Anything else, Jonas?"

"Nah. I'm stopping in to see the coach. I'll talk to you later."

"Can't wait," Cal muttered as his agent walked away.

FRANKIE WAS STILL SHAKING when she left the building housing the DCFS offices. She made her way to her car and sat in it until her breathing steadied and her heart slowed. She didn't want to go to FreeZone yet—she'd just sit and think or pace and think, and she'd done too much of that already. She needed to be distracted.

She needed her brothers.

Thirty minutes later, she opened the door to Mama's Place, the family restaurant in Chicago's Wildwood neighborhood. The rich scent of simmering sauces drifted over her. She was home. The restaurant wouldn't open for several hours, but she knew her brothers would be here.

Nathan managed the restaurant, and Marco was the chef. Frankie and all three of her brothers had grown up in the restaurant, walking there after school and doing their homework at the big round table in the corner of the dining room. Nathan and her second brother, Patrick, had worked as busboys, then as waiters.

When their parents were alive, she and Marco had been too young to work. But they'd been at the restaurant every day after school, helping to set up, doing homework, harassing the cooks.

The short hallway to the hostess table was lined with pictures of local celebrities, taken with her beaming mother and father. Yellowing reviews, raving about the food, were interspersed with the pictures.

As she always did, Frankie refused to look at the last laminated newspaper clipping, closest to the hostess station. It was her parents' obituary, complete with details about the car crash that had killed them. A garland of green, red, orange and white flowers were tucked into the top of the sheet, put there by friends and neighbors.

She'd begged Nathan to get rid of it, but he told her that everyone expected to see it. It would be disrespectful to take it down.

Sunlight had faded the flowers almost to white.

Nathan looked up from the table where he was working on his laptop. "Frankie!" He stood and enfolded her in a hug. "What are you doing here?"

She clung to him for a moment, inhaling his familiar smells of minty soap and coffee, then eased away. "I had some extra time and thought I'd see how you and Marco are doing."

"We're good." He frowned as he held her shoulders. "You look worn-out."

"Long couple of weeks." She managed a smile. "Lots going on."

"You seem thinner." He pushed open the swinging door to the kitchen and yelled, "Marco! Frankie's here. And she needs food."

"I'm not hungry, Nate." She hadn't been hungry for the past two weeks. And after her confrontation with Bascombe, her stomach was still in turmoil.

Before she could protest, Marco came bounding out of the kitchen holding a plate of ravioli in arrabiata sauce. He knew exactly what she liked.

"My favorite sister," Marco said, setting the plate on the table and hugging her tightly. His hands smelled like garlic, as they usually did. "Missed you, babe," he said, giving her a smacking kiss on the cheek.

"I missed you guys, too."

Nathan pressed her into a chair, and he and Marco sat down on either side of her.

"I made a few adjustments to the arrabiata," Marco said. "See what you think."

As she and Marco talked about cooking and Nathan chimed in with gossip and news about Mama's Place, the tension in her stomach eased. This was exactly what she needed—time with her family. No pressure. Just acceptance, love and food.

She sliced off a corner of a ravioli, swirled it in the

spicy sauce, then let the cheese filling explode in her mouth. When her stomach didn't object, she tried another. "So what do you think?" Marco asked eagerly, watching her.

"It's great. What did you change?"

"I upped the number of capers and added a little anchovy paste to the sauce."

"It's a winner," she said, eating another ravioli. She was actually hungry, she realized.

"Want a glass of wine?" Nathan asked.

"I'm going to FreeZone after this," she said, gesturing with her fork. "I can't drink."

"You work too hard, Frankie," Nathan said.

"Like you don't? That's what you do when you love your job."

A shadow crossed Nathan's face, and she set her fork on the plate. "Nate? What is it?"

"I need to take some time off, Frankie. Reevaluate stuff."

She'd never noticed the lines around her oldest brother's eyes. The mouth that used to smile constantly now turned down. "What kind of stuff? What's wrong, Nate?"

"Nothing in particular." He sighed. "Mama's Place. My life. The usual."

So much for her plan to talk to her brothers about Bascombe. "How can I help?"

"You want to move home and manage Mama's for a while?"

"I can't do that, Nate." She ached to help her brother, but she couldn't leave FreeZone. What would happen to her kids?

"I know, Frankie." He rubbed his hands over his face. "But I need a break."

Nathan had been in charge of Mama's Place for fourteen years. He'd been twenty-two when their parents were killed. He'd dropped out of college and come home to run the restaurant and raise his three younger siblings.

"We'll hire someone to manage Mama's, then. Unless Marco wants to do it?" She glanced at her younger brother, who held up his hands.

"Not me. I'm the food guy, not the business guy."

Nathan closed his eyes, then opened them and leaned toward her. "I wish you could do it, Frankie."

"Not in my skill set," she said, pushing the plate of food away. "I make cupcakes and take care of a bunch of teen-agers."

"If you ever need a break from those kids, let me know."

She slung an arm around his shoulders and hugged him. "What do you want to do?"

"Not sure. Travel, for one thing. Maybe go back to school. I always wanted to be a lawyer," he said wistfully.

"So go do that. You've raised us all, and we turned out okay." She grinned when Marco rolled his eyes.

"We turned out *awesome,* Bunny, and you know it," he said.

The old family nickname made her want to weep. When she'd been released from juvie, all three of her brothers had been waiting for her and hugged her fiercely. Called her Bunny.

She'd broken down, sobbing, in their arms.

She couldn't break down now. It was Nathan's turn to be comforted. Helped. She had to be strong for him.

"We'll figure this out, Nate," she said. Guilt flickered, and she tried to ignore it. Clearly, he wanted *her* to manage Mama's. But he would never insist.

Nathan had sacrificed so much for all of them. She should be willing to help out.

But what would the FreeZone kids do without her?

She had the Bascombe situation to deal with.

And Cal had four more weeks of CS.

As much as she wanted to step in and help her brother, she couldn't do it.

And that sucked.

As FRANKIE HEADED BACK toward the city, all she wanted was to go home. To hide in her apartment and lose herself in some mindless activity, like cleaning.

She didn't want to talk to anyone. To be in charge, to make decisions.

For the first time since she'd opened FreeZone, she didn't want to walk through that door.

She wanted to block all of it out, including Bascombe.

She couldn't do it, though. She'd promised the kids that she'd be there for them, no matter what. It was a promise she intended to keep.

And she was responsible for Cal, for making sure he got his community-service hours.

For the past two weeks, he'd pissed her off at least once a day, but he'd been charming about it. He didn't want to be there, but he managed to hide the fact from the kids. He'd become the go-to guy for math help, and for that alone she was grateful.

He also played basketball with the boys every day. She'd even seen Ramon smile once when Cal had made a hot-dog move and actually hit the basket.

Since he was doing what he was supposed to do, she needed to do her part. Which was get him out of FreeZone in time for his training camp.

As she got closer to the center, she turned on the car's CD player to get herself psyched for the afternoon. By the time she swung by the bakery for the cupcakes, Adele and Neko Case had helped her settle. She was an expert at compartmentalizing. She would put Bascombe and her brothers' problems in a box and bury it for the afternoon.

Ten minutes later, she parked her car in the church parking lot across the street and grabbed the white bakery box from her trunk. As she hurried toward FreeZone, she faltered when she saw Cal in front of the building, microphones stuck in his face.

That hadn't happened since his first day. Why now?

He spotted her before she reached them. "Here she is," he said. He shouldered his way through the reporters and took the bakery box from her hands. "We have a problem," he said in a low voice.

He set the box on the hood of his Escalade, then put his hand on her back to steer her through the crowd. She sighed when the reporters moved aside.

Red-and-black gang signs were spray-painted across FreeZone's windows. The symbols of the Insane Street Vipers.

Ramon's old gang.

CHAPTER SIX

THE PERFECT TOPPER to a crappy day.

Frankie had dealt with this before. Calmly. Rationally.

But she couldn't be calm or rational now. Anger rose in a choking wave. No one else was going to intimidate her today.

She drew a deep breath and closed her eyes. She couldn't let the reporters see her fury. They fed on emotion like sharks on chum. But before she could get control, Cal placed his hand on her waist and bent his head.

"I'm mad as hell, too, but don't let them see it," he said quietly. "It'll be on the news, and those ass-wipes will know they got to you."

"You think I don't know that?" she said under her breath. "They may not follow me around like dogs after a pork chop, but I've dealt with reporters before."

His hand was warm and heavy on her waist. "A pork chop? Really, Frankie? Come on, I'm at least a T-bone steak. Probably a filet."

She stifled a laugh and her anger began to ease. "Thank you," she murmured with a small nod.

She turned to face the reporters. Instead of letting go, Cal tightened his grip and his fingers pressed into her hip. She should have brushed them away, but she didn't want to draw the reporters' attention. She needed to stay on message.

"As you can see, a gang has targeted FreeZone. They

did so because we're a threat to them. FreeZone gives kids an alternative to joining a gang. It's a safe place for them to come after school, do their homework and meet their friends." She nodded at Cal. "Mr. Stewart and I will clean this up, then we'll welcome the kids. It's not the first time this has happened, and it won't be the last. We'll survive."

Cal's hand twitched when she mentioned other incidents, but he didn't speak. One of the reporters shoved a microphone in Frankie's face.

"The two of you look pretty comfortable together," the woman said, her gaze measuring the distance between Frankie and Cal, then drifting to where he touched her. "I guess it doesn't bother you to have a felon working with kids."

The burned-toast-and-stale-beer smell of the neighborhood grounded her. It reminded her what was at stake. "Mr. Stewart isn't a felon." She tried to step away from Cal, but he kept his hand in place. Her mind went blank for a moment.

"But he *has* been convicted of a crime," the reporter insisted.

Frankie forced herself to concentrate. She'd prepared for this question—had known someone would bring it up sooner or later.

"The judge agreed to expunge Mr. Stewart's conviction after he completes his community service. Many of our community-service volunteers come to us via the justice system, so this is no different. Yes, it was an act of violence, but Mr. Stewart didn't start the fight. He was trying to protect a woman. So I have no reservations about having him around the kids."

"Thank you," murmured Cal, still standing too close.

His hand lingered a moment longer, then he stepped away. Good. She didn't need to lean on anyone.

After a few more questions about gang activity in the Manor neighborhood, and additional photos of the window, the reporters began to drift away. Frankie shut the door firmly behind her and Cal, and slumped against the wall.

"Thank you for distracting me," she said quietly. "I was furious, and that's not the way to talk to reporters."

"They didn't see it," he said, his tone cool and distant. "You handled yourself like a pro."

She looked at him carefully for the first time. "You're angry."

"There's *gang graffiti* on your window. And when you said it was no big deal, you meant it."

"Of course I meant it. This is a gang neighborhood." Suddenly bone-tired, she sank to the floor. "There's always graffiti around."

He scowled down at her. "How can you be so casual about it? This is a teen center." She heard the reporters milling around behind the blinds. "Thank God they followed me today. Maybe they'll run a story about it."

Did she want that? No. Not with Bascombe in the background.

But there were a lot of reporters out there, and some carried video cameras. A sexy football player working at a community center was bound to get airtime. Just another reason to want him gone.

Sexy? She must be more tired than she'd realized.

"The gang signs. They're from Ramon's gang, aren't they?"

She pushed herself upright at the anger in his eyes. "Ramon's *former* gang. The Insane Street Vipers."

"Clearly, they haven't given up on him."

"That's not his fault." Even when she stood ramrod straight, she had to look up at Cal. She refused to back down. "Ramon isn't the problem here. T-Man and Speedball and the rest of their buddies are the problem."

"They targeted you because of Ramon."

"Yes, they did. Because he's trying to get away from them." Her head pounded as though someone had taken a sledgehammer to her temples. "And instead of arguing about it, we need to clean it up before the kids get here."

"Good luck with that," Cal said. "We have fifteen minutes."

"And that's about what it will take." She hurried into her office and grabbed a box from the bookcase, then hustled out the front door. The last of the reporters were leaving as she set the box on the sidewalk.

"See, this is what I'm talking about." Cal pointed at the plastic container. "You have a *kit* for cleaning up graffiti."

"Yes, I do," she said, her voice even. "Gangs like to tag buildings. We've been tagged before, and we will be again."

"Are you going to call the police?"

"There's no point." She rubbed her forehead. "They'll write it up, file it away and resent me for making them do the paperwork. I'll tell Don when he stops by today. He'll have the patrol cars do some extra drive-bys." She snapped on a pair of gloves. "So why are you pissed off?"

"Ramon is why I'm pissed off. You're inviting problems by letting him stay."

"I've known him for two months." She grabbed the bottle of paint remover and sprayed the window. The sharp scent of the solvent made her nostrils burn. "In the two weeks you've been here, Ramon has done nothing to deserve your anger. So drop the caveman routine. This is a gang neighborhood. Gangs tag buildings. Get over it."

"'Caveman'?" Cal swiped a pair of gloves, picked up a razor and began scraping at the symbols as she sprayed the solvent. "I'm not going to forget what happened during that confrontation on my first day here. I've spent my life around violence. I can see who likes it and who doesn't." The paint came off in red-and-black curls that looked like devilish cake decorations. "I don't care what bull Ramon has fed you, he likes violence."

Cal made another swipe and jerked his head toward the door. "I'll take care of this. You go get things ready for the kids."

"Fine." She grabbed the box of cupcakes off the hood of his car and went inside.

FreeZone was cool and quiet. She opened the blinds, switched on all the lights and put the bakery box in the display case, then circled the room, making sure everything was ready.

Instead of heading into her office, though, she leaned on one of the battered tables and watched Cal through the window. The paint was peeling steadily away, lying on the sidewalk in giant spirals. There were only a few smears left on the window.

She couldn't leave this tension simmering between them. The kids would pick up on it immediately. She headed toward the door, but before she got there, a group of girls appeared.

They stopped to talk to Cal, and he smiled at them as he worked. There was no sign of anger or unease as he chatted, and the girls giggled as they pointed at the window. Their smiles faded when he spoke, but he nodded toward the door, and they scampered in.

"Hey, Ms. Devereux," Harley Michaels called as they entered. She was twelve, and one of the youngest kids who came to FreeZone. The three girls with her were fourteen. "T-Man and Speedball came back, huh?"

"I'm not sure who it was," Frankie answered. "But the graffiti is gone, so it doesn't matter."

"Ramon's gonna be mad," one of the older girls said with relish. "I bet he'll fight them."

"Ramon isn't fighting anyone," Frankie said. "He gave that up when he quit the gang." Did he know what the Vipers had done? Could Cal possibly be right? Had he been part of it?

Damn it, she wouldn't let Cal poison her mind against the teen.

"You girls are early today," she said.

"We didn't stop by the mini-mart for a snack," Harley said. "We came straight here." She glanced out the window at Cal, and the other three girls giggled.

Oh, God. Of course the girls would crush on Cal. They put their heads together and whispered, then turned to stare at him again.

Fighting a smile, Frankie herded them toward the homework area. "I'm glad you didn't stop at the mini-mart. You can get a head start on your homework, then you'll have more time to just hang out."

"Okay," Harley said. The group settled at the end of one table, but there was more giggling and whispering than homework being done. Frankie finally sat next to them.

"Harley, do you have English homework?" When the girl nodded, Frankie asked, "You need help?"

"I'm good today, Ms. Devereux," she replied. She glanced at Cal again. "If I have a question, I'll ask Mr. Stewart."

"He's focusing on math," Frankie answered.

"I have math homework," Kerrie said.

Frankie didn't have the energy to deal with teenage

crushes today. "Why don't you get started while he's finishing with the window? He'll be out there for a while." She hoped.

CAL TOOK ONE LAST SWIPE at the glass and tried to avoid watching Frankie. She was sitting with the four girls, talking to one as they bent over a textbook. Her hair wasn't as spiky today, as if she'd tried to tame it. The rings were gone from her ears. And she was wearing a business suit rather than her usual cargo pants and tank top.

Where had she been? And what had she been doing?

Not that he cared. He was here for four more weeks, then he wouldn't see Frankie or FreeZone again.

He was just curious. Anyone would be.

The business suit had a short jacket and a tight skirt that hugged her ass, unlike those baggy pants. He always appreciated a nice ass.

Frankie's was world-class.

He flung a curl of paint away and it landed on his car. As he wiped it off, he glanced over his shoulder again. Frankie was bending over the table, helping the redheaded girl with something, and her skirt pulled taut.

Damn it. He crumpled the paper towel and heaved it toward the box. He'd been thinking about Frankie way too much lately.

The only think he needed to think about was the Cougars' playbook. Memorizing the new plays. The only thing he should be doing was getting his knee stronger.

Not working in this crummy place in a crummy neighborhood. Not thinking about the woman who wouldn't take his money and free up his time.

Not even if the anger that had flashed in her eyes when she saw the gang tags made them an even brighter blue.

He could still feel her hip beneath his fingers, firm muscle and bone that fit his hand perfectly.

He wiped the window one more time, then dug the dust-pan and brush out of Frankie's graffiti kit. Soggy curls of paint scattered as he swept, and he forced himself to calm down.

His knee ached when he straightened, reminding him of what Jonas had said. Reminding him of what he needed to focus on.

When he opened the door, Frankie pushed away from the table and hurried over. She'd been watching him.

"Thanks, Cal. I appreciate you cleaning up that mess for me." She was brisk and businesslike, as if heat had never sparked between them.

"I need to get rid of this mess," he said, more abruptly than necessary. "I assume there's a bin in the alley?"

"Yes, there is. Thank you."

"I'll be right back." He walked through the center to the back door, aware of Frankie and the girls watching him. He had to grit his teeth, but he managed not to limp.

In spite of what he'd said to Jonas that morning, his knee hurt like a son of a bitch. His agent was right—playing basketball with the boys was a dumb-ass thing to do. Even icing it at night didn't prevent the stiffness and pain when he got out of bed every morning.

Today he should help with homework and avoid basketball, but he knew he wouldn't. The minute he declined a pickup game because of his knee, someone would tweet about it. Or post it on Facebook.

The door opened behind him as he headed toward the bin in the alley, and by the time he finished cleaning up and putting everything away, another large group of kids had arrived. They looked older than the first four girls.

Cal sauntered over to Frankie. "So what's the plan, boss?"

Her pen bounced on the table, as if she was jittery. Nervous. Which made no sense.

Unless she was thinking about that moment in front of the reporters, too.

"Why don't you see who else needs homework help? Maria and I are working on her English paper."

"I need math help, Mr. Stewart," Kerrie said, then actually fluttered her eyelashes at him.

Cal froze.

Frankie touched the girl's arm and bit her lip. "You're almost done with your math, Kerrie. If you still need help when I finish with Maria, I'll help you."

"Yeah," he said hastily. "Ms. Devereux was just saying how she was hoping to work on some math today."

Frankie glanced at him, her gaze full of both amusement and something more private. Then she turned back to the dark-haired Maria.

He spun around too fast, and his knee reminded him that wasn't a good idea. What the hell was wrong with him? Women didn't stir him up. They didn't make him lose his cool. He was always calm with women. Charming and a little mysterious.

He'd been off balance since the moment he'd walked into FreeZone two weeks ago.

He didn't like it.

Didn't like anything about this place.

He glanced over at Frankie. Other than her ass in that suit.

She sat down, and Cal spotted Joey with a math book open in front of him and a puzzled look on his face. Okay, this he could handle. This he understood. "Need some help with that?"

"Yeah," the kid said with a sigh. "Algebra is so bogus."

Cal took a deep breath and glanced at the page. Equations. He could deal with that. "So what's giving you trouble?"

After helping two more kids with their math, Cal began to relax. He'd get through this day, then he'd have less than four weeks left. He could do this.

Although he hadn't looked, he knew Frankie was still helping the group of girls with their homework.

He stood up to find another kid with math trouble just as the door opened and Sean walked in.

His backpack was as huge as it had been on Cal's first day. But today, instead of appearing ready to take on the world, Sean looked as if the load was grinding him into the ground.

Before he could reach the table, Frankie intercepted him. She put a hand on his shoulder and asked him a question, but Sean shook his head. It didn't take a mind reader to know he was telling her everything was fine. His body language screamed *leave me alone.*

Frankie stepped back, then nodded, but glanced over her shoulder at him as she walked away.

Sean took a seat far away from the other kids. His hand shook as he pulled a stack of textbooks out of his pack, opened one and began flipping pages.

He was barely looking at the book.

This wasn't Cal's responsibility. He wasn't a damn social worker. But the kid looked upset. Scared, almost.

Before he could stop himself, Cal strolled over and slid into the seat next to him. "Hey, dude. What's up?"

Sean didn't look at him. "Hi, Mr. Stewart."

"Need some help with your homework?"

"No, thanks. I have to read a chapter in my history book." He kept flipping pages.

"You're late getting here."

Sean's hand froze for a moment, then he continued flipping. "Yeah. I was talking to…to one of my teachers."

Cal put his hand on the book, forcing him to stop. "Sean. What happened?"

The boy didn't answer, so Cal leaned closer. "If you don't want to tell me, that's cool. I'll go get Ms. Devereux. You can talk to her."

"No," he said quickly. "I don't want to tell her."

Cal cleared his throat and wiped his suddenly sweaty palms on his thighs. "Listen, I know sometimes there are things a guy wants to talk to another guy about." Jeez, could this be any more awkward? "If it's, uh, guy stuff, I'm cool with that." His face burned. He should have stayed at the other table. Ignored the kid.

"It's nothing like that." Sean looked horrified. "I mean, I don't have any guy problems or anything."

Thank God.

Sean played with the edges of the pages, then slammed the textbook shut. "Three guys from Ramon's gang stopped me when I was coming here. They told me they needed a smart guy, that I should join."

Cal fisted his hands beneath the table. "Yeah? What did you do?"

"I told them I wasn't interested, and walked away. I heard them talking behind me. I didn't look back, though. I just kept going."

"That took a lot of guts, Sean," Cal said quietly. "To just walk away." Sean smoothed a page of the book and didn't look at him. "Are you sure about which gang it was?"

He nodded. "I know the gangs in this neighborhood. It was the Vipers."

Cal wanted to tell the kid that it would be all right, that the gang would leave him alone, that he would be safe. But probably none of that was true. "Can your dad or mom drive you over here after school?"

Sean gave him a withering look. "If they could, I wouldn't have to come here, would I? My dad works. My mom…my mom passed two years ago."

"I'm sorry," Cal said gruffly.

The boy lifted one shoulder. "It's okay."

Cal had no idea what to suggest. Why had he gotten involved? He had no experience with this.

As he scanned the room, his gaze landed on the four younger girls who'd arrived early. "Do you think this happens to other kids?"

Sean shrugged. "I don't know. Maybe."

"Those girls over there." He nodded at the group. "They're younger than you, right? Do you think the gangs bother them?"

"They've never said anything."

"Maybe you should walk them to FreeZone after school." A group might give all of them some protection. "I don't like the idea of the gang hassling the younger kids."

Sean was maybe a year older than the girls, but he sat straighter. "No. They're too young to deal with that sh… stuff."

"Should I ask them?"

The boy suddenly looked unsure. "They go to the junior high next to the high school. They get out before me."

"I bet they'd wait for you."

He stared at the book. "I don't know."

Cal tapped Sean's biceps with his fist. "Let me work it out."

He felt the boy watching as he walked over to the girls. He'd lost his mind. He'd rather face a smirking middle linebacker than these girls, who watched him with bright, eager eyes and blushes.

"Hey, ladies," he said, and all of them giggled. "I need to ask you something."

Five minutes later, the girls had agreed to wait for Sean after school, and Sean was working on his homework, his shoulders finally relaxed. But Cal needed to talk to Frankie. There had to be something they could do to stop the damn bangers from harassing these kids.

He began to search the room for her and stopped. When had this become his problem? Then he caught Frankie's eye and she nodded at him, as if she approved of him talking to Sean.

Cal wasn't doing it to get her approval. He'd gotten sucked in, was all.

Then he saw that shadow in her eyes again. Sadness.

About Sean? Did she know what had happened? Had it happened before?

If so, why hadn't she done anything about it?

Before Cal realized it, he was walking toward her.

CHAPTER SEVEN

FRANKIE WATCHED CAL stand up and head her way. Anticipation skittered over her nerves and she stood, too.

"What…?" He stopped, apparently noticing that all the kids were watching them. Waiting, as if they expected a show. "Can we talk in your office for a moment, Ms. Devereux?" He smiled through gritted teeth.

She led the way. He followed too closely, and she could have sworn she felt the heat of his hand near her back. But he didn't touch her.

He closed the door behind him once they stepped into her cramped office. "You knew, didn't you?" The accusation was clear in his tone.

"Knew what?" she asked, drawing herself straighter.

"About Sean. And the gangs."

"Oh, God." She sank onto her desk and gripped the edge. "What happened?"

Cal paced her tiny office. It took him three steps each way, and he was so close that he brushed against her leg. She drew her feet up and wrapped her arms around her knees.

"A couple of bangers stopped him on his way over here today." Cal braced his hand on the wall above her head, and the photos on her bulletin board fluttered. "They wanted him to join their gang."

"Which gang?" she whispered, dreading his answer.

"The Vipers." His eyes narrowed, and she saw the dark

ring around his green irises. "But you knew that, didn't you?"

She rubbed the heel of her hand over her forehead, trying to push the headache away. Why did everything have to happen at the same time? "I didn't know they'd approached him today. But that's the reason why he's here."

"What?" Cal straightened.

"Sean's father, Robert, came in and talked to me a few months ago. Sean was getting pressure to join the Vipers. Older teens stopped him at school, followed him home, waited for him in the morning. Robert was scared, and he didn't know what to do."

"Did you tell him to have their asses arrested?"

Of course she had. She'd been just as angry as Cal. "It's not that simple. It was never the same kids. They didn't threaten him. They didn't do anything that could be construed as menacing. All they did was offer him membership in their 'club.' That's why Sean started coming here. Now his dad drives him to school every morning and picks him up here at six. We've got him covered."

"Not completely." A muscle in Cal's jaw twitched. "Do they harass all the kids this way?" He flexed and released his hands, over and over, as if he was imagining them around one of the Vipers' necks.

"No, Sean was a special target."

"How come?"

She slid off the desk, brushed past him to peek out into the main room. Julio was playing basketball. The four younger girls were whispering together. Everyone else was doing homework. She closed the door again and turned to face Cal.

His evident frustration made her want to touch him. Reassure him. She crossed her arms over her chest. "A couple of reasons. He's a smart kid, and everyone in his school knows it. He wants to be a doctor."

"Yeah, he told me that."

"He did?" An ugly worm of jealousy wriggled beneath her skin. She was supposed to be the one the kids confided in.

Cal shrugged. "Came up in a conversation."

This was *her* center. They were *her* kids.

Frankie swallowed the resentment. It was good Sean had confided in someone. That was probably why he'd talked to Cal today, after brushing her off.

"So what does him wanting to be a doctor have to do with the Vipers trying to recruit him?" Cal asked. "Even those losers can't be stupid enough to think Sean can be their medic."

"Gangs are a business, and every business needs smart people. Especially smart people who are good at math. The other kids say Sean's practically a math genius."

Frankie looked at a photo of Sean with his mother and father. She had a picture of every one of her kids up there. The family shot was the one Sean had given her.

"Besides being smart, Sean is vulnerable," she said quietly. "That's who the gangs pick on. He's quiet. Shy. He doesn't have a lot of friends at school. Some kids in this neighborhood are suspicious of smart kids. Excelling in school, going to college…those aren't part of the culture around here. Sean is different."

"That sucks." Cal slammed his hand against the bookcase, which shuddered against the wall.

"Yeah, it does." She slumped against the door. "He's been safe so far. And we'll make sure he stays that way. Don knows what's going on. He's keeping an eye on Sean."

Cal bent and rubbed his left knee absently, as if he didn't even realize he was doing it. When he straightened, he shifted his weight off his left foot. "Sean, Harley, Lissy, Kerrie and Maria are going to walk here together after school. I thought a group would be safer for all of them. But maybe I shouldn't have done that. Maybe I just made it *less* safe for the girls."

"No, it was a good idea. But I can't believe you actually talked him into it." Jealousy was squirming again. "I tried to get Sean to walk with a bunch of the other kids, but he wouldn't do it. I figured he didn't want them to think he was a sissy."

Cal shrugged. "I framed it as him watching out for the younger girls. Appealed to his male ego." He smiled, and suddenly all the oxygen rushed out of the room. "Men are stupid like that. Stroke our egos and the large brain disengages."

"No kidding. I'm just surprised you admit it." He hadn't taken his gaze off her face, and she couldn't look away.

"I'm familiar with my own operating instructions." He leaned closer and his smile faded. "Where did *you* learn how to handle men, Frankie?"

Her heart was pounding so hard she was certain the sound was bouncing off the office walls. "Three brothers. It was figure them out or get crushed."

"I can't imagine anyone crushing you."

It felt as if he'd moved closer, but he was still leaning against the desk.

"No one does. Not anymore."

"But someone did." Cal's eyes hardened.

"Tried. Didn't succeed. Ancient history." The words conjured Bascombe in his expensive suit and fancy office. He wouldn't succeed this time, either.

To steer the conversation away from this dangerous topic, she said, "I've been wondering something. Why did that guy in the bar keep poking at you? Didn't he know what would happen?"

She hadn't thought Cal's eyes could get any more distant. "He wanted to be a tough guy. Show what a big man he was by fighting with a football player."

"Is that why he started shoving his girlfriend around?" she asked, horrified. "To get your attention?"

"Who knows what was going on in his peanut brain? The woman was half his size, and I wasn't about to stand there and let him whale on her." Cal leaned closer. "Anyone who picks on someone smaller or weaker is a worthless piece of trash. Trash needs to be disposed of. Like the guys who hassled Sean."

Cal's eyes glittered. "The guy who tried to crush you?" His voice dropped. "I would have done the same thing to him."

"I, uh, managed by myself," she said. "But I appreciate the sentiment." Maybe she shouldn't have asked about Cal's club incident.

"You shouldn't have had to." He touched her cheek, then slid his hand through her hair to cup her head. His palm was warm and strong. Huge. But his fingers were gentle. Tentative. Careful not to hold too tightly.

His eyes darkened as they stared at each other. A hint of blond whiskers gleamed on his cheeks, and she wanted to reach up and feel them rasp against her fingers. She wanted to touch his mouth and see if it was as soft as it looked.

Slowly, he lifted his other hand to her head. He touched her hair, rubbing his palm over the ends, then caressed her scalp. Heat rushed through her, and she swayed toward him.

"Frankie?" he murmured, and his voice broke the spell. She backed away abruptly, and he let her go. They stared at each other for another heartbeat, before she spun around and yanked open the door.

"Frankie, wait," she heard him say, but she focused on the kids still bent over their homework. Not on the man behind her.

She and Cal had been in her office less than five minutes.

It felt as if she'd been gone for hours.

Cal was still in there. Was he tweeting again?

Maybe he was shaken up, too, an evil voice whispered. *Maybe he's trying to compose himself.*

Which was ridiculous. Cal knew better than to try to start something with her.

She knew better, too.

But he'd handled Sean perfectly. He'd made sure Sean would be safer, and did it in a way that made the boy feel good about himself. She had to respect that.

She didn't want to. It was easier to think of Cal as a publicity hound with the depth of a puddle. She wanted to assign him simple chores and dismiss him.

It was one moment, she reminded herself. One time he'd stepped up. If it happened again, she'd have to rethink her opinion of him.

Until then, he was just the guy doing community service at her place. A guy who'd even tried to bribe his way out of it.

A guy who was sexy as hell.

But no more than that.

Voices rose from the computer area, and she turned to see three kids arguing over who got to use the two computers. By the time she had sorted it out, her head was pounding.

As she watched the teens settle down, she felt Cal come up behind her.

"Everything okay?"

She sighed. "I put in a grant request for three more computers over two months ago. Damn DCFS is dragging their feet."

"Anything I can do?"

"If there was something to do, I'd be doing it," she said, watching Jesse's fingers fly over the keyboard while Lissy hovered, waiting her turn.

"Well, if anyone's ass needs kicking, I'm your man."

She spun around, appalled, to find him grinning.

"I'm going to find another victim," he said. "You're way too easy."

He strolled away, and she watched him go. *Easy?*

CAL FELT FRANKIE'S GAZE follow him, but he wasn't going to look back. He'd managed to lighten things up, and that's the way he wanted to leave it.

What the *hell* had he been thinking in the office? He'd been ready to devour her.

She hadn't seemed interested in stopping him.

Exactly what he needed right now—do something stupid with the woman supervising his community service, get tossed out of her teen center, go directly to jail. Do not pass Go. Do not make it to training camp.

Not going to happen.

He knew what was important.

Football. It was all he had, all he knew how to do.

Nothing could make him screw that up.

FOR THE NEXT WEEK, Cal kept his eye on the prize. Training camp. He got to the weight room even earlier than usual, did more reps than usual. He put in his time at FreeZone, left as soon as the kids did.

He kept his distance from Frankie, too.

She'd gone back to her baggy pants and T-shirts. Her hair was spiky again, and the hoops were back in her ears. He could almost believe he'd imagined the business suit. But the memory of her bent over the table in that tight skirt was burned into his brain.

He stayed out of the office. There would be no repeats of that too-intimate moment.

Not that she showed any inclination to repeat it. She'd been distracted all week. On the phone more than normal. And she'd spent a lot of time on that laptop of hers, with the office door closed.

Her eyes were shadowed, as if she wasn't sleeping at night.

As he helped another kid with homework, only a small part of his mind was on the math. The rest of him wondered what was going on with Frankie. What had taken her intense focus off the kids? What had turned her fierceness into weariness?

He wasn't going to try to find out. Getting closer to her was a slippery slope that could end only in disaster. No matter how hot she'd looked in that suit.

Three more weeks. That's all he had to survive. Then he'd be gone, and Frankie would be a distant memory.

As he stood up to move to another kid, a basketball rolled to a stop against his foot. Angry that the thought of not seeing Frankie again depressed him so much, Cal picked up the ball and threw it back at Julio, who turned with a nod and began shooting again.

The kid was pretty good, but basketball was all he did. He needed to diversify a little.

Why? a tiny voice asked. Cal hadn't diversified. He'd been as single-minded as Julio, and he'd made it.

For a moment, Cal let himself wonder what would have happened if he'd tried something else besides football. Another sport, maybe. Or avoided athletics altogether. What would his life be like today?

He couldn't imagine it. And he didn't need to. He was a star. Millions of people knew who he was. The cheers from the crowd on Sunday afternoon were all he needed.

Three weeks. Three weeks and he'd hear those cheers again.

The door opened and Ramon came in. He hadn't shown up since the day the windows had been tagged, and Cal had taken that as an admission of guilt.

What was he doing here now?

CHAPTER EIGHT

WHILE LISSY WORKED on a take-home history test, Frankie sat beside her and waited for the girl's questions. Lissy was a smart kid, but she had no self-confidence. Frankie spent time with her almost every day.

Today, though, she was distracted. Her gaze kept drifting to Cal as he moved from one teenager to the next, helping with math homework. Every time he stood, he winced ever so slightly. When he was standing, he often shifted from his left foot to his right, and it seemed as if he wasn't bearing much weight on his left knee. His bad knee.

Frankie had looked him up on the internet and seen a gruesome YouTube video from the game where he'd been injured. He'd leaped up to make an interception and had been tackled from the side. The two men had hit the ground, tangled together.

Cal hadn't gotten back up.

She'd found the details of his injury, descriptions of his surgeries and status reports from the Cougars. She'd read everything and wondered if he'd be able to play football again.

It hadn't been snooping. He was working for her, after all, and it was her responsibility to find out as much as possible about him. She was entrusting him with her kids.

She'd found pictures of him at rehab, as well. The photos had been snapped with a cell phone, but they'd been clear enough to see the sweat rolling down his face and his mouth twisting with pain. Feeling like a voyeur, she'd shut down her computer.

"I think I got them all right, Ms. Devereux," Lissy said, and Frankie dragged her attention back to the girl.

"Great. I knew you could do it, Lissy. You're a smart kid. Do you have any other homework?"

"I have to read a short story for English."

Frankie put a hand on the girl's shoulder. "Good. Why don't you finish that?"

As Lissy opened another book, Cal pushed away from the table again. Because Frankie was watching for it, she saw the tiny wince when he put his weight on his left leg. Her chair scraped against the old linoleum as she stood, and the door of FreeZone opened at the same time. Ramon walked in.

Cal intercepted him before she could. She reached them in time to hear Cal say in a low voice, "You hear what I'm saying, man?"

"You crazy, dude," Ramon said, holding up his hands. "You gotta chill."

"You better chill, too." Cal leaned forward just enough to make Ramon retreat. "Dude."

Cal's back blocked the light from the door as the man and the boy stared at each other. Then Ramon glanced at her. "I ain't a Viper no more. Tell him, Ms. D."

Cal hadn't moved. She stepped between him and Ramon, and the tension burned. "Lay off, Cal. Ramon, you go sit down."

Cal widened his eyes. "Ramon and I were just getting reacquainted. Right, *dude?*"

"Whatever." Ramon began to shuffle away, keeping up his baggy pants with one hand.

Frankie held Cal's gaze for a long moment, but he merely raised his eyebrows.

She turned to Ramon. "Where have you been? We haven't seen you for a week."

"I got stuff to do," he said, avoiding her eyes.

"What kind of stuff, Ramon?" she asked, dreading his answer.

"Family stuff." He scowled. "I ain't gone back to the Vipers. I promised, Ms. D."

"Yes, you did." She studied his expression, wondering if he knew about the graffiti. If he did, he was good at hiding it. Finally she said, "Okay, Ramon. Get started with your homework."

"We still good for tonight?" he asked in a low voice.

"I'll be there."

Ramon nodded, smirked at Cal, then sauntered off. Red boxers showed above his waistband, and the laces on his basketball shoes were untied. When the youth sat down at the end of a table, Cal turned his gaze on Frankie.

"Are you going somewhere with him tonight?" he asked, his voice rising as if he thought she was insane.

"No, I'm not."

He stared at her, as if expecting her to explain what Ramon had said, but she just waited. Finally he said, "Do you have a job for me, Frankie?"

"What did you say to Ramon?"

"I was welcoming him back."

"A friendly chat." She narrowed her eyes.

"Yep." Cal didn't say anything more, but she was aware of the kids watching them curiously. She grabbed Cal's arm and dragged him to the corner of the room beyond the couches. As soon as they were far enough away to avoid being overheard, she let him go.

"You've been doing a good job here," she said, trying to keep the anger out of her voice. The disappointment she didn't want to acknowledge. "You figured out what Sean needed last week. The kids think you're some kind of math genius. Then you went all Neanderthal on Ramon. What's wrong with you?"

"*Neanderthal?* I told him I'd be watching him. That's it." He rocked back on his heels. "I didn't threaten him. Didn't accuse him of anything. I simply pointed out that he'd been gone, and welcomed him back."

Frankie closed her eyes and massaged her temples. "Butt out, Cal. I'm handling Ramon and the gang thing."

"Sure you are." His expression cooled. "That's why they're tagging you. Targeting your kids. Showing up here to talk to one of their 'former' members." Cal edged closer, using his foot to shove aside a wastebasket in his way. "You're handling it just fine."

"I know what I'm doing," she said through clenched teeth. "I live in this neighborhood. I've been on the str—" She snapped her mouth closed, horrified at what she'd almost revealed.

That's what happened when you didn't keep a tight rein on yourself.

His gaze sharpened. "You've been where?"

"Never mind. It's not important. What I'm trying to say is I know about the real world. I have no illusions."

He didn't take his gaze off her face. "That's not what you were going to say, Frankie."

"It's all you're going to get."

After a long moment, he nodded. "Fair enough. I'm here because I don't want to go to jail. You're letting me stay because you need help. We both know where we stand."

His expression changed to the one he'd worn when he arrived at FreeZone. Impersonal. Unruffled. His celebrity face.

The private person she'd seen earlier had vanished. It was as if the man who'd been angry about the graffiti, worried about Sean, having a serious conversation with one of her kids, had never existed.

All that was left was his public persona. The football star.

"I'll see if anyone needs help with their math."

He moved past her toward the kids, but she grabbed his wrist. It was thick and muscular, and the fine hairs on his arm tickled her palm.

He glanced down at her hand, then slowly met her gaze.

She let him go. "Cal, I... Never mind." She closed her eyes. "Math help is great. Thank you."

He strolled over to the kids without looking back, then paused with his hands on his hips. His chest rose and fell too fast.

The kids had been watching them, but when Cal stood there, motionless, they all bent their heads to their books. Even Ramon.

Finally, Cal glanced at the textbooks open on the table and sat down next to Alysha. He said something to the girl, and they began poring over the page together.

Half an hour later, when homework time was almost over, the kids had calmed down. Frankie wished she could say the same for herself.

As she worked with the teens, she always knew where Cal was. Whenever she glanced at him, he was listening to what a kid was saying, explaining something in a low voice or scribbling on a piece of paper.

Willing. Helpful. Apparently knowledgeable about math.

Impersonal.

He didn't have conversations about anything other than math, as far as she could tell. He didn't joke with the kids or even look at them as if they were individuals.

He was doing his job.

That was it.

All because of her slip of the tongue. And her refusal to tell him what she'd been about to say.

She didn't tell *anyone* about her past. Her brothers knew some of it, but even they didn't know everything.

Now that past had come back to bite her, and there was no way she was sharing it with Cal.

For the first time that she could remember, she wasn't enjoying her afternoon with the kids. She wanted the day to be over.

She glanced at her watch. "Okay, everyone. Time for snacks."

Chairs scraped as the teens pushed away from the table, and the thuds of textbooks closing filled the air. Alysha and Julio went into the back for the milk, carrots and fruit. Harley opened the cupcakes. Tyrone got the glasses and napkins.

Cal glanced at her from the other side of a table. "You've got a well-oiled machine."

"It's good for them to have responsibilities."

"Yeah." He shoved his hands into his pockets.

The silence grew heavy, and she wondered what he was thinking. "Help yourself to a cupcake," she finally said. "Or some fruit or vegetables."

"I'll wait until the kids have had theirs."

"Trust me, there are enough cupcakes to go around."

As Cal strolled over to the case, Lissy passed him, heading toward Frankie. He said something to her, and she started, then juggled the cupcake she was holding.

Lissy glanced at Frankie, then said in a low voice, "They're usually a lot better. But they're still pretty."

Ouch.

Lissy had been practically whispering, but sound echoed in the huge room. And she was right.

Today, the cupcakes were ordinary. She'd been too distracted to concentrate at the bakery lately. Even her never-fail designs had deserted her.

A week had gone by since her confrontation with Bascombe, and she hadn't heard a thing from him. She'd give him a few more days, then she'd start researching some local reporters.

As the kids ate, Frankie gathered scraps of paper left on the tables. Out of the corner of her eye, she watched Cal wait until all the kids had taken their snack, then he selected a cupcake. Blue-and-violet piping crisscrossed the top of the icing.

Really boring.

He took a big bite as he headed toward her, then stopped dead. He stared at the dark brown cake, white icing and stupid piping for a moment, before taking another bite.

"Exceptional cupcakes," he said when he reached her. One more bite and it was almost gone. "You know how to bake." His words were polite. Well mannered. He could have been speaking to anyone.

"Glad you like them."

"I do. You ever think of setting up one of those fancy cupcake shops?"

"Nope. I bake in order to keep FreeZone open. If I had my own bakery, FreeZone would disappear."

"Maybe—"

She held up her hand. "Don't start. Please. I'm glad you like the cupcakes, but I'm not interested in my own bakery. And I have too much on my plate right now to argue about it."

"What are you talking about?"

She shook her head. "Forget it. I spoke without thinking."

"You've been doing a lot of that today." Cal turned away and headed toward the basketball area.

Tyrone hurried over. "You playing ball with us, man?" He held up a fist for Cal to bump.

"Sure." He touched his fist to the boy's.

Frankie knew Tyrone hadn't noticed Cal's slight hesitation. But she had. "Sorry, Tyrone, not now. I have something Mr. Stewart needs to do."

The lanky teen grinned. "Too bad. We'll have to kick Julio's a…butt without you, dude."

Cal watched him hurry away, then turned to her. "What do I have to do?"

"I have several more thank-you letters to get out, and since you rewrote my last one, I know you know how to do it. I'd like you to take care of that this afternoon."

"I'll stay later and do it then."

Did the idiot have no sense of self-preservation? "No, I need to leave on time tonight."

Cal's gaze narrowed, and she saw the question in his eyes. *What are you doing with Ramon?* Finally, he nodded. "I'll take care of the letters." He glanced at the boys playing basketball, then disappeared into her office.

CAL FOUND THE MANILA FOLDER on her small, messy desk. He sat in the chair and glanced at the list of donors and amounts.

Did she think he was out of control? Was she afraid he'd pound Ramon into the ground? Pick a fight? Lay him out on the scuffed floor?

The laptop almost tipped when he opened it. He might want to straighten that banger out, but he wouldn't do it like that.

No one had more self-control than Cal.

What had she almost said?

It didn't matter. She'd caught herself before the conversation could get too personal, and that was all the reminder he needed. He didn't belong in this world. He knew crap about working with kids.

He worked steadily through the donor list, feeling adrift. Lonely.

He'd known he shouldn't play basketball, but wanted to do it, anyway. He'd started because he wanted the kids to like him. He continued because he'd had a good time.

And wasn't that the height of irony? He actually enjoyed playing ball with a bunch of snot-nosed high-school punks.

He was still pissed off when a current of air brushed his neck and he inhaled Frankie's scent. He spun around to find her leaning against the door frame.

"Thanks for getting those letters ready." She plucked them off the desk and stuck them into a deep black bag, then pulled them out with a frown. "I didn't realize there were so many. Thank you." Holding his gaze, she tucked them back into her bag. "That's a huge help."

"It also kept me away from Ramon, didn't it?"

"What are you talking about?"

"You think I don't know why you sent me to my room? You were afraid I'd get into it with him, weren't you?"

She slung the bag over her shoulder. "You did say you'd be my enforcer." There was a tiny smile in her eyes that disappeared when he stood up.

"Do you really think I'd be that stupid? I'm here because I don't want to go to jail, Frankie. I'm not going to jeopardize that by hitting a teenager. I may be a dumb jock, but I do have some impulse control."

"You're not a dumb jock, Cal. And that's not why I asked you to finish the letters."

"Why, then?"

The bag started to slip off her shoulder, and she shoved it back into place. "I saw you rubbing your knee. Keeping your weight off it. I didn't think playing basketball was a good idea for you."

It had been a long time since someone thought about what would be good for him. Since anyone had cared. Because he didn't want to examine the pleasure that moved through him, Cal went on the attack.

"I'm not one of your kids, Frankie. I don't need a do-gooder to help me make the right decisions." The psychobabble came out with a snarl, and he felt a flash of satisfaction when her face paled.

"Maybe you do. You would have played with the boys if I hadn't asked you to do this instead."

"It would have been my choice."

"Fine." She adjusted the bag on her shoulder again. "Ruin your months of rehab. Stretch those rebuilt ligaments too much. You're right. It's none of my business."

Another ripple of pleasure moved through him. "I didn't know you were a football fan."

"What are you talking about?"

"You know a lot about my injury and rehab."

"I read the papers," she said. "It's not like it's a big secret." She avoided his gaze, focusing instead behind him.

She turned abruptly and walked out of the office. A few moments later, the lights went off. "Come on, Cal. I need to get going."

"What about cleaning up?"

"I'll come in early and do it tomorrow. You're welcome to join me, if you want more hours. But I have to be somewhere at seven tonight."

Somewhere with Ramon.

Cal slammed off the lights in the office and walked

across the center to where she waited by the door. He didn't limp. He wouldn't give her the satisfaction.

"Where do you have to be?"

She shifted the bag to her other shoulder. "None of your business."

"You're not walking in this neighborhood, are you?"

"I live in this neighborhood. I walk here all the time."

The sun was a huge orange globe sliding behind the buildings across the street. He moved between her and the door and blocked her way. "It's getting dark."

"Not for another hour," she said impatiently. "Out of my way, Cal. I can't be late."

She wasn't going to tell him where she was going.

He was determined to find out, anyway. Only because he didn't trust Ramon as far as he could throw him.

Frankie was too trusting. Someone needed to make sure she was safe.

"Fine," he said. "What time should I be here tomorrow?"

"Two-thirty should be plenty of time."

"I'll see you then."

He walked her to her car, and neither of them spoke. She wrenched open the door, tossed her bag onto the passenger seat and slid behind the wheel. "Good night, Cal," she said, then slammed the door without waiting for a response.

As soon as she started the engine, he headed for his SUV. When she drove past, he made a U-turn and followed her.

CHAPTER NINE

THE PLUME OF BLUE EXHAUST spewing from Frankie's rusted tailpipe made it easy to follow her car.

Cal scowled as he watched her weave in and out of traffic. Apparently, she took stupid chances while driving, too.

He slowed as she pulled into the gated parking lot in front of an aging three-story building. The sign above it said High School, but the actual name was blacked out. There were gang signs above the smear of paint.

Why the hell hadn't the staff gotten rid of the tag as soon as it happened? A gang couldn't be allowed to claim a school.

A gate swung open and a guard waved Frankie through. Cal waited until she'd parked before he pulled up to the gate.

The guard eyed his Escalade, and Cal rolled down the window. "I'm with Ms. Devereux."

"She didn't say anything about someone with her."

"You know Frankie," Cal said with what he hoped was a fond smile. "She's too focused on her kids to think about anything else." Or notice someone following her.

The guard's face relaxed. "Yeah, that's Frankie. Woman needs to get a life."

Cal winked. "Working on it."

The man laughed. "Don't work too hard. This neighborhood needs FreeZone. Don't know what our kids would do without it."

"Wouldn't dream of taking her away. Just giving her something else to think about."

The guard raised the gate. "We all need that," he said. He glanced over his shoulder. "You better hurry. Doesn't look like she's waiting for you."

"Like I said. Absentminded." Cal waved to the guard and drove into the lot. The asphalt was broken and crumbling, with weeds growing through the cracks. He parked next to Frankie's beater and hurried after her.

He caught up with her as she opened the heavy metal door to the school. "Hey, Frankie."

She spun around and let the door close with a hollow bang. One of the boarded-up windows in the door shuddered. "Cal? What are you doing here?"

"Following you. And it wasn't easy. You drive like a maniac."

"You *followed* me?" Her voice cut through the cool evening air like a knife. "Why the hell would you do that?"

"I was worried about you. You talked about doing something with Ramon this evening, and I didn't think that was safe. I thought you might need help with him."

"As you can see, I'm fine." She stepped closer, and her eyes sparked. "Still in one piece."

"So far." He gestured toward the door. "You haven't gone into the school yet."

"There are only teachers left here. And there's a security guard inside. So you can leave with a clean conscience."

"Can't do that. I promised the guard at the gate I'd keep an eye on you. He's worried, too, you know."

"George?" She frowned. "Why would he be worried about me?"

"He knows you need to get a life."

She scowled. "And you're so qualified to give me advice

about that?" A gust of wind blew around the corner of the building, plastering her cargo pants and bulky blue sweater against her body. It emphasized how small she really was. How vulnerable.

She stood taller, and all sense of fragility vanished. "What's in your life, other than football?"

He ignored the twist of dread. "For the next fifty hours, my life is all about FreeZone. So I have to make sure you're okay. If you can't keep FreeZone open, I'm screwed. I don't finish my CS, I don't get to training camp." He'd always been good at keeping his eye on the prize.

And thinking on his feet.

"Are you *kidding* me? You think you're my...my bodyguard or something?" She yanked open the door so hard it bounced against the brick wall. The squares of wood replacing three of the panes of glass shuddered again.

He grabbed the door and held it steady. "Or something."

"Or nothing. Get lost, Cal. Go find a life for yourself. I don't need your help."

"Are you meeting Ramon here?"

"That's still none of your business." Her eyes flickered toward the door.

"You are," he said with satisfaction. "How come?"

"In what universe is this any of your concern?"

"I already told you. I have a vested interest in keeping you safe."

"You are such a pain in my ass. Leave now and I'll pretend this never happened." She turned into the doorway so quickly that her bag swung around in a weighted arc. The thing looked heavy enough to knock a person out.

"Frankie." He stopped the door from closing with one hand.

She stopped. Took a deep breath. Turned around. "What?"

"Why are you here?" He was careful to keep his tone neutral this time, avoiding all hint of accusation.

She studied him for a long moment. Finally, she said, "I'm meeting with Ramon and one of his teachers."

"Why you?"

"Because his homeroom teacher wants to talk to him about his failing grades and told him he had to have an adult with him. Ramon asked me if I could be here."

"Where are his parents? Or his guardian?"

"His father took off years ago. His mother is a junkie."

Cal squashed the flicker of compassion; no matter what his story was, the kid had chosen to join a gang. "So you came here after FreeZone? By yourself?" She had to have been up before dawn to work at the bakery. She'd spent several difficult hours at FreeZone. Now she was here for a frigging parent-teacher conference.

"Cal, I'm perfectly safe." Her irritation had disappeared, replaced by weariness. "Thanks for your concern, but you should go home. Sit on your couch. Ice your knee, or whatever it is you do to it. I'll see you tomorrow."

"I'll sit in the meeting with you."

"What?" Her forehead wrinkled, as if he was speaking a foreign language. "Why?"

"United front," he said. "Show of strength. Let the teacher see there are two people who care about this kid."

"But you *don't* care about Ramon," she said quietly.

"I don't trust him. But I'm here now. You might as well use me." Cal stepped closer and let the door close behind him.

Frankie glanced at her watch and shook her head. "I don't have time to argue with you. I'm already late."

She stopped at the glassed-in booth near the second doorway and smiled at the uniformed security guard. Then she took off at a fast walk, but Cal kept up with her easily.

There were some lights in the halls, but they weren't full strength. Lockers lined the walls, like soldiers on watch and on alert.

It looked nothing like the clean, well-maintained suburban high school he'd attended, and the inequity was disturbing.

Unjust.

Frankie stepped into a stairwell and hurried up to the next floor. The place smelled like every high school he'd ever been in—overripe bananas, the faint stink of unwashed gym clothes, the aroma of books.

When they emerged on the second floor, a wash of light spilled from a room halfway down the hall.

"Keep your mouth shut," she said in a low voice as they got closer. "Sit there and just…be quiet."

"Yes, ma'am. I'll be the silent but menacing presence."

Her mouth twitched. "Exactly what I need when I'm trying to sweet-talk Ramon's teacher."

"Hey, I'm good at sweet talk. Maybe you should be the menacing presence."

FRANKIE BENT HER HEAD to hide her smile. Cal had managed to make her laugh, and she hadn't thought that possible tonight. She'd been dreading this meeting. Afraid of what Ramon's homeroom teacher was going to say.

She bit her lip, composed her expression and walked into the classroom.

Ramon was sprawled in a chair in front of the teacher's desk, staring out the window into the twilight. The teacher was younger than Frankie had expected, probably just out of school. Or maybe Teach for America. He had that preppy, elite-college look—buttoned-down collar on his dress shirt, which he wore with a tie. Expensive haircut. Plain eyeglasses, but she'd bet her last dollar they were a designer brand.

"Mr. Connors," Frankie said, too aware of Cal behind her. "I'm sorry to keep you waiting." She turned to Ramon. "I apologize for being late. I was held up."

Ramon straightened. "What's *he* doing here?" He nodded at Cal.

"With three of us, we'll remember what Mr. Connors says more easily." And didn't that sound like a crock. But it was the best she could come up with on short notice. "Mr. Connors, this is my colleague Cal Stewart."

Cal reached around her to shake the teacher's hand, and the young man narrowed his eyes behind the tortoiseshell glasses. "Aren't you the Coug—?"

"I work with Ms. Devereux at FreeZone," Cal interrupted. "And Ramon."

The boy watched them with his flat, unreadable gaze. Frankie claimed the other chair near the teacher's desk and sat down. Cal dragged one of the desks over, then slid into it.

"So, Mr. Connors," she said briskly. "What can we do to help Ramon?"

The teacher was still staring at Cal. "Mr. Connors?" Frankie said sharply.

"Um, yes. Ramon." He shuffled a stack of papers in front of him. "Ramon hasn't been turning in homework assignments. His grades are dangerously low, and I'm concerned."

"What happened when you asked him why he wasn't doing the work?" Frankie inquired.

Connors cleared his throat. "His answer wasn't, ah, helpful."

She swiveled on the hard wooden seat. "Ramon? What's going on? You used to do your homework every day."

He shrugged. "Don't have time for that shit."

"Why not?" Frankie leaned closer and Ramon sat up a little straighter. "Have you been hanging with the Vipers again?"

"No! I promised you I wouldn't, and I'm not."

"Then what's going on?"

Ramon's gaze darted toward the teacher, then Cal. He stared down at his shoes.

"Tell me," she said. Mr. Connors leaned forward and opened his mouth, but Frankie shot him a sharp look. He leaned back in his chair.

"Ramon?"

"My mama's sick," he finally said, squirming. "I got to take care of her after school." He glanced up at Frankie, then back at his shoes. "I don't got time for homework. Or FreeZone."

"Oh, Ramon," she said softly. She took his hand, and the boy curled his fingers around hers. "Has she seen a doctor?"

"Ain't no free clinics around here. Last one closed a few months ago."

"Then we need to get her to Cook County Hospital. After we're done here, I'll drive you both over there."

"I don't know, Ms. D. She don't like that place." He jiggled one leg. "She's afraid they gonna put her in rehab."

"Maybe that's the best place for her right now."

"She don't want to go."

Ramon was too young to be dealing with this on his own. "I have a friend at DCFS," she said. "Her name is Emma Sloane. You've probably seen her come into Free-Zone to talk to Harley Michaels. I'll give her a call and see if she can meet us there. She knows how to deal with the system."

"DCFS? My mama ain't no kid."

"Emma would be there for you, Ramon."

"I ain't no kid, either," he said, staring at her with too-old eyes.

"We'll get this figured out," Frankie assured him. She turned to the teacher, but before she could say anything, Cal leaned forward.

"You'll speak to Ramon's other teachers and explain the situation, Mr. Connors. Won't you?"

Connors stared at Cal. "Yes. Yes, of course." He glanced at Ramon. "He can make up his homework after… after everything is settled at home." He cleared his throat. "But it's important that he keep coming to school."

"He will." Cal leaned around her. "You've been going to school, haven't you, man?"

Ramon lifted one shoulder. "My mama mostly sleeps during the day."

"There you go," Cal said to Mr. Connors. "Is there anything else you need to discuss with Ms. Devereux?"

"No, that was it." The teacher looked at the teen. "You get your mama taken care of, Ramon. I'll handle things here at school."

"That's tight." He stood, hiking up his baggy jeans. "I gotta go."

"We're coming with you, Ramon." Frankie shouldered her purse, then walked into the hall, with Ramon behind her. She turned to see Cal leaning over the desk, talking to the teacher.

"Absolutely, Mr. Stewart," the man said. "I'll make sure of it." Connors shook Cal's hand a bit too enthusiastically.

After a moment, Cal gently extricated himself. "I'll check back with you on that."

"Good. Great." Connors sank back into his chair and watched him leave the room.

Once they were clear of the door, Ramon shuffled along

beside her, holding up his jeans with one hand. Cal was silent. It made her wonder what he was thinking about.

And what he'd said to Ramon's teacher.

The sky had darkened to purple when they emerged from the school, and several more cars had left the parking lot. Her vehicle and Cal's were the only two left in the middle row. Her tiny foreign compact looked like a toy beside Cal's monster.

Who needed a car that big, anyway?

"Ramon, you can wait in my car while I have a word with Mr. Stewart," she said.

"No, get in my truck, Ramon. We'll be taking it to the hospital."

Ramon's eyes actually brightened. "Yeah? That's a chillin' ride."

As he hurried toward the SUV, Cal pressed his fob to unlock the doors.

"You don't have to drive us to the hospital," Frankie said.

Cal looked genuinely puzzled. "Why wouldn't I?"

He was trying to be helpful, and she appreciated that. "Fine, you can drop us off."

"What, you think I'm going to open the door at the E.R. entrance, kick you out and keep going? Leave you to get home on your own?" He shook his head. "Not happening."

"No, I figured you'd actually stop first."

"I'm staying, Frankie."

The simple words sent a shiver down her spine. None of her other volunteers had gone this far for one of the kids. Cal didn't even like Ramon, but he was putting himself out for the boy.

"This is Cook County Hospital. We'll be in the emergency waiting room for hours. It could take all night." She didn't want to sit next to him in the cramped emergency-room chairs, where he'd undoubtedly hog the armrest and all the leg space. She didn't want to watch him and Ramon posturing, both trying to be the alpha dog.

All of it would be too damn tiring.

Too personal.

"Not up for discussion, Frankie." He nodded at the white Escalade, where Ramon was leaning forward to examine the dashboard, and smiled. "Besides, he's already in my truck. You want to get him into that POS of yours? Good luck with that."

"This isn't your problem, Cal," she said, even though she knew it was a losing battle.

"It is now." His smile disappeared, and the charmer was gone. "Who knows, Frankie? I might actually be helpful."

"Helpful or not, it doesn't feel right to take your time."

He watched her for a moment, his face in the shadows. "You don't want to accept my help? Fine. You can count these as CS hours."

"Cal, I—"

"This is what we'll do," he said. "Give me your address. I'll drop Ramon at home to help his mom get ready, then pick you up. We'll double back to Ramon's and pick up him and his mom."

"You already thought that through?"

"I play games for a living. It's all about strategy."

"You're good at it," she said, but he didn't react. He merely watched her while she took out a piece of paper and wrote down her address.

"Your cell number, too, in case there's a problem."

She hesitated a moment too long, then wrote it down.

"Don't worry," he said as he slid the piece of paper into the pocket of his dress shirt. "I won't be scribbling it on men's room doors."

Her face heated. "I know that. I just…I don't give out my number to many people."

"Then I'm a lucky guy, aren't I?"

Without waiting for her to answer, he strode to the SUV and swung himself into the driver's seat. He said something to Ramon, and the kid snapped on his seat belt.

They were halfway to the gate by the time she got into her car.

CHAPTER TEN

CAL WATCHED in his rearview mirror as Frankie hurried to her car.

She truly believed all the stuff she spouted. She cared about those kids of hers, the ones who'd gotten the short end of the stick. And she backed up her words with action.

Did those kids have any idea how damn lucky they were?

Frankie was real. There was no BS about her. He didn't think he'd ever met anyone like her. Someone whose confidence came from knowing she was doing the right thing.

Someone who was in control of herself and her life.

She hadn't been completely controlled tonight, though. Maybe he made her nervous.

He stepped on the gas, and the truck leaped forward. Hell, ever since that moment in her office last week, she'd made *him* damn nervous.

Ramon reached for the radio. "What kind of stereo you got in this thing?"

"Turn it on and see," he said.

Ramon tuned the radio to a rap station, and the pounding rhythm blared from all ten speakers. Cal turned down the sound. "Sorry, kid. I don't want to shatter any windows."

Ramon shrugged, then stared at him. Cal rolled to a stop at a traffic light. "What?"

"What's going on with you and Ms. D.?"

Cal froze. "What do you mean?"

"You heard me. You doing her?"

Control. He controlled himself. Always. But he wanted to grab the kid's T-shirt and shove him up against the windshield. Instead, he tightened his hands on the steering wheel as he stared at the little turd.

"Don't you ever disrespect Ms. Devereux like that again." He leaned toward Ramon, and the kid had the good sense to slide toward the door. "If I hear you say *anything* like that about her, I will take you apart. Piece by piece. When I'm done, there won't be enough left to scrape off the pavement."

Ramon held up his hands. "Just asking, dude. 'Cause you look like you're doing her."

"What the hell is that supposed to mean?"

"You watch her, man. I know what that look means."

"I look at her because I work for her, you jerk."

The car behind him honked, and Cal saw that the light had turned green. The truck lurched forward. "Why is her personal life any of your business, anyway?"

"Ms. D.'s been good to me. I watch out for her." The kid scowled. "She don't need trouble like you."

Cal couldn't help asking, "What kind of trouble would that be?"

The teenager kept his eyes stubbornly on the road in front of them. "You got arrested for beating the crap out of some dude. Ms. D. don't need that."

"You think I would hit her?" Cal asked, appalled.

Ramon snorted. "Don't matter. I seen a lot of guys like you, think they're some kind of hot shit. Ms. D., she's real. She don't need what you got to give."

Translation: he wasn't good enough for Frankie.

In the opinion of a gang banger.

Cal's knuckles hurt as he gripped the steering wheel.

Even a loser punk like Ramon could see the emptiness inside him.

Not that Cal was interested in Frankie that way. She was a do-gooder hippie chick. Serious. Intense. Everyone knew Cal Stewart was all about the flash and not the substance.

"Turn here." Ramon pointed at a one-way street. "There."

Cal pulled up in front of a brown brick three-flat. The landscaping consisted of bare dirt. The bottom floor had plywood where the windows had been. The second floor had sheets over the windows. There were no curtains at all on the third floor.

"I'll tell my mama what's up," Ramon said as he opened the car door.

"Ms. Devereux and I will be back in fifteen minutes or so," Cal replied.

The kid walked into the building without looking back.

Cal programmed Frankie's address into his navigation system and drove several blocks to a quiet side street. The houses and apartments beyond the retail stores were in better shape, but it was still a down-on-its-luck neighborhood. There were beaters on the street that made Frankie's car look like a Rolls-Royce. When the voice navigation lady said, "You have reached your destination," he found himself in front of a closed bakery. There were lights on in the apartment above it.

So Frankie lived where she worked.

The curtain rippled, and a few moments later she appeared in the doorway next to the bakery. She jogged to the car, still carrying that damn huge bag.

"Hey," she said, dropping her load on the floor. She buckled her seat belt, then reached into the bag and pulled out two sandwiches in clear plastic containers and a bottle of water. "Here." She held them out to him.

"You made me sandwiches?" He stared at them without moving, and she finally dumped the sandwiches and bottle of water into his lap. The bottle was ice-cold against his thigh, even through his jeans.

"I was starving," she said, rummaging in her bag. "I figured you must be, too." She pulled out another bottle of water.

"Thank you, Frankie." He looked from the jumble in his lap to her and caught her watching him. Even in the darkened truck, he saw color rise in her face.

She held his gaze for a moment too long, then opened her bottle and took a gulp. She yanked another sandwich out of her bag. "You might want to get going. Ramon and his mother will be waiting."

Instead of pulling away, he opened one of the bags, and the scents of freshly baked bread, cheese and turkey wafted out. "Did you make this bread?"

"I might have." She opened her own bag and took a bite.

"You 'might have'? I didn't think you were the coy type, Frankie."

She swallowed and took another drink. "I'm not being coy. I don't remember which bread I made this morning. Might have been the wheat. Might not have been."

"You make more than cupcakes?"

"Once the cupcakes are done, I work on everything. Some days it's bread, some days it's pastries, some days cakes." She waved her sandwich toward the street in front of them. "Go."

"Yes, ma'am." He pulled away from the curb and looked at the sandwich again. It had been a very long time since someone made food for him.

He'd mistaken Frankie's kindness for condescension.

She was trying to take care of him, just as she took care of the kids. "It's delicious," he said, without taking a single bite.

FRANKIE WAS FINALLY ABLE to relax when they picked up Ramon and his mother. She and Cal had been busy eating, and neither had said anything. But she knew he glanced at her every few moments. And when he wasn't looking, she glanced back.

When Ramon and his mother got into the car, Frankie busied herself with handing them food and water, asking Ramon's mother how she was doing and reassuring Ramon.

By the time they got to Cook County Hospital, Ramon had inhaled two sandwiches and put one carefully aside for his mom. "She's not hungry right now," he explained.

Ramon's mother, Yolanda, was stick-thin, with brittle dark hair and haunted eyes. Even though it was a warm, early-summer evening, she shivered in a heavy coat, clutching it around herself as if it were the dead of winter.

When they pulled up to the door of the emergency room, Cal said, "You go in with them. I'll park the car."

The waiting room was crowded. Mothers rocked crying children, elderly men and women stared at the two ancient televisions with dull eyes, and three pregnant teens held huge bellies as they clung to the hands of middle-aged women.

A bored-looking staffer took Ramon's mother's name and directed them to triage, where they sat down in the hard plastic chairs that lined the wall. Ramon helped his mother onto the chair, then wrapped his arm around her shoulders and whispered in her ear. She shook her head and tried to stand, but he tugged her back down.

Frankie touched Ramon's shoulder. "Can I get your mother a cup of coffee or soda?"

"She's good. She don't like hospitals."

Frankie didn't like them, either. She stared at the registration desk, willing the woman to hurry.

The crowded waiting room, the misery and anguish that hung in the air like a bad smell, brought back memories of the night her parents had died. She and Nathan and Marco had huddled in a smaller version of this room, waiting for doctors to tell them if the rest of their family were alive or dead.

Patrick had survived the auto accident.

Her parents had not.

Trying to insulate herself from her surroundings, Frankie wondered dimly where Cal was. Maybe he'd decided to just drop them off and go home, as she'd told him to do.

No, Cal wouldn't do that. After three weeks, she knew him better than that.

Finally, the woman at the desk called Ramon's mother's name. The boy helped her up, then supported her as they approached the door to the registration stations. Just as they disappeared around the corner, Cal slipped into the seat next to Frankie.

"They got in fast," he said.

She glanced at him, startled to see him wearing sunglasses. "It's just triage and registration. Trust me, it'll be a while before they see a doctor." She gestured toward his face. "Why the shades?"

"I need to protect my eyes." He shifted in the chair. "What's wrong?" he asked, setting his palm on her thigh to still her leg. She hadn't realized it was jiggling.

"Nothing. I'm fine. Worried."

"That all?"

"What else would it be?"

Cal studied her for a moment, then turned away. He sat upright in the chair, even though the slippery plastic made most people slouch, and stared straight ahead.

She opened her mouth to tell him that hospitals freaked her out, then bit her lip. *TMI,* she told herself. Cal didn't need to know that.

After a few minutes, she became aware of a murmur rippling through the room. When a young African-American man approached Cal, she finally understood.

"Hey, man. How's the knee doing?" he asked.

"It's good, thanks," Cal replied. He smiled at the man, then looked away.

The murmurs grew louder, and several more people came over. Some offered scraps of paper for autographs. Some just wanted to shake his hand. Almost all asked about his knee.

That was why he wore sunglasses, she realized. He didn't want to make eye contact with anyone.

"Do you want to leave?" she asked him quietly. "I would, if I were you."

"I'm good, Frankie."

She couldn't see his eyes through the dark lenses. He was hiding from her, too. And why wouldn't he? It wasn't as if she'd been so open with him.

Finally a middle-aged man approached him. "Did you hurt your knee again?" he asked in a loud voice. "Is that why you're here?"

"My knee is fine," Cal said with a tight smile. "Thanks for asking."

A few people approached with cell phones and took pictures. The woman behind the registration desk scowled and picked up a telephone. A few minutes later, a gray-haired woman in a suit appeared from behind the triage door and walked over to Cal.

"Mr. Stewart?" she said in a pleasant voice. "Would you come with me, please?"

Cal stood up. "Where are we going?"

"I'm going to get you checked in so you can have some privacy."

Cal pulled Frankie to her feet, then held on to her hand as they followed the woman. As soon as they were behind the triage door, he let go.

He took off the sunglasses and slipped them into his pocket. "Thank you for bumping us to the head of the line," he said with a smile. "Our friend's mother is in triage. She'll appreciate the fast service."

The woman's lips tightened, but she nodded. "What's her name?"

An hour later, Frankie stood with Cal in the doorway of a hospital room. Ramon's mother was lying on the bed closest to them, an IV in her right arm to pump in antibiotics. Her infected, grotesquely swollen left arm was scarred with needle tracks and ugly red-and-purple streaks.

She'd been very close to septicemia.

Emma Sloane was sitting in a chair off to the side. She'd assured Frankie she'd take care of Ramon. And she would. Emma was as good as her word.

"Thank you, Emma," Frankie said.

She nodded. "Glad you called. Ramon will be safe tonight."

"Ramon?" Frankie said softly.

The boy looked over his shoulder. "Yeah?"

"You can trust Emma. I'll check with you tomorrow."

He shrugged, then turned back to his mother.

Cal slung an arm over Frankie's shoulders and steered her down the long corridor. The scent of disinfectant hung in the air, doing little to mask the smell of illness. Soft beeps bled out of several rooms, along with the sounds of quiet sobbing.

Frankie walked faster.

Cal tucked her closer. She should have shrugged off his arm, but it was oddly comforting. Reassuring.

Once they were in the elevator, she moved away. "Thank you," she said quietly.

"For what?"

For not asking me again what was wrong. "For getting Yolanda in to see a doctor so quickly." She should have objected to getting bumped to the head of the line, but she couldn't. She hadn't wanted Cal to stay in that waiting room, watched by so many strangers.

He shrugged. "There are benefits to being a celebrity."

That's what he'd meant when he'd said he might be helpful. "You knew that would happen, down in the waiting room."

"People in Chicago love their football."

"Does that happen everywhere you go? The people looking for autographs? Asking intrusive questions?"

"It's no big deal, Frankie. It comes with the territory."

"It can't be fun." Her skin had been crawling in that waiting room, and they weren't even looking at her.

"I get paid a lot of money to do what I do. It doesn't take much effort to smile and be nice to the fans."

The elevator stopped and the doors opened with a quiet ping. As they left the building, cars flew by, going too fast. She and Cal walked down a dirty sidewalk and into a dim parking garage. Their footsteps echoed in the harshly lit stairwell, which smelled faintly of urine and stale beer. Cal's knuckles were white as he gripped the handrail.

"We should have taken the elevator," she said.

"For two floors?" He raised his eyebrows. "Wimp."

The sunglasses were gone, but he was still all celebrity—charming and remote.

As remote as she had been earlier.

"I hate hospitals," she said abruptly. "That's why I was freaking out in the waiting room."

He paused on the steps and looked at her. "How come, Frankie?"

"My parents were killed in a car accident when I was thirteen. Every time I'm in a hospital, I remember being there with my brothers, waiting for the doctors to talk to us. To let us know if they were alive."

His hand slipped into hers, warm and comforting. Protecting her. "I'm sorry," he said, his voice quiet. Real. The celebrity was gone. "That's awful."

"It was horrible, but I survived," she said. Barely. She'd gone wild afterward, eventually running away from home.

She'd ended up in juvie.

They stepped onto the landing, and Cal turned to face her. "Kids shouldn't have to survive the loss of their parents," he said, still holding her hand.

"No one promised that life would be fair."

"But you try to change that, don't you?" he murmured. "That's why you opened FreeZone."

"That's part of it, I suppose." She took a deep breath. "It's more about my experiences as a runaway."

His hand tightened on hers. "That's what you almost said earlier, wasn't it? That you'd been on the streets."

"Yes." She searched his gaze, but didn't see any censure there. Any disgust. "I know what a lot of my kids face."

"Frankie is such a hard name," he murmured, edging closer. "But you're not hard at all, are you?" He dropped her hand and cupped her face. "You're soft, Francesca."

His hands, slightly callused, were warm on her skin.

But when he brushed his thumbs over her cheeks, she shivered. Swallowed. "Cal…"

"What?" he whispered.

"What are we doing?" She gripped his wrists, but wasn't sure if it was to push him away or to hold him still.

"I don't know," he said, and his eyes gleamed with hunger. Desire. "Let's find out."

He lowered his head to hers, infinitely slowly. As if waiting for her to object.

Instead, she pulled him close and pressed her mouth to his.

CHAPTER ELEVEN

WHEN CAL'S MOUTH TOUCHED HERS, Frankie lost her nerve. She tried to back away, but he followed, his lips clinging to hers. She bumped into the wall and braced her hands on his chest.

He didn't try to overwhelm her. Instead, he nibbled at her lower lip, giving her a chance to get comfortable. She flexed her fingers into the hard muscle beneath his shirt, and his shudder vibrated through her palms.

Had all that passion, that smoldering need, been hidden by his laid-back, take-nothing-seriously exterior all along?

The cold wall chilled her back, but Frankie was suddenly overheated. She wanted to believe it was Cal, that his body was warming her, but she knew better.

She was generating plenty of heat on her own.

He drew away, watched her, waited for her to decide. His fingers lingered on her face, but she wanted to feel the power and strength of his body against hers. She wanted to kiss him again.

She slid her hands to his back and pulled him closer. He groaned as he lowered his mouth, and she opened for him.

Instead of deepening the kiss, he slid his tongue along her lower lip, as if he wanted to savor every taste. Learn every texture of her mouth, study every nuance of her response. She hadn't known a simple kiss could be so seductive. A small, helpless sound blossomed deep in her throat.

He wrapped his arms around her and fitted her against him, her chest to his, his hard thighs pressing into her. His hands traced the bumps of her spine, drifted over her ribs, then dipped lower to palm her rear. And the whole time, he kissed her. His tongue danced over hers, tasting of the coffee he'd gulped in the E.R. and the Snickers bar he'd shared with her.

He stroked her tongue, moved in and out of her mouth, flexed his hips against hers. Desire swept through her, obliterating any caution, any hesitation. She'd never been so aroused by just a kiss.

Wrapping one leg around his, she yanked his shirt out of his jeans and slid her hands across his hard, muscled abdomen. He sucked in a breath, then bent his head to her neck. As he sucked lightly, his hands burrowed beneath her sweater.

In the stairwell below them, a door banged open. The landing vibrated with the force of several feet, and she and Cal froze. He let her go, smoothed her sweater back into place and hurried her into the parking area.

He held her to his side as they walked, his hand caressing her upper arm. His Escalade was a beacon of white in the darkness.

He pressed her more tightly against him as they reached the truck. The faint click of the locks echoed hollowly in the silence. But instead of getting in, he swung her around and kissed her.

Heat shot up her spine again as Cal's mouth moved over hers with frantic need. He moaned against her mouth, or maybe that was her. Her hands roamed over him, testing the muscle in his back, his rear end, his chest. She was entering unfamiliar territory, where nothing existed besides the next kiss, the next touch. Nothing mattered besides feeling his body against hers.

His hand fumbled for the handle behind her and he pulled her forward when he found it. And then she was falling backward onto the seat. Cal stepped between her legs and reached for the hem of her sweater. Cool air touched the heated skin of her belly, followed by his hot mouth. Her muscles quivered under his lips, and she wrapped her legs around him.

He lifted his head and stared down at her. "You're killing me," he groaned as he thumbed the tiny navel ring she wore.

Memories rushed through her, and she froze.

This was Cal, she reminded herself. She was safe. But it was too late. The moment was gone, and reason took over.

She put one hand between them and grabbed his arm. "Stop, Cal." She swallowed. "I can't… This isn't the place."

His hands stilled on the buttons of her pants and he lifted his head. Desire glittered in his eyes, darkening them, and his neck was splotched red.

She'd done that, she realized. Oh, God. They had been minutes away from making love. They were in public, in a dirty, smelly parking garage, and she'd been too wrapped up in him to care.

Her hands shook as she tugged her sweater back into place. He straightened, but not completely, staying partially hunched over. Her gaze dropped to his zipper, then slid away.

He braced both hands against the roof of the truck, his breath sawing in and out. He stayed that way, his eyes closed, until his breathing slowed.

"Sorry." His voice was hoarse as he straightened. "I don't know what we were thinking."

His eyes opened and his mouth curved up. "No, that's not true. I know what we were thinking. But it was damn stupid to be thinking it here."

He helped her sit up, then went around and slid into the driver's seat next to her. "My place is ten minutes away." The tires squealed as he backed out of the parking spot. "I can be there in five."

"Cal, wait." Frankie's sanity was returning, and with it a faint edge of panic. "We can't."

"Why not?" He concentrated on the curving ramp, taking it faster than she would have thought possible.

"You know why not. I'm supposed to be supervising you."

"That's okay," he said. He glanced over at her with a tiny smile. "You can supervise me all you want. You can tell me exactly what you want me to do."

"I'm serious," she said, although his words made her quiver. "This would be a big mistake."

His smile faded. "So, what? You want to ignore what just happened?"

"We should." She closed her eyes, her body still throbbing.

"You had your hands on my ass and your tongue in my mouth. A few more seconds and we would have been doing a lot more than that. Can't put that genie back in the bottle."

"No, we can't." Suddenly chilly, she wrapped her arms around herself, her fingers clutching her heavy sweater. "But we can make sure it doesn't happen again."

"You can ignore this? You have that much self-control? Really, Francesca?"

He had no idea. "Don't call me that."

He slanted her a look. "Why not? I want Francesca. She was the one in the stairwell with me. Frankie would never have kissed me like she would die if she couldn't."

Her heart stuttered, and she almost reached for him. "Come on, Cal. We were both a little raw. Emotional about Ramon and his mom." She'd revealed a part of herself to him, something she rarely did. "It was a natural reaction. But that doesn't mean it was smart. Or right."

The truck bounced as Cal jammed on the brakes at the payment booth. He shoved a handful of bills at the parking attendant, then accelerated the moment the gate came up.

"Felt pretty right to me," he said, once they were on Lake Shore Drive. On their left, the lights of the city glittered beneath a black velvet sky. On their right, the lake was dark and choppy. He skimmed one hand over her thigh, and she closed her eyes again. "But I get your point. If I was a big disappointment in bed, things might be awkward for the next three weeks."

"I don't think you'd be a disappointment," she said, then snapped her mouth closed. He'd laid the trap, and she'd walked right in. "Take me home, Cal."

He drove too fast the rest of the way to her apartment, neither of them speaking again. The truck had barely stopped when she jumped out. "Good night, Cal. Thanks for all your help with Ramon and Yolanda."

He nodded but didn't answer. The truck rumbled at the curb as she hurried up to her apartment. As soon as she turned on the light, she heard him drive away.

THE NEXT AFTERNOON, dizzy with weariness, Frankie yanked the white box of cupcakes out of her trunk. Walking into FreeZone exhausted was *not* a good idea. She needed to be able to focus on the kids and their problems.

Not on what had happened last night with Cal.

After an almost sleepless night, she knew sending him home had been the right decision. Though she still quivered when she thought about their kiss, they couldn't get involved.

Besides the fact that she was his supervisor, she had too many other things to worry about right now.

As she walked toward FreeZone, she saw a crowd of people on the sidewalk. Reporters. She recognized some of them from a few weeks ago. Today, the group was bigger.

She pushed through the throng, ignoring the shouted questions and the microphones shoved in her face. After setting the cupcakes inside, she turned to face them.

"What's going on?" she asked. Her heart pounded. Had something happened to Cal? "What are you doing here?"

"Did Cal Stewart hurt his knee again?" someone from the back of the mob shouted.

"No." She gave the reporter a puzzled look. "Why would you think that?"

"He was at Cook County Hospital last night." A reporter close to her held out a microphone. "Are you sure his knee is okay?"

Oh, my God. She hadn't even considered this. But Cal had expected it. As soon as the first kid had approached him, as soon as the cell phones had come out, he had to know what people were going to think.

"He wasn't there for himself." She let her eyes meet every one of the reporters she could see.

"Who was he there for?" a woman asked. "You?"

"That's none of your business."

"So he *did* hurt his knee again," one of them called. It sounded like satisfaction in his voice.

"I heard he limped into the E.R." She couldn't see the speaker, but could hear his smirk.

"Does he need more surgery?"

"Will he be able to play this year?"

"You're wrong," Frankie shouted, but no one paid any attention. The reporters pressed closer and their voices beat at her in waves, breaking down her composure. She wanted to scream at them to go away, to stop harassing her and Cal.

"Knock it off, guys." Cal shoved his way through the crowd to her side and glared at the reporters in front of him. "From now on, you'll leave Ms. Devereux alone. She's not used to sharks like you. If you have questions about my recovery, you can ask me yourself."

She put her hand on his arm and felt the tension in his muscles. "It's okay, Cal," she murmured.

His eyes blazed. "No. It's not. Ms. Devereux and I took some friends to the hospital last night. That's all it was. My knee is fine." He jumped up and down a few times, lifted his knee and flexed it. Frankie was sure no one else noticed his almost imperceptible wince. She raised her hand to reach for him again, then let it drop.

"Trust me, that was not about my knee. Hell, it's not even where my orthopedic surgeon practices. No story here. All right?"

While the reporters shouted questions at him, he ushered Frankie into the center. As soon as they were out of sight of the crowd, she turned and grasped his arm.

"You knew that was going to happen, didn't you?"

"That the reporters would show up?" He shoved his hands into his pockets. "I'm not surprised. They've been here before."

"That's not what I mean. When they found out you'd been spotted at County, you knew they'd assume you'd hurt your knee again. It's probably in the papers today, isn't it?"

He shrugged. "There might have been a few comments in the gossip columns."

"I shouldn't have let you come with me." She released him and began to pace. "I'm sorry, Cal. I should have realized something like that would happen."

He grabbed her elbow to stop the pacing. "I make my own choices. Sure, I knew what might happen. But getting Yolanda to the hospital was more important." His hand dropped away. "Making sure you didn't have to handle that on your own was more important."

Everything inside her softened. "I should have insisted."

"You think I would have paid any attention? It was after hours." He watched her steadily. "Everything that happened last night was off the clock."

Her cheeks heated, but she wasn't going to be distracted by a mention of their kiss. "Why did you do it, Cal? You knew what they'd assume."

"I wanted to help you." He drew her closer. "And I'm glad I did. If I hadn't, I wouldn't have kissed you. At least not for another day or two."

"We agreed to forget about that."

"*I* didn't agree, Francesca."

Her name sounded intimate when he said it like that. The way a lover would. Her belly tightened as she remembered the way he'd touched her, the way he'd kissed her. Nuzzled her neck and told her how soft she was.

"Don't call me that."

He let her go and smiled. "Francesca."

"You're not going to drop this, are you? You're going to keep reminding me."

He leaned closer again. "Do you want me to drop it?"

She opened her mouth to say yes, but nothing would come out. He smiled. "I didn't think so."

The reporters outside were buzzing again. Grateful for

the distraction, she brushed past him. "What are they up to now?"

"Probably interviewing each other. I think that's what they do when no one else will talk to them."

She heard a single voice, then the reporters again. "They better not be bugging my kids!"

She ran outside, only to stop at the sight of a man in a suit, his back to her, holding court in front of the reporters. He was average height, with thinning brown hair carefully combed to cover the bald spot in back. When his suit jacket fluttered in the breeze, his shirt was too tight over the spare tire around his waist.

"As the head of DCFS, I'm pleased to see all of you here," he said. "We need more press coverage of the wonderful things volunteers are doing for our children in Chicago."

Frankie froze, her hand on the door. He'd come here. To FreeZone.

She was sure it wasn't to tell her he was resigning.

Why was Doug Bascombe here?

What did he want?

CHAPTER TWELVE

CAL WATCHED FRANKIE RUN outside, full of righteous fury, then rear back as if someone had hit her. He leaped forward, ready to defend her from whatever or whoever had hurt her.

No one was even close to her. But her face was sheet-white as she stared at the pompous, pudgy guy spouting off. Cal hid a smile as he watched the reporters' eyes glaze over. A few of them exchanged WTF looks.

When they saw Cal, they surged forward, pushing the pudgy guy back. He stumbled, bracing himself on the window, and Frankie recoiled. Cal dragged her inside, away from the door.

"What's wrong?" he asked, gripping her upper arms.

"The guy out there. He's…" She closed her eyes and sucked in a ragged breath. "He's the new head of DCFS."

The man's voice rose again, but Cal didn't hear any questions. "Thinks he's pretty important, too."

"He always has."

Frankie stared out the window, a combination of loathing and fear on her face. He'd never seen her afraid of anything.

"You know him?"

"We've met."

They'd more than met. No casual acquaintance could make her shut down like this. "What's the deal?"

She turned to face him. "I don't like him. And he has no reason to show up here. I want to know why he has."

"Guy like that? My guess is he figured the media would be here and he's looking for face time on the news."

"How would he know that? I didn't expect them."

"I did. And I'm sure an attention seeker like that would, too."

"He'll come in here." She looked around, and Cal saw the mess they hadn't cleaned up last night.

"So? FreeZone isn't a DCFS program, is it?"

"No. I started it and I run it. But I've gotten grants from them. And I have more in the pipeline."

"If he doesn't like what he sees, screw him. We'll find another way to raise money."

We? Was he planning to stay involved after his CS time was up?

"Cal." Her face softened and her shoulders relaxed. "You're right. Thank you for reminding me. He has no power over me."

"Damn straight." He glanced around the room. "But we still need to clean up. The kids will be here before long."

"Right." She took a deep breath. "I'll wipe off the tables. You sweep the floors. Okay?"

"Got it."

He kept one eye on her as he swept. Her hands shook as she cleared off the tables, but she worked steadily. The fear was gone from her expression, replaced with resolve. *Good for you, Frankie.* She wasn't going to let this guy intimidate her, no matter what his job was.

After she finished with the tables, she tied up the garbage bag and dragged it out the back. Cal wanted to do it for her, but he suspected she needed to keep busy. So he stored the broom in the closet, picked up her bakery box and set it in the deli case.

The door opened and the head of DCFS walked in. His hair was brown, his face bland and ordinary. An anonymous bureaucrat. But his expression as he looked around the room was assessing. And a little angry. Did he resent Frankie's success with FreeZone?

Cal had met plenty of men like him.

He plastered a smile on his face as he walked over. "Can I help you?"

"I'm Doug Bascombe, the new director of DCFS. I'm looking for Frankie Devereux. You must be Cal Stewart, her community-service volunteer."

"That's right."

"You're the Cougars' quarterback. How are you enjoying working at FreeZone, Cal?"

"I'm not the quarterback. I'm a safety." He managed to keep the scorn out of his voice for Frankie's sake. "And I'm pleased to be here. I like the kids. I like working with Frankie. This place is needed. It's a good thing for the neighborhood."

"That's great. I came by today to see if you'd like to talk about your experiences here with the media." He turned to glance out the door at the few reporters who were still there. "We need to publicize places like this to get them more outside funding."

He was right about that, at least. "I agree. People need to know about FreeZone." Before Cal did anything with this guy, though, he'd discuss it with Frankie. Especially after seeing her reaction to the man.

"Excellent." Bascombe beamed and held out his hand. "Give me your card and I'll call you. Your CS hours would be better spent doing public-service announcements and visiting more of our volunteer centers. You're wasted in a small place like this."

Cal had no interest in making this officious bureaucrat

look important. He glanced at the man's hand, but didn't shake it. "The judge placed me here at FreeZone. I don't think she'd agree to change my service."

Bascombe dropped his hand, but his smile didn't dim. "I can take care of that."

"I'd prefer you didn't. I enjoy working at FreeZone."

Bascombe's eyes hardened. "How many teenagers come here? Fifteen? Twenty? You could help so many more."

"There are twenty-two kids," Cal said coolly. "Kids I can *personally* help." Bascombe wasn't interested in attracting donors to places like FreeZone. The scumbag wanted to milk Cal's celebrity and bask in the reflected spotlight.

Cal would be damned if he let that happen.

Bascombe opened his mouth again, but Cal heard the back door slam. Frankie was coming in from Dumpster duty.

When he glanced over his shoulder, she was leaning against the door frame, her eyes shuttered and impossible to read. "Hello, Doug."

Bascombe nodded to her, his expression calculating. "Devereux. I need to talk to you."

"Fine. Let's go into my office. The kids will be arriving soon."

She walked toward her office without looking back. Frankie shoved her hands into her pockets, but not before Cal saw them trembling.

He looked from her to Bascombe. What was the real story here? Why was this guy making Frankie shake?

FRANKIE KEPT HER SPINE straight. Bascombe would see no weakness in her. No fear.

Men like him thrived on fear and weakness.

When they reached the office, she leaned against the

desk and gestured for him to close the door, even though it would trap her in the too-small room with him.

Show no weakness.

As he took a seat, he said, "Devereux. So good to see you again."

He smiled, and revulsion rippled through her. She crossed her arms over her chest so he wouldn't see her reaction. "I can't say the same. And it's *Ms.* Devereux, Doug." He needed a reminder that she wasn't a child anymore. That they were equals now.

The slight narrowing of his eyes told her he'd gotten the message.

"I hope you're here to tell me you're resigning."

"As I've already told you, that's not going to happen. I came to get your community-service volunteer."

It was the last thing she'd expected him to say. "You want Cal? Why?"

"I have better uses for him than sweeping floors in this place. He can draw attention to all of DCFS's programs, rather than just your center. He's wasted here."

"Are you kidding me?" Frankie stared at Bascombe, shocked. "First of all, *Doug,* this isn't a DCFS place. I started FreeZone and I run it. I don't have any connection with your agency."

"We fund you."

"No, you don't. I fund myself. DCFS has given me a few grants, which I've applied for, following your guidelines. Just as I've applied for grants at dozens of other agencies. None of them have the right to dictate how I run my program."

"As I said a few weeks ago, I can make life very difficult for you. So I'd suggest you play ball."

"You tried to force me to play ball with you once before,

remember?" She felt a vicious kick of satisfaction when he paled. "Didn't work then, either.

"Besides, you're in no position to make demands. This time, I hold all the cards."

"You think so?" He smiled, and Frankie's stomach twisted. Bascombe didn't look as if he was afraid of exposure. "You have no proof of anything. So you can go public whenever you want. It's not going to change anything.

"And just to remind you of that, I'm taking the football player."

"So this is supposed to be a warning."

"Be grateful he's all I want. I could do a lot worse."

Frankie hadn't expected Bascombe to be quite so explicit, but she shouldn't be surprised. He hadn't risen to the top of DCFS without knowing how to play the game.

"Even if I was willing to give you Cal, I couldn't. It's here or nowhere for him. According to the judge."

"As long as Stewart agrees, I can get the judge to change her mind."

Frankie doubted Sarah would do that, no matter what this self-important bureaucrat believed. "I think it's up to Mr. Stewart, don't you? And he's apparently already made his choice."

"Give him up, Devereux. Or…"

"Or what?" She leaned forward, knowing she was in control. "There's nothing you can threaten me with, Doug. Because if you do anything to FreeZone, I'll go to the press immediately." She smiled, although it was hard. "I'll be going to them eventually, anyway, unless you resign. So it's your choice. Now or later?"

"Those reporters are still out there, Devereux. How do you think they'd react if they found out you're a felon?"

"Who would care? Not the parents of anyone here. It

might make them *more* eager to send me their kids. I'm a woman who managed to turn her life around.

"And you forget, I'm not a felon." She smiled. "You fixed that for me, remember?" She leaned a little closer. "I'm sure you remember why."

He sucked in a breath. "Don't screw with me, Devereux. I'm not resigning, and you're not going anywhere with your bullshit stories that no one would believe. If you do, I will shut this place down. The health department will be here. So will the building department. Sanitation. The city will be so far up your ass they'll need flashlights. And not only will FreeZone disappear, I'll make sure you never open another place like this again. I'm the head of DCFS. I can make it happen."

Doug Bascombe was the kind of person who collected favors. As the head of DCFS, he'd no doubt collected a lot of them. "Go ahead and try. We'll see who comes out on top."

Bascombe leaned closer, just as she had earlier, and she had to force herself not to recoil. "Your brothers run a restaurant. The health department can pay them a visit, too."

"Don't threaten my family, Doug." Frankie kept her face cold. Expressionless. But inside she trembled. Business at Mama's Place was slow. If the health department closed them down, they might not recover.

"I won't need to, as long as you keep your mouth shut."

"I can't do that."

"Be very sure before you take that step, Devereux. I usually get what I want."

She held his gaze. "Not this time, Doug," she said softly.

His mouth thinned as he reached for the door. "I'll be watching you."

He jerked the door open so hard that it bounced off the bookcases beside it. His footsteps echoed as he walked out of the center.

Frankie sank onto her desk. She shouldn't be surprised. She should have known he wouldn't cave easily. But he'd threatened FreeZone.

Her brothers.

The only thing that kept her from going public immediately was that he wasn't working directly with children. She'd checked with Emma and found out he'd stopped all visits to juvie and teen centers a couple of weeks ago. Right after Frankie had paid him a visit. Now he sat in his fancy office and issued orders. Cut deals. Preened for the press.

But he still made decisions that affected thousands of children.

She couldn't ignore this and just hope it went away. She needed to do something. Tell her story.

Your brothers run a restaurant.

She couldn't let Bascombe destroy her family's business. The restaurant her parents had built and her brothers had saved.

She would talk to Nathan and Marco. She'd call them right now, before she lost her nerve.

There was a brisk knock at the door. Cal.

"Come on in," she said.

He paused in the doorway. "What's wrong, Frankie? You look like you've seen a ghost."

She had. It was a ghost she'd buried deep and tried to forget. But like all ghosts, it refused to stay buried.

She couldn't let Cal see how devastated she was. He'd push and probe and try to get her to spill her guts.

She couldn't tell him about Bascombe. She couldn't expose herself that way.

And she knew Cal. Knew he'd go ballistic. Do something he might regret. She couldn't let that happen.

"A disagreement with a bureaucrat," she said, struggling to keep her tone matter-of-fact. "Not the first time, and it won't be the last."

Cal threw himself into the chair next to her. Their legs nearly touched, and she drew hers onto the desk. "It was more than that," he said quietly. "I saw your face when you first spotted him."

Damn it. Her life would be simpler if Cal really was the dumb jock she'd assumed he would be. "He's been around DCFS forever. I've crossed paths with him before." She needed to steer Cal away from her history with Bascombe. "He wants you to work with him instead of here at Free-Zone. I told him no, but that's not fair to you."

Cal studied her, a hint of heat in his gaze, and she squirmed. She should never have kissed him.

If they hadn't connected like that, she wouldn't be so distracted by him. It would have been easier to let him go with Bascombe and buy herself a little time.

"Is that what you want, Frankie? Do you want me to leave?" He leaned forward. "Is it because I kissed you last night?"

"If I remember correctly, Stewart, I kissed you first. So it would be a little hypocritical of me to toss you out because of it." She slid off the desk. "Doing what Bascombe wants would be better for you. You'd get more of the media attention you said you needed."

She paced the office so she wouldn't have to look at him. He stood, and she edged past him, trying not to touch him.

He grabbed her hand and stopped her. "Is that what you want, Frankie?" he repeated.

"Publicity is important. You've said it often enough."

He drew her closer. "As if I'm not getting enough already."

"Being Bascombe's mouthpiece would let you spend more time training. Rehabbing your knee."

"How do you know I need to spend more time doing that?"

She tried to tug her hand away, but Cal wouldn't let go. He twined his fingers with hers and held on. She was close enough to feel his heat. Close enough to smell the sharp, fresh-scented soap he used. There was a gleam in his eyes as he watched her, waiting for her to admit she'd paid attention to him.

She stared resolutely into the main room. "There's stuff in the newspaper," she muttered.

"You're reading about me in the *Herald Times?*" His smile widened. "I'm flattered that you're interested." He tried to draw her closer, but she stiffened her arm.

"You're part of my kids' lives, at least for a while. Why wouldn't I be interested in what's going on with you?"

"So it's all about the kids?"

"What else would it be about?"

He laughed. "You're tough, Frankie. I like that about you. You're not going to give me anything, are you?"

She put her hand on his chest to shove him away. "Do you want me to beg you to stay? Sorry, Cal. I'm not doing that. Yes, you're helping. Yes, the kids like you. Last night was…it was more than anyone could expect of you. But the bottom line is you're going to be gone in less than a month."

"A lot can happen in three weeks. Ask me to stay, Frankie." He still held her hand, and now his thumb traced a small circle on her palm. His touch shot through her nervous system and made her jumpy.

"It's your decision."

Another circle. "Ask me."

She tried to back away, but he wouldn't let her. He held her gaze and stroked her hand. "I can't tell you what you should do," Frankie muttered.

"Yes, you can." He leaned forward. "Would you ask me if I kissed you?"

He watched her with half-closed eyes.

Bedroom eyes.

"Fine. Stay." She took a breath. "Please."

"Yes." He squeezed her hand. "Why would I want to work with a tool like Bascombe when I could be here with you and the kids?"

Cal had made her forget about Bascombe, but now it all came rushing back. Frankie yanked her hand away. "The kids will be here any second. We should get ready."

His eyes weren't teasing anymore. They narrowed, and she knew what was coming next. Questions about Bascombe.

Questions she had no intention of answering.

"I have to make a phone call, Cal," she said without looking at him. "Would you mind closing the door on your way out?"

CHAPTER THIRTEEN

SHE FELT CAL HESITATE in the doorway, so she picked up her phone and pushed speed-dial one. When she realized her hand was shaking, she gripped the receiver more tightly.

"Hey, Nate," she said when her brother answered. "How're things going? How are *you* doing?"

"I'm fine, Frankie," Nathan answered. "Sorry I dumped on you last week. I shouldn't have said anything."

"I'm glad you did," she replied as the door shut behind her. "Who else are you going to dump on?"

She heard the air-hockey puck crashing against the side of the table in the other room. Again and again. Then the clatter as it went into the slot. Cal was taking out his aggressions on the hockey game.

Better than on Bascombe.

"Not you," her brother said. "You have enough problems of your own."

He had no idea. "Actually, there's something I want to talk to you and Marco about. You guys mind if I stop by tonight?"

"We'd love to see you," Nathan said, his voice brightening. "Marco will be excited, too. He's got a bunch of ideas for new dishes, and he's always looking for a victim…I mean a test subject."

She heard Marco say something rude in the background, and Nathan laughed. "See you tonight."

"You will. Love you, Nate."

"Love you, too, Bunny."

WHO THE HELL was she talking to?

Cal carefully set the plastic disk on the air-hockey table. He wasn't trying to eavesdrop on Frankie's conversation. But the office door hadn't latched properly, and her low, intimate tone drifted out.

"Love you, Nate."

Cal froze, his hand tightening on the side of the table. Then he relaxed.

Frankie wouldn't have kissed him last night if she was in love with someone else. He was sure about that. But he still wanted to know who Nate was. What he was to her.

Cal cracked the puck into the slot again. He had no claim on Frankie. No right to know who she was talking to.

He wanted to, though.

And that was stupid. He couldn't get tangled up with a woman like Frankie. She was nothing like the celebrity groupies he usually dated, women who knew the score. Frankie was real. Complicated.

The kind of woman he avoided at all costs.

Last night, he'd kissed her on a whim. Just because he'd wondered what she tasted like? How she would feel?

If she would kiss as passionately as she did everything else.

A couple of kisses in a filthy parking garage. That was all it had been. But once his mouth touched hers, he hadn't cared where they were. He hadn't thought about anything but Frankie.

He wanted more. A lot more. Today, at rehab, he hadn't worried about the new safety the Cougars had drafted. He hadn't noticed the pain in his knee.

The only thing he'd thought about was Frankie.

That was dangerous. He didn't have room in his life for a woman like her.

He was happy with his life the way it was.

No more after-hours excursions with her. No more trading intimate bits of their lives.

No more letting her distract him from what he had to do, which was get ready for the football season. Finish this community service and go back to his real life.

Even if it was beginning to look a little barren.

When she walked out of her office, he was shoring up the short leg of the Ping-Pong table. He heard her approaching, but didn't turn. Finally, she stepped into his space, her scuffed black boots less than a foot from his head.

He stood, moving so that the table was between them. "Hey, Frankie."

She gestured. "Thanks for fixing that."

"That's why I'm here, right? My superior engineering skills."

"Absolutely." Her smile looked forced. "Listen, Cal. Before the kids come, I just want to make sure we're clear on something." She swallowed, and he watched her pulse jump in her neck. "If you need to work with Bascombe, I'll understand. No hard feelings."

Cal knew he should take what she was offering. It would be a lot easier than spending another three weeks here. He opened his mouth, but couldn't force the words out.

Finally he shrugged. "If I had to work with Bascombe, I'd get arrested again. Because sooner or later, I'd knock the snot out of that pompous ass. So I'll stick around here."

She smiled, a genuine one this time, and her shoulders

relaxed. "Good. Thank you. But it's okay if you change your mind."

"Got it."

They stared at each other a beat too long, then Frankie spun around and hurried away. "The kids will be here in a few minutes."

Thank God.

It would give him something else to think about.

"GODDAMN IT, FRANKIE!" Nathan jumped up from his chair at the corner table in Mama's Place, and a diner at a nearby table dropped her fork.

Frankie yanked him back into his chair. "Settle down, Nate," she said in a low voice. "I'm not telling you this to get you worked up. I need your help."

"I'll help. I'll kick his ass for you, Frankie," Marco said with gritted teeth.

What was it with her and aggressive men? "You settle down, too, Marco," she retorted. "I appreciate the sentiment, but we need to solve a problem here. Not go off half-cocked."

"Oh, I'd be completely cocked," Marco promised.

"Dude! Focus!" She cleared her throat when another diner glanced at them. "Look, maybe we should discuss this later." She'd timed this badly. She should have done it during the afternoon, when there weren't so many witnesses. "I'll come back tomorrow, before FreeZone opens."

"No." Nathan stood abruptly and pushed his chair back. "You're right, we can't talk about this here. We'll go to the house." He waved to one of the waitresses, a short, slender woman with auburn hair. "Hey, Darcy," he said when she arrived. "You know my sister, Frankie, right?"

"Sure. How are you?" Darcy said with a smile.

"We need to go home for a while," Nathan said. "Could

you seat people for an hour or so and keep an eye on things?"

"No problem, Nate."

She moved away, and Frankie looked at her brother. "You trust her to take over for you."

"Yeah, she's smart. Organized. Pays attention to every detail."

"Maybe you should let her manage Mama's while you take some time off."

He stared at Darcy, who was leading a couple to a table with a smile. "I never thought about that."

"You should." Frankie watched Nathan track his employee's progress through the dining room. "You interested in her?"

"God, no." He turned horrified eyes on Frankie. "She's like another sister. And don't try to change the subject. Let's go."

Ten minutes later, they were home. Nathan's home now. The cheerful yellow walls and old wooden table in the kitchen were familiar. Comfortable. Frankie inhaled a deep breath and outlined for her brothers what had happened. She didn't give them details. She didn't want to make them even more angry.

She didn't want to think about the details herself.

She looked down and realized that Marco was holding one of her hands, Nathan the other.

"I went to see him a few weeks ago," she said. "I told him he had to resign or I'd go to the media. He didn't, of course. He showed up at FreeZone yesterday and demanded Cal. Just to show me who had the power."

"Who's Cal?" Nathan asked.

"My community-service volunteer."

"Why would he want your volunteer?" Marco asked.

Frankie felt heat creep up her face and tugged her hands

away. "He's a football player. Kind of a celebrity. Bascombe thought he could use him for publicity."

"Hang on. You're talking about Cal Stewart," Nate said, his mouth flattening. "That guy was arrested for breaking a guy's jaw in a bar fight. And he's working with your kids?"

"The guy was pushing a woman around," Frankie retorted. "After he'd been hassling Cal all night."

Nathan's eyes narrowed. "You're defending him? Ms. Peace and Nonviolence, Frankie Devereux?"

"Not the subject, Nate," she said, her face burning. "Cal isn't the issue here. Bascombe is."

Marco leaned forward. "You can't be the only one he molested. There are other women out there. You have to find them."

"How do I do that? I can't just put an ad in the newspaper."

"Let's talk to Patrick on Skype," Nathan said. "I bet he would know."

Ten minutes later, Frankie was telling the story again. Patrick's expression got darker and his eyes glittered. "We'll nail him, Frankie," he said from his home in Detroit. "He's not going to get away with this."

"I wish I'd told you guys about this when it happened," she whispered. "But I was too scared. Too ashamed."

"That's what sexual predators count on," Patrick said. He looked every inch the dangerous FBI agent. "I'll do some checking on him. Maybe he has a prior arrest or complaint."

"Thanks, Paddy," she said. "But Marco's right. What we really need is to find other women he's molested. Can you get some names of girls who were in juvie around the time I was?"

"Those records are sealed, Frankie."

"I know the FBI can get them if they need them."

"Not for personal reasons."

"But he has to be stopped. I'd file charges if I could, but we all know it's too late for that. Can't you bend the rules a little?" she begged.

Patrick shook his head. "Sorry, Bunny, but I can't do that. Not only would I be breaking the law, but those records are sealed for a reason. The women would freak out if you approached them with questions."

"Then, what am I going to do?" she asked.

"Hold on for a while longer," Patrick said. "Let me see if I can find anything through legitimate channels."

"Because God forbid you take one step off the straight and narrow," she muttered.

"I heard that, smart-ass," Patrick said. "I'm sworn to uphold the law, and I won't go against that unless every other option has been ruled out. I'll call you as soon as I know anything, okay?"

"Thanks, Paddy," she said. They turned off the computer, and she pushed herself away from the table. "And thank you, too, guys. Let me know if you think of anything else."

Nathan enfolded her in a hug. "I wish we'd been able to protect you back then," he said.

"You *did* protect me," she answered, kissing him. "I put myself in juvie, but you got me out."

A COUPLE DAYS LATER, an attractive blonde woman walked into FreeZone. It was the social worker Cal had met the other night at the hospital, the one who'd taken charge of Ramon. He hadn't noticed much about her that night; he'd been too focused on Frankie.

Today, he saw that the woman's hair was a wavy cloud around her face. She wore a colorful skirt, red Chuck Taylors and dangly earrings that looked like fishing lures. She swept Harley into a hug, then gave one to Frankie.

It figured that Frankie's friends would be as unconventional-looking as she was.

The social worker—Emma, that was her name—spoke to Harley for a few moments, then absently smoothed her hand over the girl's hair as she nodded toward the office, clearly signaling that she needed to talk to Frankie in private.

The two women were halfway there, heads together and talking, when Frankie grabbed Emma's arm. Then she looked for Cal and jerked her chin, silently asking him to join them. When he arrived, Emma was perched on the desk, watching her pace.

"Ramon has disappeared," Frankie said.

"He's probably at the hospital." The way the kid acted around his mom the other night, Cal was surprised the social worker had been able to convince him to leave her.

"No, he's not." Frankie put a hand on her friend's shoulder. "I'm sorry. You remember Emma Sloane, right? She took charge of Ramon that night."

"Of course. Nice to see you again, Emma," he said, shaking her hand.

"Cal." She glanced at Frankie. "Are you sure we want to—"

"Yes," Frankie interrupted. "Cal is just as invested in Ramon as I am."

He wouldn't go that far, but for Frankie's sake, he wanted the kid to be okay. "Yeah, I want to help. What's going on?"

"I placed him in a foster home." Emma's knee jiggled beneath her skirt. "It's a family I know well. I've used them before in emergency situations, and they're good people."

"And…?" Frankie asked.

"Ramon left this morning and said he was going to school. But he never showed up. I checked with Yolanda, and he was at the hospital early—probably right after he left the foster home. But he didn't stay long, and she has no idea where he went." The social worker's mouth thinned. "Or at least nothing she's willing to share."

The two women exchanged a long look. Then Frankie sighed. "You think he's gone back to the Vipers."

"Where else would he go? He has no family other than his mother. I went to their house, but he wasn't there. The attendance office made a few phone calls, but they couldn't find a thing."

"He promised me he wouldn't."

"Where else would he be?" Emma retorted.

"Okay, I'll see what I can find out," Frankie said.

Cal stepped in front of her as she paced. "What are you going to do?"

"Go to where the Vipers hang out, of course. We need to find him before he gets hurt. Or worse."

"Are you out of your mind?" Cal took a step toward her. She barely reached his shoulder, but she didn't back down.

"I know a few of the kids in that gang. They know who I am. It'll be fine."

"The hell it will." He glanced at Emma. "Tell her she can't do that."

The woman gave him a strained smile. "Haven't you realized no one tells Frankie she can't do something?"

"This is whacked."

"You have a better idea?" Frankie asked.

"Yeah. Do nothing. Or go wait at the hospital until he shows up to see his mom."

"That might be too late. He's been trying to leave the Vipers, and gangs don't like it when their boys leave. There's no telling what they'll do to him."

"Then he'd be smart not to go there, wouldn't he?"

Frankie paced again. "He's upset. Lost. His mom is sick and he's living in a stranger's house. He might go back to the Vipers because they're familiar." She pressed her lips together. "If they get hold of him again, we won't get him back."

"Frankie." Cal stopped her as she brushed by him. "If he really left, he won't go back. He'd know what would happen."

"*If* he left?" She bristled and yanked away from him. "You think it was all a ruse?"

"Until the other night, I was sure it was. Now? I don't know." Cal took her hand and absently rubbed his thumb over her palm. The calluses he felt reminded him again that she was nothing like any other woman he knew. "But barging into a group of gangbangers isn't smart. It's dangerous."

"Frankie, I have to agree with him." Emma acknowledged their joined hands with a tiny smile. Cal let go. "We'll figure out where he's gone without poking a stick into the Vipers' hole."

Frankie looked from one to the other with resolve. "I'm going to try and help Ramon."

"I want to help him, too, but maybe we need to cool off and think this through," Emma said, sliding off the desk and pausing with her hand on the doorknob. "I have to go. Don't do anything rash, Frankie."

She glanced at Cal, and the question in her eyes was easy to read.

He nodded once. He might not be able to stop Frankie

if she was determined to do something stupid, but he'd make sure she didn't do it by herself.

Emma's shoulders relaxed. "I'm heading over to Ramon's foster house. If I hear anything, I'll let you know."

Cal watched her leave, uneasiness stirring again. Emma had assumed he'd be able to reason with Frankie. Protect her.

"Listen, Frankie," he began, but she held up her hand.

"Not now, Cal. The kids are waiting for us." She closed her eyes and took a deep breath.

"What?" he asked. "What's wrong?"

She opened her eyes and stood straighter. "Just wishing for the impossible."

"What would that be?"

"That we could limit the crises to one per week."

"We've had more than one?" He studied her more carefully. "That would be Ramon and…?"

She pressed her lips together. "Bascombe."

"Hey, I'm staying right here. You can cross him off the list."

"Yeah." She shoved her hand through her spiky hair and avoided his eyes. "Let's get back to the kids."

FRANKIE LOCKED UP after the last two kids had gone, then rested her forehead against the door.

She had to get rid of Cal before she went looking for Ramon. Judging by the mulish expression on Cal's face when they'd discussed it with Emma, he was going to be stubborn about this.

The sound of running shoes on linoleum approached, and she lifted her head. Cal was only a few feet away.

"You okay?"

"I'm fine." She straightened and smiled. "Long afternoon."

"Yeah, it was. More drama around here than on a soap opera."

"That's normal with teens," she said, hoping her voice sounded ordinary. As if she wasn't planning to go to a sketchy neighborhood tonight to search for Ramon.

Cal waited, as if he expected her to say more. When she didn't, disappointment flickered over his face. "So I'm learning."

"You can go on home. I'm not staying late tonight."

"I know you're not. You're chasing gangbangers, aren't you?" He rocked back and forth, as if preparing to fight. Or gather her close. Her heart began to thud, and her toes curled in her shoes.

"I'm not going to do anything stupid."

"Says the woman who wants to walk into the Vipers' headquarters. What are you doing, then?"

"Maybe I'll stop by a pub and have a beer. I'm in the mood for mindless conversation and a few laughs." She shrugged as if it was a spur-of-the-moment thought.

"Sounds like a great idea. Where is this place?"

"You're not invited." Her heart beat even faster. She didn't want Cal anywhere near the Town Tap. It would ruin everything.

"I could go for a beer. And if you want mindless conversation, I'm your man."

Cal's innocent expression was completely misleading. His eyes swept over her, head to feet, as if he wanted to devour her. She swallowed. "I don't think there's anything mindless about you, Cal."

He tilted his head. "Is that an insult? It sounded like a compliment, but you never know."

His voice was lower than usual, a rough growl that made her shiver. "Good night, Cal." She walked past him, closing her eyes when she caught a whiff of the spicy aftershave he used. She didn't need this tonight. She had too many other things to worry about.

She heard the sound of the dead bolt sliding back as she went into her office. After she'd grabbed her bag and turned off the lights, she walked out, and Cal was gone.

She scowled when disappointment trickled through her. He would only get in the way. Prevent her from doing what she had to do.

She relocked the door a little more forcefully than needed, then headed for her car. And found Cal leaning against his truck.

He didn't smile as she approached. "So are you going to tell me how to get to this place, or do I have to follow you again?"

CHAPTER FOURTEEN

"DIDN'T I MAKE IT CLEAR that I don't want company?" Frankie didn't have the energy to deal with Cal, too.

"Oh, you did. But I don't care. Someone has to pick up the pieces after you get your ass kicked."

"You're such a sweet-talker." It would have been easy to keep walking away from the Cal who hid behind his charm and fame. This Cal, the one who got involved even though he obviously didn't want to, was much harder to resist.

And the woman who'd kissed him last night didn't want to resist. She kicked a chunk of broken sidewalk into the gutter, barely missing his truck. "How does going to a bar and having a beer mean I'll get my ass kicked?"

"It doesn't, if that's all you're going to do. I'm betting it's not."

"You think you know me so well? After a few weeks?" He shouldn't. But judging by the grin tugging at his mouth, he did. And that scared her.

She lifted her chin and tried to stare him down.

His grin widened. "Am I wrong?"

"Oh, for God's sake, Cal. Go. Leave me alone."

"Sorry, Frankie." He straightened, moving away from his truck. "I promised Emma."

"You did no such thing." They'd barely spoken to each other.

"Our eyes met across the room, and we communicated

without words." He tried for soulful, but the twinkle in his eye ruined the effect.

Frankie scowled in exasperation. "You're a piece of work."

"Could say the same about you." He slung an arm over her shoulders. "So are we walking to this bar?"

"We're driving," she said, shrugging him off. "I mean, *I'm* driving."

"Give it up, Frankie." He opened the passenger door. "Hop in. Let's get a beer."

"I'll drive myself."

"I'll drive you back here to get your car later. Quit stalling. I'm coming with you, one way or another. Let's get this over with."

"'Get this over with'?" She slid onto the leather seat, still warm from the sun. "Nice words from someone who wants to have a beer with me."

He braced his hands on the roof of the truck and leaned in. His gaze dropped to her mouth. "Let me be clear. 'Get this over with' referred to whatever idiotic plan you have. Not the rest of the evening."

"Let *me* be clear. There *is* no rest of the evening."

"We can discuss that over our beer."

He shut the door before she could answer.

"Where are we going?" he asked, once he was behind the wheel.

"A few blocks north, then left on Hutchinson." She knew she sounded sulky, but she wasn't used to being steamrollered. Both tonight and the other time with Ramon, Cal had done it effortlessly.

Once his truck was moving, he scanned the street constantly, as if expecting trouble.

Her neighborhood wasn't *that* bad. People spilled out

of bars and sat at tables in front of the small restaurants. Couples and groups jostled on the sidewalks.

But security grills glinted in the streetlights, and the alleys were dark, scary places.

Everything changed a few blocks after they'd turned onto Hutchinson. Cal frowned. "*This* is where you were coming by yourself?"

"It's okay during the day." Even to her own ears she sounded defensive.

There were as many boarded-up storefronts as viable businesses. The ones still there were poorly lit, menacing bars, payday-loan stores and the occasional dirty window displaying strange odds and ends. Every shop had a security grate across the front. Half the streetlights were either burned out or broken.

Small groups of young men loitered in the alley entrances.

A few people sat on their front stoops, and the occasional couple strolled down the sidewalk. All of them stilled when Cal and Frankie drove past, making her very aware that they were intruders.

This area made the neighborhood around FreeZone look upscale.

Fear and desperation hung heavy in the air. She didn't remember this neighborhood being so bad.

"You were right." She glanced at the gloomy street, the hostile people, the shadowy alleys. "It would have been dangerous to come here alone. I'm glad you're with me."

"Damn straight." He pulled away from the stop sign too fast, pressing her back into the seat.

It was more than just wanting support in a dangerous neighborhood. Bascombe showing up the other day, making demands, had shaken her.

She'd needed someone to lean on tonight.

And Cal was the only one she wanted next to her.

That made her edgy. Unsettled. She wasn't used to needing people.

She was bone-deep scared that she needed Cal.

As if he'd read her thoughts, he said, "We all need help once in a while, Frankie. It doesn't make you weak."

No, but needing *Cal* made her an idiot. He was a temporary part of her life, here for a few weeks, then gone. But she still wanted to reach for his hand.

She curled her fingers into her palms.

A few minutes later, she pointed to a bar that looked like all the others they'd passed—seedy and run-down. The *o* and *n* on the Town Tap neon sign were burned out, and the rest of the letters flickered. The greasy film on the windows blurred the interior. "There," she said.

Cal pulled to the curb, but made no effort to get out of the truck. "This is the bar." There was no inflection in his voice.

"Yeah." Swallowing, she began to open the door. He reached across her and yanked it shut. Then he pressed the button to engage the locks.

"I know you're not a stupid woman," he said, staring out the window, watching everything. "Why are you determined to have a beer in that dump?"

She shifted so she could look across the street. That building's windows were painted white, and indistinct shadows moved behind them. The door was fitted with two huge, impossible-to-ignore locks—a clear warning to stay away.

She looked at the Town Tap again and realized she was out of her depth. "You see the building across the street? The one with the whited-out windows? That's the Vipers' place. Their headquarters, if you want to call it that. I thought if I sat in the bar and kept an eye out, I might see Ramon."

Cal didn't say anything for a few seconds. He studied her, his face hidden in shadow. Finally, he took her hand from her lap, uncurled her fingers and meshed them with his. "We'll wait in the car instead. Okay with you?"

She tore her gaze away from the storefront and focused on Cal. "That's it? No lecture? No making fun of me for being naive and foolish?"

"No lecture. Although it's tempting as hell, and I reserve the right to change my mind." He pressed a kiss into her palm, and she trembled as heat swept through her.

Cal watched the building across the street, brushing his mouth over the back of her hand almost absently. As if it was the most natural thing in the world to be holding her hand. Kissing it.

As if they were connected.

She twined her fingers with his, and his grip on her tightened. As if he felt the connection, too.

He glanced at her. "How many people would be willing to come to this neighborhood and spend an evening in that hole, waiting for a kid who might not even show up? Damn few. You have several loose screws, but you also have guts, Frankie. And a lot of heart. The least I can do is sit here with you while you wait."

The blue lights from the Town Tap sign flickered across his face, making it difficult to read his expression. His hand was warm and comforting, and she clung to it. "Thank you," she said softly. "I know you have lots of things you could be doing tonight besides sitting here waiting for a kid you don't even like."

"I'm not here for Ramon." The flickering sign briefly lit Cal's face, and his expression was tender. Compassionate.

Unguarded. Frankie was certain not many people saw him like this.

The ever-present knot in her stomach loosened slightly, and she put her hand on Cal's face. His whiskers tickled her palm, and she traced one finger over his dimple. "You're a remarkable man, Cal Stewart. You keep saying you're just a football player, but you're so much more."

He froze momentarily, then eased away and let go of her hand. "Yeah, I'm also the guy who's doing community service at your place because of a bar fight." He stared at the Vipers' den. "Saying that a sow's ear is a silk purse doesn't make it so."

She reached for him, but he shrugged her off. Wrapping her hand around the muscle of his forearm, she leaned on the console between them. "Why do you want everyone to think you're a dumb jock?"

His jaw tightened. "Don't use your social-worker psychobabble on me. Sometimes things are exactly what they seem to be."

"I'm not a social worker." *Stupid.*

"You're pretty good at faking it. The kids at FreeZone think you can solve all their problems."

"Of course they don't. I'm a refuge for a few hours after school. That's all."

"You're a lot more to those kids than that, and you know it." He gestured toward the painted windows. "If you weren't, we wouldn't be sitting here."

Cal had turned the conversation away from himself and back to her. He'd done it so smoothly that she'd leaped at the bait he'd tossed out. She studied his crossed arms, his bland expression that gave nothing away. "Do you ever take off your sunglasses, Cal?"

His detached expression disappeared, and he frowned. "What are you talking about? I'm not wearing sunglasses."

"Yes, you are. Emotional ones. They're just like the shades you put on at the hospital, preventing anyone from seeing the real you."

He snorted and turned away. "More psychobabble."

"Cal." She reached for him, but before she touched him, he tensed.

"You were right," he said. "There's Ramon."

CAL COULD HAVE KISSED the kid for saving him from treacherous waters. Give Frankie the smallest opening and the next thing you know she was trying to get into his head.

At the sound of her seat belt being unfastened, he swiveled and reached for her. Too late. She was already out of her seat and walking in front of his truck, intent only on the kid skulking along on the other side of the street.

"Damn it!" He jumped out, but not before Frankie stepped in front of Ramon.

The kid looked up, something shiny in his hand, and froze when he saw Frankie. By the time Cal reached them, whatever Ramon had been holding had disappeared.

"Ms. D., you crazy? You shouldn't be here."

"Neither should you, Ramon." Frankie's voice was calm. As if she was standing in FreeZone instead of a dangerous street.

Cal moved to stand between Frankie and Ramon, ready to protect her.

The kid glanced at and dismissed him. He shuffled his feet as if trying to figure out how to get into the building behind her. "I need their help," he finally said.

"You don't need anything from them." She put her hand on Ramon's arm. "You have other people who can help you. Cal and me. Emma. The family you're staying with."

The boy's face hardened, and the vulnerable kid from

the other night disappeared, replaced by a cold, lethal gangbanger. "None of you can do what I need done."

Frankie didn't seem to notice Ramon's transformation. She rubbed his shoulder. "What's that, Ramon?" she asked softly.

"Business," he said flatly. "*Gang* business."

Cal shifted so that he could intercept if the kid tried to push Frankie out of his way. But Ramon paid no attention to him.

"I thought you were out of that business," she said.

"Not anymore."

Frankie put both hands on Ramon's shoulders. "Why?" she said, her voice as gentle as a mother talking to her child. "Why are you going back, when you tried so hard to leave?"

Ramon was a kid again, with a hunted, desperate look on his face. He swallowed once and turned to Cal, as if expecting Cal to save him from Frankie.

Cal didn't react. Frankie was the only person he was interested in saving.

"Ramon? You can tell me."

The kid hunched his shoulders. "I need to find my mama's dealer," he muttered. "The one who sold her the bad junk. That's why she's so sick."

Frankie frowned. "I thought she had an infection from using dirty needles."

Ramon rolled his eyes. "My mama ain't stupid. She knows what to do. The doctor told me this morning that the stuff she injected was contaminated. All kinds of germs and shit in it. That's why she's so sick."

"How is she doing today?"

"Sick." With one word, the boy was gone and the banger was back in his place.

Cal tugged Frankie out of Ramon's reach. "What are you going to do when you find the dealer?" he asked.

"What do you think?" Ramon held his gaze, letting Cal see the truth in his eyes.

Before he could respond, Frankie reached for Ramon. "Don't do this," she said. "Go to the police. Let them find the dealer and arrest him."

He snorted. "Police help a banger? Ain't gonna happen. But my boys will know what to do."

"You're upset and angry. I get it. But this is a mistake." She glanced at Cal. "Tell him."

"She's right, man," Cal said. "You want that scumbag dealer in a cage. You want to think about him in there, every day. Getting the shit beat out of him. Eating the crappy food. Being the bitch of the baddest guy in there." He paused to let his words sink in. "You don't want him in the ground. That'll put *you* in the cage."

"You don't know nothing about it."

"You think that's what your mama wants when she gets out of the hospital? To visit you in jail?"

"She's not gonna care. She'll start using again." Ramon swiped a shoulder across his face, and his eyes glittered. Cal wasn't sure if it was from anger or tears.

"Maybe not," he said. "Maybe this scared her."

"That's why I quit the Vipers," the boy said, his focus moving to the building again. "Me and Mama made a deal—I'd quit the Vipers and she'd get clean." A muscle in his jaw twitched. "Guess the deal's off now."

"It doesn't have to be," Cal said. "We'll get her into rehab when she's better. They'll help her clean up."

"I told you before. She don't want to go to rehab. It's nothing but a lot of crap."

"We'll find someplace good. Someplace that will help her." He'd make sure of it.

"Ain't no place can help my mama." Ramon shoved past him and strode to the entrance, tapped out a complicated pattern. The door opened, spreading a rectangle of light onto the sidewalk. Ramon stepped inside and the locks clicked back into place.

Voices rose from behind the whitewashed windows. It was hard to tell if they were welcoming or threatening.

Frankie stood next to Cal, her fist pressed against her mouth as if she was trying to hold back a scream. "We have to get him out of there," she said, her eyes pleading.

She was practically vibrating.

Cal needed to get her out of this world of gangs and violence. He needed to keep her safe.

He curled his arm around her shoulders and steered her toward the truck. She resisted, as if she intended to stand on the sidewalk until Ramon walked out again. Cal held on more tightly before lifting her into the seat. She weighed next to nothing, and he held her close for a moment before he set her down.

Once she was safely in the truck, some of the tension in his shoulders eased. He scanned the area again, saw no one, then went around to the driver's seat.

He started the engine, but she grabbed his arm. "We can't leave," she said. "Not while he's inside."

"We can't sit here all night, Frankie." Cal brushed her cheek with his thumb. "All we can do is hope some of what you said sank in. That he thinks twice before he goes gunning for the dealer."

Cal put the truck in gear, made a U-turn and headed toward FreeZone before she could convince him to stay. If she used those blue eyes on him and begged him to wait, he might give in.

She was staring over her shoulder, as if her gaze could draw Ramon outside.

"I'll go to the hospital in the morning and see if he shows up," Cal said.

At that she turned around. "You can't. You have to do your rehab."

"I'll do it afterward. My knee is getting better. I don't have to do as much every day."

That was a lie, but once he said he'd try to find the kid, he couldn't take it back.

She frowned. "You're still limping."

"The hell I am."

"I've seen you."

"After rehab. Of course my knee's sore then."

"Cal." She laid her hand on his arm, and he felt the pressure of every finger. "I can't let you do that. I'll go myself."

"You have a job."

"I'll start early and go to the hospital when I'm done."

They turned onto Broadway, and Cal relaxed a little more. There were people on the sidewalks, and a couple of bars were doing good business. Noise and light spilled into the street.

They were coming up to the church where she parked her car, and he slowed down. He didn't want to drop her off and drive away. Part of him was afraid she'd go right back to the Vipers' place.

Mostly he didn't want her to be alone.

"You want to get—" he began, but she grabbed his arm.

"Pull over. There's someone at the door of FreeZone."

CHAPTER FIFTEEN

"IT'S PROBABLY a homeless guy," Cal said. But he pulled over, anyway. "Stay here and I'll go check."

"Like I've never seen a homeless person before? I'm coming with you."

"Damn it, Frankie! Do you ever look before you leap? You have no idea who that is. What if he's a drunk? Or high? Or trying to break into FreeZone? I don't want you to get hurt."

"It might be one of my kids," she said calmly.

"If it is, I'll call you over. Let me handle this one, Rambo."

Cal stared at her until she nodded reluctantly, then he climbed out of the truck.

It was quieter on this block. There were fewer stores, fewer pedestrians. A fast-food wrapper blew by in the wind. It tumbled over the curb and into the gutter in a splash of dirty yellow.

The person in the doorway of FreeZone had huddled as far away from the sidewalk as possible. Whoever it was wore a ragged, dark blue knit cap and a brown jacket several sizes too big.

As Cal got closer, he saw the young face, as well as long hair spilling from the cap. It was a woman.

A girl, he realized. She clutched a backpack to her chest, her arms wrapped tightly around it. Her eyes were closed and her head leaned against the door frame at an uncomfortable angle.

The kid's neck would be sore when she woke up.

He turned to the truck and motioned for Frankie.

She hurried over and studied the young woman. "Someone you know?" he asked.

"No. She's never been here." Frankie crouched a couple of feet away from her. "Hey," she said softly. "Are you okay?"

The girl stirred, but only straightened her head. She was thin and gaunt. The hair exposed by her cap was tangled and greasy-looking, as if it hadn't been washed in ages. Her fingernails were dirty and broken.

"Hey, sweetie," Frankie said. "Wake up."

The girl awakened with a start. When she saw Cal and Frankie, she leaped to her feet and tightened her grip on the backpack, holding it in front of her. "Leave me alone," she said in a hoarse voice. "I'll scream."

"We're not going to hurt you," Frankie said. "What are you doing here?"

The girl looked from one of them to the other, her eyes fearful. "Waiting for this place to open." She sounded defiant. Scared.

"This is an after-school program," Frankie said gently. "It won't be open until tomorrow afternoon. You need a teen shelter. There's one a couple of blocks away."

She shook her head vehemently. "I'm not going to that place. This is where I need to be. Someone told me they help kids. I need help."

Frankie sat on the sidewalk in front of the girl. She glanced at Cal, and he read her perfectly. She wanted him on the sidewalk, too, where he'd be less threatening. But his knee wasn't going to cooperate. If he managed to get into that position, Frankie would have to help him stand up again.

No way would he humiliate himself that way.

He moved away slightly so he wasn't in the girl's space, but still close enough that he could react if Frankie needed him. She glanced at his knee, gave a tiny nod, then turned back to the girl.

"What kind of help do you need?"

She looked from him to Frankie, her hands scrabbling on the backpack. She flexed her ankles, getting ready to run.

"What's your name?" Frankie asked.

The girl licked her lips. "Martha."

"Okay, Martha. I'm Frankie, and this is Cal. What can we do for you?"

The girl's glance dropped. Then, bracing her hand against the door, she lowered the backpack to her side.

Revealing a very pregnant belly.

FRANKIE SUCKED IN A BREATH. Homeless and pregnant? And she couldn't be older than sixteen. "Oh, honey," she said softly. "How far along are you?"

Martha touched the bulge of her belly through her heavy jacket. "I think six months."

She thought? So she hadn't seen a doctor. "And how long have you been on the street?"

The girl looked down at the pavement and fingered the backpack. "About a month."

The memories crashed over Frankie in a wave. Cold. Hungry. Lonely.

Scared. She'd been tense and frightened every minute she'd been on the street.

Above everything else, she could still taste the fear.

"You should go to the teen shelter," she told Martha.

"They have resources to help. They'll get you to a doctor, contact your parents if that's what you want, find you a place to stay." She glanced at Cal, who'd shifted closer to the girl, as if trying to protect her. "We'll take you there, if you like."

Martha shook her head emphatically. "I'm not going there."

"How come?" Frankie forced herself to maintain a conversational tone. "Did someone there…hurt you?"

"I'm not going to the shelter," Martha repeated, her eyes darting back and forth as if searching for an escape route.

Something bad had happened at the shelter. Frankie consciously relaxed her fists. "Okay, sweetie. No one's going to force you."

"Is there anyone who can take care of you?" Cal asked.

"No." The girl slung her backpack onto her shoulders, pulled her hat down over her ears and stepped away from the door. "A guy told me I could stay here, but I guess he lied. So I'm good. I don't want to bother you."

Frankie stood and moved into Martha's path to prevent her running away. "You're not bothering us," she said. "This is my center. That's why we stopped. We saw you and we were concerned." She took a small step closer. "It's not an overnight place, but we'll do what we can for you. What about your baby's father? Is he someone you can trust? Maybe stay with him if he has somewhere safe?"

Martha suddenly looked far too old. "No."

She gathered herself, as if preparing to run, and Cal leaned against the window, clearly trying to be as non-threatening as possible. "You look hungry," he said. "You want to get something to eat?"

Martha licked her lips. "I'll, uh, get something down the street."

"Frankie and I haven't had dinner yet, either," Cal said. "We were thinking pizza. That sound okay?"

The desperation in the girl's eyes was painful. "Pizza?"

"There's a good place a few blocks from here," Frankie said, flashing Cal a silent thank-you.

"Lenzoni's." Martha licked her lips. "Sometimes, if we go to the back door, the cooks give us pizzas they burned, or that someone didn't pick up."

Cal nodded. "Tonight, you can sit in the front and order whatever you want."

"Maybe." Martha looked from Frankie to Cal, hope blooming slowly in her expression. "But I'm *not* going to the teen shelter. Got it?"

"We won't make you do anything you don't want to do, Martha."

"We're parked right up the street," Cal said.

Martha clutched her backpack closer. "I'm not getting in any car."

Cal opened his mouth to argue, but Frankie cut him off. "I understand. We'll walk."

Excuse me, please. I need to use the restroom."

Martha got up from the table, grabbed her backpack and headed for the ladies' room. Just before she rounded the corner, she glanced over her shoulder at Frankie and Cal.

Frankie watched until she disappeared, then turned to him. "I know this isn't the way you wanted to spend your evening. Thank you."

"You think I'd let a pregnant kid sleep in a doorway?"

"Of course not. But you convinced her to come and eat with us. She was getting ready to run when you mentioned pizza."

"Probably not the healthiest food for the baby. But no

teen can resist pizza." He shrugged, as if it was no big deal. "It was better than letting her take off. She needed to eat."

Frankie looked at Martha's plate, where five crusts were neatly lined up. "She was hungry."

"Poor kid." While they'd waited for the pizza, Martha had guzzled two glasses of milk and told them a little bit about being on the street. She and two other girls and four boys had been staying in an abandoned building, scavenging food and struggling to survive. When Frankie asked her why she'd come looking for help tonight, she'd bent her head and concentrated on the pizza.

Cal glanced toward the bathroom. "So what do we do now?"

"I know the woman who runs Hope House. It's a shelter for runaway pregnant teens. She might not have room, but it's the kind of place Martha needs. Annie is the kindest soul in the world and completely nonjudgmental."

"If you can convince Martha to go there."

"If I can't, I'll take her home with me," she said. Her couch would seem luxurious to someone who'd been sleeping in an abandoned building. Frankie knew exactly how uncomfortable and scary an old, run-down structure could be.

"No way." Cal swiveled to face her. "You know nothing about this kid. You can't take her into your apartment."

"I can't leave her on the street, either."

He sighed and slouched in his chair. "Have you heard anything sketchy about that teen shelter?"

"No, but I probably wouldn't. None of my kids are homeless. Doesn't matter, though. I can't force her to go there."

"I hope this woman has room for her, then." The tiny

lines around Cal's eyes seemed deeper. As if he was exhausted.

And why wouldn't he be? He'd spent the morning doing rehab, been at FreeZone all afternoon, then dedicated his evening to chasing Ramon and now feeding a homeless kid.

Frankie touched his hand. "I'm glad you were with me tonight, even though you're probably not."

He turned his palm up, joining their fingers. "So am I." Their shoulders brushed, and she wanted to lean into him. To absorb some of his strength.

As if he could read her mind, he gripped her hand more tightly. Frankie realized she was swaying toward him. She drew her hand away.

Cal cleared his throat and nodded toward the restrooms. "Hasn't she been in there a long time?"

"Damn it." Frankie jumped up and ran along the hallway. At the end of it, Martha was trying frantically to unlock the dead bolt on the alley door.

"Martha." She stopped several feet away from the girl, who spun around, her back pressed against the wall.

"Hey, thanks for the pizza. It was awesome. But I need to split." She attempted a smile, but her eyes were desolate. "The guys where I'm staying will be worried about me."

"This place you're staying. Is it safe?"

She lifted one shoulder. "Safe enough." But she didn't meet Frankie's gaze.

"You get to choose where you go, Martha. We're not going to force you anywhere." She took a careful step closer. "But have you heard of Hope House? It's a home for pregnant girls who have nowhere else to stay."

"No." Martha's expression was wary. "I know most of the places around here."

"It isn't in this neighborhood. It's farther west."

"Who runs it?"

What had happened to Martha? On the street, there were predators waiting to pounce on the weak and vulnerable. But this was worse. Martha didn't trust the people whose job it was to protect homeless kids.

Frankie thought of Bascombe. Sometimes the predators come disguised as friends.

"Her name is Annie. She's about a million years old, but she takes good care of her girls. She gets them to the doctor for their appointments, makes sure they eat well and helps them with school." Frankie waited, watching the myriad expressions flit across the girl's face. Fear. Wariness. A faint hint of hope.

"I don't know," Martha said.

"Why don't you let me and Cal take you there? We won't leave until you're sure it will work for you. If you don't feel comfortable there, we'll think of something else."

"Maybe."

"We'll have to drive," Frankie said carefully. "It's too far to walk."

Martha played with the backpack strap. "You'll leave the car doors unlocked?"

"Absolutely."

She bit her lip, then nodded. "Okay. I'll check it out."

Frankie's shoulders relaxed. "Good. Let's go tell Cal." As they walked toward their table, Frankie saw Cal massaging his leg above his knee. He'd been shifting it while they ate, as if it was bothering him. And he hadn't been able to sit on the sidewalk earlier.

She wasn't about to let him walk all the way back to his car.

When Martha sat down, Frankie put a hand on Cal's

shoulder. "Martha would like to meet Annie. Why don't you stay here with her and pay the bill, and I'll get my car so I can drive her over there. You can go home if you want."

Cal's shoulder tensed beneath her hand, but he gave her a lazy grin. "You trying to dump me?" He glanced at Martha and winked. "Martha wants me to stay. She thinks I'm big and dumb, but cute and maybe marginally helpful." He flashed his dimples at the girl. "Right?"

Martha's giggle shocked Frankie. "Yeah. I want Cal to come, too."

"Um, okay." Was there a woman alive who was immune to Cal's charm? "But I'll still get my car."

Cal started to rise, but she pressed on his shoulder to hold him in place. When he looked up, she nodded toward his leg.

His mouth tightened, but she held his gaze. Finally, he pulled the keys to his truck out of his pocket. "Get mine instead. Martha would be embarrassed to be seen in that heap of yours."

He was letting her help him. Acknowledging he needed help. Frankie's heart fluttered, but she managed an easy smile. "My car will be insulted, but I guess she'll survive. I'll be right back."

AN HOUR LATER, as Cal drove away from Hope House, Frankie watched the streetlights illuminate him in tiny bursts. "Do you think she'll stay?" he asked.

"I hope so. She'll be safe with Annie." The grandmotherly African-American woman had taken one look at Martha and opened her arms. To Frankie's surprise, Martha had stepped into her embrace and exhaled, burying her face in the shoulder of Annie's faded blue bathrobe.

After Martha told them she wanted to stay, Frankie had promised to keep in touch, then watched as Annie led the exhausted girl to a bedroom.

"Annie needs a bigger house," he said.

"She also needs ten more arms and twenty more hours in a day. None of that is going to happen."

"Is your life always like this, Frankie?" he asked. "Staggering from one crisis to another, missing meals, scrambling to help the next kid who shows up?"

"You make it sound like FreeZone is a hotbed of intrigue and trouble," she said. "Mostly, the kids come after school, they leave, I go home. That's it."

"That sounds boring." He touched her hand, a quick brush of his fingers that made her skin burn. But instead of moving away, he lingered. Let his hand hover over hers.

"Right now, boring would be good." It would mean she wasn't worrying about Ramon and now Martha.

It would mean she didn't have to think about Doug Bascombe.

Cal stopped at a red light, the truck rumbling gently beneath them. "Really, Frankie? You like boring?"

She glanced at him. Big mistake. Even in the dim light, she recognized the heavy-lidded expression on his face.

Parts of her life could be very exciting. If she wanted them to be.

"You're too rich for my blood, Cal."

His slow, sexy grin emphasized his dimples and curled her toes. "Funny, I was just thinking the same thing about you."

She snorted. "Immune to charm, remember? Even if I wasn't, you're way out of my league, and you know it." She didn't want to be immune, though. She wanted what Cal was offering—flash and heat and mindless pleasure. A distraction from the problems trying to consume her.

Someone to lean on, at least for a little while.

He'd leave, and she'd go back to her life. But until then, she wanted to throw caution to the wind.

He pressed a kiss to her palm. "What's going through that fascinating brain of yours?"

I figured out that I need somebody, and it's terrifying. "Just admitting that I'm too tired to think rationally tonight."

They were almost at FreeZone again, and Cal pulled into the parking lot where she'd left her car. It was the only one there, almost hidden in the shadows of the church.

He stopped, but left the truck running. "Long night for everybody. Tons going on."

Both on the surface and beneath it. She'd learned some things about herself tonight. That being the Lone Ranger wasn't always the best approach. Or the smartest.

That she liked having a shoulder to lean on.

Specifically, that she liked leaning on Cal.

"Yeah. I'm glad we found Martha."

He nodded slowly, his face in the shadows. "She didn't want to ask for help. But I'm glad she did. Glad she's safe."

"Me, too."

"Thanks for bringing the truck to the restaurant," he said quietly. "My knee was killing me."

For a moment, Frankie was too shocked to speak. Finally, she murmured, "Thank you for letting me get it."

"You didn't give me much choice." He sent her a lazy grin, and serious Cal was replaced by the Cal who took nothing seriously. "I'm gonna have bruises on my shoulders where you held me down. Probably need PT."

She opened her mouth to offer to kiss them and make them better, but caught herself just in time. "Poor baby."

He moved a little closer. "You pack quite a punch, Francesca."

Her stomach fluttered and her mouth went dry. *So do you.* "Frankie's pretty tough. Francesca? Not so much."

"You have no idea how wrong you are." He was close enough for her to see the bristles of his beard, the tiny indentations in his cheeks where his dimples came out when he smiled, the laugh lines at the corners of his mouth. The desire in his eyes. "Francesca terrifies me."

"I didn't think you were scared of anything, Cal."

"You'd be surprised."

"Tell me," she whispered, afraid to breathe.

She expected him to back away, tell a joke to deflate the tension growing between them. Instead, he gripped her hand.

"I'm afraid I won't make the team. Don't have a clue what I'll do if that happens." He ran one finger down her face. "And I don't understand what you're doing to me."

Had Cal said this to anyone else? Admitted his football life might be over? She doubted it. She wasn't sure he'd even admitted it to himself.

She wanted to reassure him. Tell him he could do anything he wanted to. Instead, she leaned over the console, grabbed his shirt and pressed her mouth to his.

He stilled for a moment, then swept his tongue over her lips. Her eyes fluttered shut as she fumbled with her seat belt, then knelt on the seat to lean closer to him. His hands shook as they moved restlessly down her back, curved over her hips, dipped into her waist.

He lit fires beneath her skin wherever he touched her. Desperate to feel more of him, she stretched across the console. Her hands were still fisted in his shirt, and she opened them and pressed her palms to his chest.

He was so much bigger than she was. Solid. Hot. As her fingers explored his sculpted muscles, he shivered. When she touched the hard nubs of his nipples, he froze.

Then he lifted her as if she weighed nothing. He swung her over the console and settled her so that she straddled his thighs.

She was wedged between his chest and the steering wheel, barely able to move. His erection pressed into her thighs, and she undulated against him.

"Stop that," he muttered, nipping her earlobe. "Or I'll embarrass myself."

She moved again.

He groaned. "I'm losing my mind. And you wonder why I can't resist you, Francesca?"

"You can't?" She leaned back to look at him. His eyes were hooded, his face taut with desire.

"Are you kidding me?" He swept his hand down her spine, slid one finger between her waistband and her skin. "I haven't made out in a car since high school."

"I never have." She wriggled again. "I like it."

"You're a devil," he muttered as he fumbled with the button of her pants. When he'd popped it loose, he slid his hand down to cup her rear. "I'm going to make you pay for every one of those squirmy things you're doing."

He kissed her again, and she smiled as she welcomed him into her mouth. She'd never teased a man while making love.

No man had teased her, either. Sex had always been a rush of desire and heat. Never just fun.

She began to unbutton his shirt. His blond chest hair was coarse against her palm, and she wanted to feel it against her own chest. She tugged at the hem of his shirt, trying to pull it out of his pants, and he put his hands over hers.

"Not here," he murmured. He let her go slowly, his fingers releasing her one by one. His palm brushed down her back, as if he couldn't bear to break contact with her.

Finally, he scooped her up and set her in the seat beside him. "Buckle your seat belt. I'm not paying attention to any speed limits."

CHAPTER SIXTEEN

FRANKIE FUMBLED with the seat belt. "My car," she panted. "I need to drive it home."

"Later." His hoarse voice slid over her skin like velvet. He pulled out of the parking lot, tires squealing, then raced toward her apartment. As he turned onto her block, scanning for a parking spot, she said, "Down the alley. Behind the building."

He wrenched the steering wheel and shot into the dark mouth of the lane. The side mirrors were only inches from the brick walls, and the truck jolted as he hit the potholes. Frankie dug her nails into the leather seat, as desperate as Cal to get to her apartment.

He slowed as he reached the small parking area. "There." She pointed to the spot next to the bakery door, in front of the wooden staircase that led to her second-floor apartment.

She slid out of the truck before he could open her door, then wrapped an arm around his waist as they headed for the stairs.

He gripped the railing worn smooth by countless hands. As they started up the stairs, he leaned heavily on her. He probably weighed twice what she did, and her head barely reached his shoulder. But instead of objecting, she braced herself to keep from stumbling.

Cal would be mortified if he knew how much of his

weight she was supporting. *My knee was killing me.* She shifted to take more of it.

At the top of the stairs, he accidentally kicked the metal water bowl she kept for the neighborhood cats, propelling it into the dish of dry food. "You have a cat?"

"A couple of strays hang around."

He nodded at the small plastic box in the corner of the porch—a pet carrier with the door removed. "They're not your cats, but they have a house?"

"Winter is hard on them."

He tightened his arm around her shoulders. "So it's not just stray kids you take in."

"I'm a sucker for the lost ones," she said lightly.

"Yeah," he said. "I noticed."

Are you one of the lost ones, Cal? Their gazes met, and neither of them looked away. The yearning in his expression made her want to hold him close.

When her chest was too tight to breathe, she fumbled with the door. She flicked on the kitchen light, stepping aside so he could enter.

As she locked the dead bolt behind them, she watched him take in his surroundings. The stove beside the door was old, but immaculate. The compressor in the avocado-green refrigerator next to it wheezed and struggled to pump out cold air. The slow drip, drip, drip from the sink on the far wall echoed loudly in the small room.

Her battered kitchen table wobbled, even with a piece of folded-up paper under one leg. But the yellow tiles on the bottom half of the wall were cheerful, as were the bright yellow, blue and red flowers on the wallpaper above it.

His kitchen was no doubt equipped with the latest appliances, granite countertops, fancy cabinets. Her shabby apartment was a reminder of how different they were.

She rubbed her palms down the sides of her pants. "Um, want a beer?"

He turned and slid his hands over her shoulders. As he backed her toward the wall, he said, "What do you think I want, Francesca?"

She wanted to tear off her clothes to feel his hands on her bare skin. She gripped the front of his shirt to hold herself steady. "Not a beer."

"Smart woman." He ran his hands down her arms and crowded her closer to the wall. No other part of him touched her, but his shoulders blocked out the overhead light, and she flattened her palms on his chest. She usually stayed away from big men. They made her edgy. Made her feel boxed in. Trapped.

Not Cal. She wanted to touch him, feel the strength of his muscles, the power in his limbs. She wanted to wrap her arms around him and hold him close.

"What can I give you instead?" she whispered.

He stared down at her, his cheeks flushed. Then he fitted her against him. "Everything," he said, his voice a low rumble that made her shiver. "I want everything, Francesca."

He finally kissed her. This time, his kiss was soft, asking instead of demanding. He nibbled at her lower lip, ran his tongue along the seam of her mouth. Tasting. Testing. He was holding back, trying to go slowly. But his quivering muscles, the way his hands gripped her as if they'd never let go, betrayed his need.

His chest was solid against hers, his muscles hard. Unyielding. His erection pressed urgently into her belly. He was all about power. Strength. Aggression.

But he was gentle with her.

She curled one leg around his, and he groaned into her mouth. Their kiss became harder, more demanding, as he cupped her rear end and lifted her. She struggled to get closer.

His grip tightened and he thrust against her. Needing more, Frankie opened her mouth in invitation, and he swept in.

He lifted her higher, and she wrapped her legs around his waist. "Bedroom," he managed to say.

With her mouth fused to his, she waved toward the hallway. He held her tightly and lurched through the door to her bedroom. He laid her on the bed and followed her down.

The security light from the courtyard filtered through the curtain, spilling over his head. The planes of his face were sharply defined. When he opened his eyes, she saw raw need in them.

"Cal," she murmured against his mouth.

He eased away and stroked her face. His thumbs caressed her cheeks as he asked, "You sure you're okay with this?"

In spite of the desire that smouldered between them, he was careful. Respectful. "I'm sure." She brushed her mouth over his. "You?"

"I've been sure for a long time."

He kissed her again, and as his tongue tangled with hers, she tasted the coffee he'd had at Hope House. She lifted her hips, and he pressed against her.

"I need you," he murmured into her mouth. He swept his hands down her sides, over her belly, as if trying to learn her by feel alone. When he cupped her breasts, she arched up.

A seam ripped as he tore the T-shirt over her head, then stared down at her. "*This* is what you wear beneath those ugly-ass T-shirts?"

She glanced down at the black scrap of nothing that was her bra. "You don't like it?" she asked, raising her eyebrows as she tugged his shirt out of his jeans.

He rolled over, lifting her on top of him. "Oh, sweetheart, I like it. I like it a lot." He drew one finger down the edge of the bra, thumbed the clasp, let it fall open. He sucked in a breath as he stared at her breasts. Then he lifted his head and took one nipple into his mouth.

Arousal shot through her blood like lightning, all flash and heat, making her burn. She could feel his erection through the thin material of her cargo pants, and she rocked against him. She clawed at his shirt, trying to undo the buttons, but her hands were shaking too badly. Finally, she ripped it over his head.

His muscles weren't bulky, but they were defined and chiseled. His abs rippled down his belly and the dark blond hair on his chest was wiry against her fingers. She touched him everywhere, entranced by his body, trying to learn every ridge of muscle, every inch of hot skin.

When she bent to put her mouth on his chest, he froze again. His skin was salty on her tongue, and he smelled like clean sweat and the outdoors. He groaned when she trailed her mouth over one of his nipples.

He reached for the waistband of her pants, opened the button and shoved them down her hips. After tossing them aside, he stared at her as she straddled him again the way she had in the truck.

He ran his hands down her sides, touched the sheer black thong that barely covered her. "I have never seen anything sexier in my life." He trailed a finger along the edge of the fabric, building a drumbeat of need inside her.

He rolled her onto the bed, cupped her and slid one

hand inside her panties. To her shock, she convulsed at the contact. She grabbed his hand and held it against her as her climax went on and on. Finally she stilled, feeling completely drained.

"Cal." She opened her eyes and reached for him. "I'm sorry. I didn't… That's never…" She brought his face down to hers and kissed him.

"Don't apologize." He swept his hand over her, chest to thighs, and she trembled. "That was amazing. *You're* amazing."

She kissed him again. Softly. Tenderly. Saving every taste, every touch, every sound to remember later. Then, as her mouth moved over his, she unbuttoned his jeans and pushed them down his legs. His penis was hot through his boxers, and she held him for a moment before she removed his shorts, too.

Then he was in her hand. As her fingers moved over him, she savored every hitch in his breathing, every jerk of his hips.

Suddenly, he lunged for his discarded jeans, fumbled a foil packet out of his wallet and rolled the condom on. "Francesca," he murmured, coming back to her, his hands twining with hers. "I can't wait any longer. I need you."

"I need you, too, Cal." She closed her legs around him, drawing him in. Their bodies fit together perfectly, and they moved as if they'd been lovers for years. She held him tightly, tangled her mouth with his, wound her legs around his waist.

Heat built again as they moved together, both of them shifting, angling their bodies as if determined to give the maximum pleasure.

Frankie didn't try to hide behind a cool exterior. She didn't worry about being in control, didn't think about what she was revealing. She opened herself completely to

Cal, let him see how much she wanted him, how he made her feel. And as her release crashed through her, she felt him join her.

WHEN CAL COULD MOVE AGAIN, he flipped onto his back, carrying Frankie with him. She sprawled on his chest, her face buried in his neck, her delicate hands still touching him. Mapping him with her fingers.

She traced gentle patterns on him, and he shuddered at her touch.

She'd given him everything, and he wanted more. He wanted to lie here with her forever, learning everything about her. Her favorite color. Her favorite food. If she cried at sad movies. What made her laugh.

She was passionate, caring, fiercely loyal. She gave all of herself in everything she did. Including lovemaking.

He'd never known anyone like Frankie.

He wanted to wrap his arms around her and never let her go.

Whoa. He tensed, and she raised her head. "What's wrong?"

Her voice was low and husky, and he wanted her all over again. Ignoring his sudden unease, he held her more tightly, her breasts against his torso, his hand stroking her back. "Only that I can't get enough of you."

The hint of tension disappeared, and she relaxed against him, boneless. "Me, either," she whispered, so quietly that he wondered if she meant him to hear.

His eyes began to flutter closed, and he opened them wide before he could fall asleep. He never stayed the night. He always charmed himself out the door after sex.

He should do the same now. But his hands wouldn't release her. He needed to feel her skin against his. So he turned and pressed a kiss to her neck and allowed his eyes to close completely.

The jangling of a phone startled him, and he felt Frankie stiffen in his arms. "Do you need to get that?"

"I don't want to. But I should." She buried her face in the crook of his shoulder. "It's my brother."

"Your brother? Calling you at eleven at night?"

"It must be important." She untangled herself from Cal and reached for her pants. The long sweep of her back was pale, the tiny bumps of her spine a string of pearls in the darkness.

"Nathan," she said. "What's wrong?"

As her brother spoke, the tightness came back to her body, erasing the glow from their lovemaking. "How did that happen?" She glanced over her shoulder at Cal, who propped himself on one elbow. "Can't it wait until morning?"

Cal heard the faint sound of a male voice. Upset. Finally, Frankie said, "All right. I'll be there as soon as I can."

She snapped the phone closed, then flung it toward the pile of their clothes. "A pipe burst in the basement of the restaurant. They didn't discover it right away, and there's a foot of water down there. The plumber is working on it, but the restaurant is a mess. It's going to take all night to clean it up. I have to help them."

"Why did they call *you?*" Why couldn't her brothers take care of it themselves?

"Because we're family." She stared at him as if he were a slow child. "When there's a problem, we help each other."

Cal's only family was his father, and it would never occur to him to call the old man in the middle of the night for anything. Maybe because the only help his father had given him had been yelling instructions from the sidelines during his childhood football games.

His old man called him for help a lot—for tickets to a game or merchandise from one of Cal's sponsors. Cal never dropped everything to get to it, though.

He was both disappointed and relieved that Frankie had to leave. He wouldn't have to worry about the awkward morning after. He wouldn't have to break his no-sleepover rule.

Frankie grabbed her shirt, fingered the ripped seam. Then she pulled on her pants. "You're not going to try and change my mind?"

"I won't make you choose. That wouldn't be fair."

She swiveled on the bed and took his hand. "Come with me."

To meet her family? He swallowed. "Why would I do that?" he asked cautiously.

She slowly untangled their fingers. "I thought you might want to hang out. The more people helping, the sooner we'd be done. We could come back here afterward."

He reached for his jeans. "I have to get to rehab early tomorrow," he said without meeting her eyes. "Otherwise, I'd love to meet your brothers."

"Okay." She slid off the bed, took a clean shirt from a drawer and found her shoes. Finger-combing her hair, she said, "Would you mind dropping me off at my car?"

"Of course not." He shimmied into his jeans and shirt, watching her as he tied his laces. She still hadn't looked directly at him.

He didn't want to say goodbye, he realized uneasily. But boundaries were important. He *had* to leave.

He drove through the alley more slowly this time, trying to avoid the potholes. There were still people on the street, but not as many as earlier. When he pulled into the church parking lot, she turned to him, one hand on the door.

"Thank you," she said. "I could have walked, but this way I'll get to the restaurant more quickly. I'll see you tomorrow, Cal."

He reached for her, not sure what he would say, but she was already jumping out. He waited while she started her car and drove out of the lot, then followed her. The blue plume of smoke from her exhaust disappeared down the street in front of him.

CHAPTER SEVENTEEN

THE CLANG OF WEIGHTS and the curses of the men in the gym echoed around Cal as he sweated and struggled. The pressure tugged on his rebuilt knee and he grunted in pain.

God, he hated rehab. He hated the pain, the boring repetitions, knowing everyone in the room was watching him. Everyone was trying to figure out the same thing—was he good to go for the season?

He would be. His aching knee was still stiff, still tentative, but he'd work harder. He'd get his leg back to where it had been before the surgery. He had three weeks until training camp, and he'd use every spare minute.

He wanted to spend his extra time with Frankie.

The weight dropped with a bang as he wondered how the cleanup had gone at the restaurant. How bad the mess had been. What time she got home.

Last night had been great. Better than great. He remembered her whispering his name, touching him as if she couldn't get enough, the sounds she'd made when she climaxed.

The damn phone call had ruined everything.

He wanted to know what Frankie looked like in the morning. If she liked morning sex. If she was crabby when she woke up, or one of those irritatingly happy people.

He wanted more of her. More of what she had to give—the unconditional support, the caring, the loyalty. The understanding. She was always ready to go out of her way for people who had no one else in their corner.

On paper, he wasn't that guy. He had money. Connections. A job most men would kill for. But he couldn't name one person who was a close friend. Who genuinely cared about him. His agent wanted to make money from him. So did the team. His friends were people who craved what he had—money, fame, access to beautiful women.

Frankie didn't want anything from him besides his help at FreeZone. That made her unique in his world. And last night, when he could have helped her, he'd run like a scared rabbit.

He hadn't wanted to leave her. He could have gone with her, met her brothers, pitched in on the cleanup. Gone back to her apartment afterward.

But he hadn't. He had to focus on his career. Get to rehab early. Work on his knee. Being with Frankie the way she deserved would compromise that.

So she'd gone on her own. She would be tired this morning. But she'd still go to the bakery, still open Free-Zone.

He'd gone home and slept.

"Hey, Stewart, you old hound dog." Remington, one of the wide receivers, grinned as he waved a rolled-up newspaper in Cal's face. Not the sports section, which was the only place Cal would be mentioned in the paper these days. He'd been conspicuously absent from the club scene since his arrest.

"What are you talking about?" No one could have snapped his picture with the latest It girl or a bunch of drunken teammates. The gossip columns had nothing to report.

Remington wiggled the newspaper in the air. "She's not

your usual style, buddy. You have a secret life we don't know about?"

The weights clattered as Cal dropped them to lunge for the newspaper. He unrolled it and saw a photo of him with Frankie at the pizza parlor. They were staring at each other, their hands barely touching. Seeing that private moment in the newspaper felt like a violation.

He hadn't noticed anyone snapping their photo. But he wouldn't have; he and Frankie looked completely absorbed in one another.

He tossed the paper onto the floor. "Yeah, I have a secret life. It's called community service."

"So who's the chick? She's pretty hot."

Cal wanted to reach over and rip Remington's throat out. "She runs the teen center where I'm doing my service."

Remington grinned as he stooped to pick up the paper. "What kind of work are you doing there, Stewart? 'Cause I'd like to get some of that myself."

Before Cal could respond, Remington strolled away with the newspaper, still looking at the picture. Cal's hands curled into fists. Before he could move, one of the coaches stepped in front of him.

"The rehab going well, Stewart?" Marty Kelleher asked.

Cal forced his attention away from Remington. Kelleher's face was lined from too many hours in the sun, his red hair was mixed with gray, and he hadn't shaved yet that day. But his eyes were sharp and observant.

"Going great, Coach." Cal lifted the weight as if he'd never been interrupted.

Kelleher put his hand on Cal's knee, stopping him from lifting again. "Got a favor to ask you," he said.

"What is it?" Cal snatched a towel from the floor and wiped the sweat off his face.

"That new safety we drafted. Tommy Grover. The kid is good. He's got the instincts and the moves, but he doesn't have the intangibles." Kelleher glanced at Cal's knee. "He needs help. Will you work him out? Spend some time with him?"

Cal smiled through clenched teeth. "Sure, Marty." He was a team player. Even if it meant training his replacement. "Is Grover here now?"

"He's doing his weights. When you finish here, grab him and work with him for an hour or so."

"Will do." He wiped the towel over his face again as the coach walked away. *Damn it.*

Cal flung the towel across the room. Asking him to put the rookie through his paces was a not-so-subtle way of finding out how Cal's knee was really doing. To see if he had anything left.

If he was through, if he couldn't pass his physical, the team would still get their money's worth as long as he taught the kid his tricks. All the knowledge he'd accumulated in his years in the league. The team could wring the last ounce of value from Cal before they cut him.

He stared at the ugly red scars on his knee, then pushed himself to his feet. Might as well get this over with.

"Hey, Cal," Marty called from across the gym. "Almost forgot. When you're done with Grover, come find me. I got a call from some guy at DCFS."

DCFS? Was it Bascombe? Whatever. He had more important things to think about right now.

Tom Grover was a nice kid, Cal thought an hour later. Eager to learn, appreciative of Cal's help. Not full of himself like a lot of the rookies. He'd asked Cal about his community service, and Cal found himself describing FreeZone as they gulped down bottles of water.

"Sounds like the place needs help," Tom said.

"Yeah." Cal tossed an empty bottle at the recycling bin, watched it drop in. "What they really need is money."

Tom rubbed his face with a towel. "The Cougars should organize a fundraiser for her. They do that kind of stuff a lot, don't they?"

"Yeah, they do. That's not a bad idea."

Grover nodded. "Thanks for the help, man."

"You're welcome," Cal murmured as he watched the kid walk away. It hadn't been as bad as he'd expected. Tom was a quick study. He was going to do well in the league. Cal had almost enjoyed teaching him.

FRANKIE ROLLED OVER when the sun woke her up. Still half-asleep, she frowned. The sun didn't shine into her bedroom window.

When she opened her eyes, she was face-to-face with a yellowing Ani DiFranco poster, which hung next to a Death Cab for Cutie poster. The heavy paper curled around the edges and the pictures were faded.

She pushed herself up to a sitting position. She was in her room at her parents' home. Nathan's home now.

Details of the previous evening came rushing back. Hauling everything from the basement of the restaurant to the first floor. Waiting for the plumber to finish, then hand washing and drying all the dishes.

Cal. At her apartment.

Sitting on the side of her old twin bed, Frankie rested her elbows on her knees and shoved her hands through her hair. He would have stayed, she told herself. If Nathan hadn't called, Cal would have stayed. They would have woken up together.

Today was her day off at the bakery. She and Cal could have slept in, made love again this morning.

She pressed her hands into her scalp. Cal wouldn't have stayed the night. She'd seen his panicked expression when she'd asked him to help at the restaurant. He'd started edging toward the door the moment the words were out of her mouth.

He'd claimed he had rehab in the morning, and she knew that was true. But even if he hadn't, he wouldn't have joined her. He didn't want to meet her brothers. He didn't want anything beyond sex.

So she'd come alone. And she'd woken up in her old bed. In her old room.

She'd hung the posters when she was twelve. The books on the shelves were the ones she'd read as a preteen—all those sad books about kids with cancer, parents dying, broken homes. God, why had she wanted to read about such heartbreaking topics?

She'd read them because she'd felt safe. Invincible. As if nothing bad could ever happen to her.

But it had.

A world of heartbreak had dragged her down, nearly drowning her. Afterward, she couldn't bear to look at the books.

When she got home from juvie, this room had been a refuge. It made her feel as if she was safe again. Back where she belonged.

Now it was a reminder of how far she'd come from that scared, angry girl. How dangerous it was on the streets, when even the protectors could turn out to be predators.

She hadn't let Bascombe win before. She damn well wasn't going to now. She'd figure out a way to bring him down.

Throwing on her clothes, she went down to the kitchen.

Nathan sat at the old family table, drinking coffee and reading the newspaper. He gave her an assessing look.

"Hey, Frankie. Coffee's made."

"Thank God for that."

He jerked his head toward the counter. "You know where the mugs are."

She knew where everything was in this kitchen. The appliances had been replaced, the walls had been repainted a cheerful yellow, but the dishes were in the same cabinets. So were the glasses. The silverware, the cooking gadgets, the pot holders and towels were all in the same drawers.

She leaned against the counter, blowing on the coffee, as Nathan swiveled in his chair. "Thanks for coming over last night, especially so late. Marco and I really appreciate it."

The gulp of dark liquid scalded her throat. "That's what families do."

"Did you leave the football player behind when I called?"

"What are you talking about?" Her heart began to pound, which was ridiculous. She was an adult. So was Cal. But she didn't want to discuss last night with her brother.

Nathan tossed the newspaper onto the table. Next to the gossip column was a picture of her and Cal at the pizza place last night. "You have something going on with him."

She tore her gaze away from the photo. "Cal is doing community service at FreeZone."

Nathan snorted. "He wasn't working very hard in that picture, was he? Oh, wait. Maybe he was. He was sure focused on you."

"Don't be crude, Nathan. Cal is none of your business."

"You're having fun. I get it. But when he hurts you, he answers to me."

"*When* he hurts me? What makes you think he will?" The image she'd tried to ignore all night leaped back into her head—of Cal, right after she'd asked him to come to Mama's with her. He'd physically drawn back. Put distance between them. She'd seen the shock on his face before he'd masked it.

Cal didn't want a relationship. He wasn't about getting involved, meeting a woman's family, making a commitment.

Nathan made an impatient noise. "Come on, Frankie. The last woman he dated was Prissy Howard. Sure, she's attractive, but she has no apparent career or talent. She's just famous for being famous. The one before that was Chloe. Again, she's a freakin' supermodel so she's gorgeous, but not the sharpest tool in the shed. You're worth a million of those two, Frankie. You deserve better than a guy that shallow."

She stabbed her finger into his biceps. "Nathan, I'm not a kid anymore. The protective chest-pounding is not necessary. Maybe I *want* a shallow guy." She flexed her finger, which had bent the wrong way. Damn it, why had she let Nathan provoke her into losing her temper? "And Cal's not shallow."

"Yeah, he's Mr. Serious. Mr. Save the World." Her brother rolled his eyes. "Cal Stewart is all about clubbing, hot women and football." When she narrowed her gaze at him, Nate added hastily, "Not that you're not hot, Frankie." He curled his hands around the back of his head. "God! I do *not* want to talk about my sister's hotness."

"Then drop it, before you shove your foot any farther down your throat. Not your business. Not anyone's business but mine."

"Mom would have said the same—"

"Mom would have agreed with me," Frankie interrupted. "She'd have told me that you can't help who you like. For God's sake, Nate. I'm twenty-seven years old. You don't have to threaten my boyfriends anymore." She pushed past her brother and left the kitchen, stopping only to grab her purse before she stormed out of the house.

Frankie clung to the steering wheel of her car as she drove east toward her apartment. She didn't want to go home. Not now, when she was raw from her fight with Nathan. She didn't want to face the unmade bed that would still hold the scent of her and Cal.

She didn't want to think about what Nathan had said, that Cal was going to hurt her.

To know that he already had.

She knew his focus was football.

Not FreeZone. Or her.

Her apartment would be easier to face later tonight. Delaying going there would give her time to calm down. Time to put last night with Cal into perspective. To file it in the box labeled "Good times that aren't going to happen again."

She'd put everything out there. Cal hadn't. Frankie wasn't going to play those games.

It had been a stupid thing to do, anyway. She was supposed to be supervising him. She could just imagine the smirks if anyone found out they'd slept together.

She didn't want to think about this now. She'd do what she always did when she needed to keep busy—she'd think about her kids. Maybe she'd go to the hospital, visit Yolanda and see if Ramon would turn up.

CHAPTER EIGHTEEN

THAT EVENING after leaving FreeZone, Frankie couldn't wait to get home. By the time she turned into the alley, she was desperate for the refuge of her apartment. But as she emerged into the small parking area, she found a sleek black car in her spot.

Parking spots on the street were rare and coveted. It would take forever to find one.

She braked hard and stopped the car. Then dropped her head to the steering wheel. It had been that kind of day.

The afternoon had gotten off to a bad start when Julio stopped shooting baskets long enough to announce that his "street agent" was getting him a shoe deal. Cal had told him he was an idiot, and the discussion had disintegrated into a shouting match.

Everything had gone downhill from there. Sean had arrived with Harley, Lissy, Kerrie and Maria, and reported that Vipers had followed them to FreeZone. Don was called, reports were taken, and the girls had sucked up most of Frankie's remaining energy as she'd struggled to settle them down.

Emma had stopped by to tell her that Ramon had called her, but hadn't shown up to meet her as he'd agreed. Frankie gave the social worker Yolanda's address, hoping Ramon was all right.

On top of everything else, she'd tried to act as if nothing had changed with Cal. Tried to forget he'd seen her naked. Pretended she hadn't jumped his bones the night before.

He'd done the same. She had smiled so hard that her cheeks still ached. She was never smiling again.

She backed out of the alley and scanned the street for a parking spot. She found one a block and a half away. Thinking dark thoughts about the car in her space, she trudged back toward her apartment.

When she was almost there, she noticed a man leaning against the building, watching her approach. Doug Bascombe.

Bascombe knew where she lived. She stumbled to a halt as fear sliced through her.

When she realized she was trembling, she drew herself straight. She wasn't a powerless child any longer.

"What are you doing here?" she asked as she strode toward him. She knew by the slight narrowing of the bastard's eyes that she'd managed to keep her voice steady. That she sounded pissed off and not afraid.

"You think I'm in this slum for my health? I came to talk to you, Devereux."

Slum? "Not interested." *Dickhead.* She took a step toward the door, but he blocked her way.

"You should be," he murmured. His voice was soft. Mild. But his eyes were ice-cold, his mouth thin with anger. "I saw the picture in the paper."

He was too close. He still used the aftershave he'd worn years ago, and the smell made her stomach roil. She swallowed to fight down the nausea.

"Good for you," she managed to say. She knew what he was referring to, but wasn't going to make it easy for him. She reached into her bag for her keys. "The picture of the new mayor at the teen shelter was great. I'm sure you applaud his priorities."

Bascombe looked confused for a moment, then his expression hardened. Frankie slipped the keys between her fingers and made a fist around them.

She fought the urge to back up as he leaned in. "I'm talking about the picture of you and Stewart. You looked very cozy. No wonder you insisted he stay at your little teen center."

"It was his choice, Doug. Too bad he refused your offer, but I guess he didn't want to work with you."

Bascombe bared his teeth, bringing memories that had lurked beneath the surface for years. Helplessness. Being trapped. Frankie pushed them back where they belonged. "I called his coach, to point out how having Stewart work for me would benefit both DCFS and the Cougars. Stewart called me back and told me to go to hell. Are you doing the football player, Devereux?" he asked. "Whispering secrets in his ear? Telling him your dirty lies? Is that why he doesn't want to help me?" Bascombe edged closer. "That would make me very unhappy."

Frankie tightened her grip on the keys until they cut into her palm. "Are you threatening me, Doug?" Of course he was—he would love to hurt her. He knew shutting down FreeZone would be devastating to her.

"I don't have to threaten you. I've talked to some of my social workers about your place. They say it's underfunded and overextended. That besides your gang problems, you have a rat infestation. Plumbing issues. There have been complaints."

"Really?" Her face and neck heated. "Funny, but I haven't heard any of that. Send me a copy of the complaints."

She tried to go around him, but he grabbed her wrist. "You were always willful and disobedient. No respect for your elders. No one could control you." His gaze drifted all the way down her body and back up. "No wonder you ended up in juvie for armed robbery."

Frankie's skin crawled and she ripped her wrist free of his grasp. It didn't matter if she couldn't find anyone else Bascombe had molested. She had to speak up. He shouldn't be in charge of an agency that dealt with children. "I ended up in juvie because I was homeless and hungry. Now get out of my way, Doug. I've had enough of your bullshit."

"What bullshit would that be, Frankie?" Cal's voice. On her left.

She hadn't heard him drive up. But his truck was in the middle of the street, door open. Cal didn't look as if he was hurrying. But he reached her in a couple of long steps.

She wanted to lean into him. To let his strength give her courage. But she didn't move. "Cal."

He touched her back in a casual caress, just enough to send a message to Bascombe. And the other man received it. He scowled as he looked from one of them to the other. "What are you doing here, Stewart?"

"I was just about to ask you the same thing," Cal said. He moved toward the other man, and Bascombe shuffled back.

"Yes, Doug. How did you know where I live?" Frankie asked.

"Information is easy to find if you know what you're doing. And I do." He looked from her to Cal. "Remember that."

He stepped around them and disappeared into the alley. Moments later, she heard an engine roar to life, then a black car nosed into view. Bascombe was the bastard who'd parked in her spot. Of course.

He slowly turned onto the street, keeping his gaze on Frankie. The threat was abundantly clear.

If she spoke up, if she told the truth about him, he'd close FreeZone. Try to damage Mama's Place.

Guilt, fear and shame tangled inside her as she watched him drive away.

"What did he want?" Cal asked as the sound of Bascombe's car faded.

"He's angry that you told him to go to hell again. Maybe you should have warned me."

"You didn't seem interested in personal conversations at FreeZone earlier." Cal touched her arm, but she didn't look at him. "What does he really want, Frankie?"

She kept her head down. She wasn't about to spill her guts to Cal. Not after last night. He didn't need to know about that raw, tender spot she carried from her experience with Bascombe years ago. About the guilt that haunted her now. "Obviously, he wants you to come to work for him."

Cal spun her around to face him. "Stop lying to me. What's going on with him?"

She was too shaken to think of a simple, plausible answer. "I have to shower." A hint of Bascombe's aftershave lingered in the air, and she needed to scrub all trace of him from her skin. "Why did you come here, Cal?"

"I want to talk to you."

"About what?"

"What the hell do you think?" He leaned against the door, invading her space just as Bascombe had.

"There's so much to choose from. Your fight with Julio? The fact that Ramon didn't show up to meet Emma? The Vipers hassling Sean and the girls?" Frankie shoved Cal aside. "And get out of my face. If Bascombe couldn't intimidate me, you certainly can't."

She yanked her keys out of her bag to unlock the outer door. Her fist was still closed around her keys, their tips protruding from between her fingers. She tried to loosen her grip, but her fingers were frozen in place.

Cal stepped behind her and took her fist in both his hands. He massaged her arm and the spasming muscles above her wrist. He pried open one finger, then another and another, until her keys fell to the sidewalk. Instead of picking them up, he stretched her fingers, squeezed them, until all the muscles relaxed.

She looked at her hand, so tiny in his. Her fingers were pale and thin. He could crush them without thinking about it. But his touch was gentle. Careful.

She pulled away and stooped to retrieve her keys.

Cal followed her up the stairs. Neither of them said anything. He stayed two steps below the landing while she unlocked her door, and he didn't enter her apartment until she stepped inside and left the door open.

He closed it behind him. "Go take your shower," he said quietly. "I'm not going anywhere."

Yeah, he was. Maybe Cal wasn't planning on disappearing from her life tonight, but he was leaving. She knew it, and he did, too.

She should have remembered that.

But if she could have a do-over, would she do anything different?

No. She would change nothing about last night. Except the ending.

So she nodded. "There's beer in the fridge. My keys are on the table by the door if you want to move your truck while I'm in the shower."

AFTER FINDING a parking spot a few blocks away, Cal returned to her apartment, heard the shower running and grabbed a beer. He took a gulp of Blue Moon as he stood in Frankie's living room. They hadn't made it this far last night. And even if they had, he'd been too wrapped up in her to have remembered any of it.

A few paintings decorated the walls, one of Lake Michigan. The water was gray and whitecaps rolled onto a deserted beach. Ominous clouds hung low in the sky.

It was a little amateurish. Had one of her kids painted it?

He'd put money on it.

There was a still life of flowers, equally amateurish, and a painting of a boy playing basketball. To Cal's surprise, the kid leaping high to stuff the ball in the hoop was easily identified as Julio.

The bookcases in the corner had lived a long, hard life. Volumes loaded the shelves, the thin wood bowing under their weight. Romance novels, mysteries, thrillers. Biographies and nonfiction. Arranged haphazardly, but Cal would bet Frankie knew where every book was.

The couch was covered by a pilled and faded blue blanket, but it was surprisingly comfortable when he sat down. A small television set with rabbit ears was perched on top of a table, flanked by two easy chairs under red-and-green blankets. Everything in the room was shabby. And also welcoming, with multicolored throw pillows on the couch and a brightly colored rug on the floor.

Frankie's living room reminded him of the house where he'd grown up—with everything old, secondhand, a little battered. She spent all her money on FreeZone.

His father claimed all his money had gone to furthering Cal's football career. Cal had been happy playing in his town's youth league, but his dad had insisted he join the expensive travel team.

Who had wanted football more—father or son?

The shower stopped, and the sound of Frankie moving around wiped all thoughts of his dad from Cal's mind. She was standing naked on the other side of that wall, dripping wet. Memories from the previous night swept over him.

Several minutes later, carrying a beer, she walked into the living room in dark green capris and a black tank top. Her feet were bare, her toenails painted red. He didn't think she was wearing a bra, but he didn't let himself check.

She threw herself into one of the chairs and drew her feet up. "What are you doing here, Cal?" She dangled the unopened bottle by its neck.

She wasn't going to dance around the subject. He hadn't really expected her to.

"We didn't get a chance to talk this afternoon. I thought we should."

The bottle swung slowly back and forth. "Fine. Talk."

He nodded at the beer. "You want me to open that for you?"

"I can open it myself." She wrapped the bottom of her tank top around the cap and twisted. The neck of her tank dipped and the cap popped off. As she took a sip of beer, a hint of cleavage showed. She didn't adjust it.

Instead, she watched him calmly. Waited for him to speak.

Cal needed a few more minutes to figure out what to say about last night. So he focused on the more recent issue. "What's going on with Bascombe? Why did he come here?"

Frankie studied her beer bottle as she picked at the label. "He wants you. And he's pissed that you turned him down." She took a sip of beer and her gaze slid away from his.

Cal's instincts had always been good, and they were screaming at him now. "There's something personal between you."

"I don't like him."

"Yeah, I got that. Why?"

"Ancient history. Nothing to do with what's happening right now."

Her foot jiggled. She tore up the tiny bits of label she'd scraped from the bottle.

"You sure about that?" Cal asked. She still hadn't looked at him.

"Why wouldn't I be? He's a detestable little worm. A bureaucrat who rose to the top because he knows how to work people. I don't like worms."

There was something else, something she refused to tell him. Cal was sure of it. But he didn't know how to pry the information out of her. "Frankie, I don't like the guy, either. But I think it's more than that."

Now she looked at him. "You want to exchange confidences? Tell each other our deep, dark secrets? What are you, a girlie man?"

"Fine. Don't tell me. But I'm kicking his ass if he tries to push you around again."

Her expression softened, the tough-girl facade melting away. "Thank you, Cal. But you know you can't do that. Sarah will throw you in jail if you get in trouble again. And trust me, Bascombe would be happy to see you behind bars. You told him no. He doesn't like that."

Had Frankie told Bascombe no about something? Was that where the tension came from?

Silence hummed between them. When Cal looked at her, curled up in that chair with her red toenails and tank top and pants that hugged her very nice ass, Bascombe faded away. All he could think about was the previous night. About how amazing it had been.

He shifted in the chair. He'd been a jerk last night. They both knew it. So why was she acting as if nothing had happened? As if he hadn't walked out when she'd asked for help?

Every other woman he knew would be yelling and throwing stuff. Why was Frankie sitting there calmly, drinking a beer?

He'd rather she threw something at his head. He knew how to deal with that.

"Um, how did it go at the restaurant last night?" he asked cautiously.

She took a drink, then set the bottle on the table next to her. "It was a mess. But between the three of us and the plumber, we got it cleaned up. They'll be able to open tonight."

"Good. That's good." The bottle knocked against his teeth as he took a swig to soothe his suddenly dry throat. "I should have gone with you," he finally said.

Frankie shrugged. "You had things to do. No problem."

He studied her, knowing she wasn't being honest. Women talked in a code men couldn't decipher. But he had to take a stab at it. "Frankie, you looked upset last night. Did I, um, hurt your feelings?"

She started swinging the bottle again. "Why would you think that? We had sex. You left. I thought that was the deal. Good times. No strings."

"Now you're making me feel cheap."

Her mouth curved up. "That's the woman's line, Stewart. I guess you *are* a girlie man."

This was the Frankie he'd met when he'd first started at FreeZone. A smart-ass. Protecting herself. Hiding beneath a tough shell.

He wanted Francesca back. She was the real Frankie, the one who had let him know what every touch had done to her. The one who didn't hide. The one whose eyes had told him what she felt.

He didn't know what the next step was. He'd never wanted to take it before.

But he wanted Francesca. To get her back, he needed to figure it out.

FRANKIE TOOK ANOTHER SIP of beer she was too distracted to taste, and watched Cal. Last night, she'd opened the door of her heart and he'd slammed it shut. She'd embraced vulnerability and only embarrassed herself. She'd made him uncomfortable. The trifecta of emotional mistakes. It would be a long time before she tried that again.

Tonight, she'd keep to safe topics. And if she let Cal stay, she'd keep it light. Fun and sexy.

"So I went to see Ramon's mother this morning," she said.

Cal paused, then nodded. The discussion about last night was over for now. "I should have gone with you."

She'd wanted him there. Which was stupid. "You were probably at rehab. I wanted to get there early and catch Ramon."

"No luck?"

"He didn't show up. But Yolanda said she'd have him call Emma. And she agreed to go to rehab. Sort of. She wants to get clean, but she said rehab didn't work."

"I'll do some checking. We'll find a place where the patients are treated like people with a problem instead of junkies."

Just when she wanted to write Cal off, he confounded her again. "That's very perceptive."

He shrugged. "Seems pretty obvious. I'll find a place that will give her a chance to succeed."

"She doesn't have the money to pay for a program like that."

"I'll foot the bill," he said impatiently, as if that was a

minor detail that didn't need to be discussed. "All she'll have to worry about is getting better."

"That's generous," Frankie said slowly.

He waved off the compliment. "I have money. She doesn't." He leaned forward. "Have you talked to Martha?"

"Not yet. When I phoned Annie, we decided it would be best to give her a few days to get used to the place. She's settling in, but she won't call her parents. She told Annie they threw her out when she told them she was pregnant."

How could parents do that? Frankie wondered. She fought with her brothers, but when it counted, Nathan, Patrick and Marco were there for her.

Cal scowled. "They should have their asses kicked."

"You're big on ass-kicking, aren't you?" she said lightly.

He shrugged. "It's generally my first option." His mouth quirked. "I should probably say I regret breaking that guy's jaw, but I don't. He deserved it. And I ended up at Free-Zone."

Cal was happy about doing a hundred hours of community service? Frankie had assumed he was a hotheaded, violent man when Sarah had told her he was coming to FreeZone. Shallow and utterly predictable. But he had depths she hadn't imagined.

Depths she wanted to explore, in spite of the fact that he'd run away last night.

She knew Cal was a player, so she shouldn't have been surprised that the words *come meet my brothers* terrified him.

She could hold a grudge and be pissy and pouty. Or she could be pragmatic and realistic. She could enjoy Cal while she had him and mourn him privately when he was gone.

He finally glanced at his watch. "I should go."

"Is that what you want to do, Cal? Leave?"

He stilled. "Of course not." Meeting her gaze with sudden intensity, he said, "I replayed last night in my head all day. I couldn't concentrate on anything. But I figured you wouldn't want me here."

"I enjoyed last night, too." She stood and reached for his hand. "I've been looking forward to repeating it."

CHAPTER NINETEEN

FRANKIE'S LEGS GRIPPED his waist and her mouth fused to his as they moved together on her moonlit bed. He needed to feel her skin beneath his hands. He flipped her on top of him, then skimmed her back. Her sides. Her breasts.

Her muscles trembled and Cal slid his fingers down her sweat-slicked arms, searching for her hands. But instead of linking her fingers with his, she gripped his shoulders more tightly and arched her back. Her eyes fluttered closed, and she moaned into his mouth as she tensed.

She shuddered around him, and he followed her over the edge. They clung together, their breath sawing in and out, and she buried her face in his neck. She inhaled deeply, as if trying to absorb his scent, then pressed her mouth to the sensitive spot beneath his ear.

"Francesca," he murmured, rolling onto his side, but keeping her close. Her hair tickled his nose, and he rubbed his face against the silky strands. The grapefruit scent of her shampoo filled his senses, and he searched for her mouth.

He fumbled for the sheet at the end of the bed and drew it around them. His eyes drifted closed as he aligned their bodies so he was touching her from chest to legs. Frankie's trembling gradually stopped. Her muscles relaxed, and the hand she'd laid on his shoulder dropped away.

Floating between awareness and slumber, he felt her

breathing slow and deepen. Cal wrapped his arms around her and let himself fall asleep.

In his dream, Frankie backed away as he reached out. She was gloriously naked, making no attempt to cover herself. "No touching," she told him. "Look all you want, but you can't touch."

He lunged for her and the real Frankie jerked, startling him awake.

"What's wrong?" he asked. He'd tightened his arms around her, and he loosened them a little.

"Nothing." She rolled onto her back, out of his embrace, and smiled up at him. Tracing the dimple in his right cheek, she said, "You should probably get going."

He brushed her hair away to see her more clearly, but her face was hidden in shadows. "I thought I'd stay with you tonight."

Her hand faltered, then she let him go and sat up. "I get up really early to go to work. The bakery is right below the apartment, and there's lots of noise. Mixers. Dishes banging together. People yelling. You need your sleep. You can't do rehab all tired out."

He was a sound sleeper and doubted noise from downstairs would wake him up. But she had no way of knowing that; he hadn't stayed with her last night.

She'd wanted him to, though. She hadn't worried about the noise then.

Before he could argue, she slipped out of bed and drew a white T-shirt over her head. It fell to the middle of her thighs.

Beneath the shirt, her curves were outlined by the light shining through the window, and he wanted to taste them again. He reached for her, but she was too far away.

He sat up reluctantly, hoping she'd change her mind. When she didn't, he threw on his clothes. She walked him to the door and kissed him, her mouth lingering on his. "See you tomorrow," she whispered, pressing herself against him.

The next thing he knew, he was in the hall, staring at the dark, scratched oak of her closed door. He heard her footsteps recede as she headed back to bed.

How had he ended up out in the hall when he wanted to spend the night with her?

Frankie had maneuvered him out of her place in a move as slick as any he'd seen. And he would know, because he'd done the same thing to her yesterday. Tonight, she'd kissed him and sent him on his way while he was still intoxicated by her.

Damn it.

Their lovemaking tonight had been fun. Sexy. She'd nibbled on his ear, whispered naughty words, touched him until he'd been ready to explode.

The sex hadn't been intimate, though. Not like yesterday.

He didn't want the same soulless sex with Frankie that he'd always looked for in the past.

No, with Frankie, he craved the intimacy.

As he headed down Lake Shore Drive to his condo, clouds skidded across the moon, splattering light on the lake one moment, leaving it dark the next. He wanted to sweep away the clouds that had filled Frankie's eyes tonight. He wanted the bright, open woman she'd been before.

He wanted Francesca.

The fundraiser he'd discussed with the Cougars' president this morning would help. Cal would make sure Free-Zone was stable, that it had the funds it needed to take care of the kids. And with the team involved, money would pour in. Hell, the silent auction alone, featuring signed jerseys, footballs and game tickets, would raise a ton of cash.

Frankie would realize that she was important to him. That he wanted to help her. Take care of her.

She would understand that he'd screwed up the night before, and that he was sorry.

AFTER CAL LEFT, Frankie hurried to the living-room window and pushed the blind aside. She saw him walking away from her building, hands in his pockets, staring straight ahead. She wondered if he'd turn around and try to convince her to let him stay, after all.

His stride never faltered. She pressed her cheek to the glass, trying to prolong her view, but he eventually disappeared.

She dropped onto the radiator cover and waited. After a few minutes, she heard the rumble of a car engine down the street. Instead of coming closer, it faded away.

Struggling to her feet, she straightened the blanket on the chair, picked up a book. She should go back to bed. The alarm went off early. Instead, she turned on the iPod connected to a set of speakers, and curled up on the couch. She didn't want to be alone with herself right now.

Shame slid through her as the sound of Adele's "Rolling in the Deep" poured through Frankie's living room. Her gut ached and her chest felt hollow. She and Cal might have had it all, too. He'd screwed up, but she hadn't given him another chance.

Instead of feeling righteous because she'd made a statement, no-strings sex left her feeling vaguely ill. Like a user.

Not very nice.

She'd tried to protect her heart, but it was a lonely way to live. Cowardly.

A braver woman wouldn't have held back with Cal. A braver woman would have let him stay when he'd asked. She would have followed her heart and given him everything.

Doug Bascombe slid into her head, smiling.

Of course he smiled. He knew what a coward she was.

The kind of coward who, to protect herself, sent a man away when she really wanted him to stay.

The kind of coward who was dragging her feet about outing a predator because she was scared.

It was time to stop being afraid and take action instead. She turned on her computer, found the name of an investigative reporter for the *Herald* and called the woman's voice mail.

As FRANKIE APPROACHED FreeZone the next day, she saw a figure in a hooded sweatshirt and baggy jeans standing at the door, peering inside. She hesitated when she saw the black-and-red shoes, the red belt. Viper colors.

Part of her brain told her to slow down. Be careful. But after a mostly sleepless night, she ignored it. She wasn't going to let the gang hurt her center.

The youth turned when he heard her coming, and her stomach dropped to her toes. This was worse than a random banger looking to cause trouble.

"Ramon," she said. The boy pulled the hood of his sweatshirt lower over his face. "What are you doing here?"

"My mama told me to come see you." He tried to look confident, but tugged again on his hood as his gaze flicked nervously over their surroundings. "She said she's going to rehab, so I have to keep my promise and get out of the Vipers. She said you'd help me."

"Take this." Frankie shoved the bakery box into his

arms and unlocked the door. "Get inside," she said. "Hurry."

She turned on the lights, but didn't open the blinds. Ramon crossed the room, heading for the deli case. He slid the box inside, then stood uncertainly, rubbing his hands down the sides of his jeans.

"It's okay, Ramon," she said, tossing her bag onto a table. "Now that you're out of sight, you're safe. Come sit down."

He walked over slowly, favoring his left leg. "Are you mad 'cause I came?" he asked quietly.

"I'm not mad." She was scared. "But you can't stay. If the Vipers knew you were here, they'd—"

"I know," he said, staring at his expensive sneakers. He rubbed a circle on the linoleum with his toe. "They'd do something bad to FreeZone."

"Yes," she said. "I can't let that happen. But I'm not going to abandon you, either. We'll figure out what to do." She hesitated. "What happened with the Vipers?"

He pushed the hood off his head. "I told them I was through."

Frankie sucked in a shocked breath at the bruises covering his face. "Oh, Ramon!"

"It ain't nothing," he said, hunching his shoulders. "Thought they could do a beat-down on me with three guys. I got away before the rest of them started."

"Where else are you hurt?"

He brushed his fingers over his left side. "Coupla places. Not important."

"Do you…do you need to see a doctor?"

"No doctors. They'd find out. Come after me and the doctor."

Frankie slid her hands beneath her thighs to keep

from reaching for the boy, who clearly didn't want to be touched. He watched her with eyes far too old for his age.

Waiting for her to figure out what to do. To help him.

"Do you have a plan?" she asked.

He shook his head. "Haven't had time."

"What about the foster family you stayed with? Can you go back there?"

"Nope." His knee jiggled. "Too close to Viper turf."

Before she could answer, the front door rattled. Then someone knocked impatiently. Ramon jumped to his feet.

"I don't think the Vipers would knock," she said quickly. "But go into the back while I see who it is."

He limped slowly toward the dark inner room. When he disappeared, Frankie cautiously parted the blinds on one window.

The painful tension in her muscles eased. Cal.

"Thank God," she said as she unlocked the door and he stepped through. "I'm so glad you're here."

His cautious expression relaxed. "Me, too," he said, reaching for her. "Frankie, I—"

"Shh." She laid a hand over his mouth, shivering when he kissed her palm. She closed her eyes and allowed herself to lean against him briefly. Finally, she stepped away. "We'll talk later. Ramon is in the back. He's been beaten. We have to get him away from here."

Her lover disappeared, replaced by a dangerous man. "How bad?"

"He won't tell me. But he looks awful."

"Let me talk to him. Maybe I can help." Cal put his hands on her shoulders, rubbed them up and down her arms. "You look terrible."

"Gee, thanks," she said, trying to smile. "You sure know how to sweet-talk a girl."

Instead of smiling back, he brushed her hair from her face. "I hate that I did that to you."

"Cal, I…"

"You're right. Not now." He pressed a hard, quick kiss to her lips, then let her go. "Are you going to call Emma?"

"I'm going to start there."

Cal grabbed her. "You're not thinking about taking Ramon to your place."

"I'm not an idiot."

"Thank God." He kissed her again and made his way toward the back.

She *was* an idiot for mooning over Cal. And stupid if she thought another kiss could make everything right. They had things to resolve. Ramon to deal with. This wasn't the time or place.

As she watched him go, Frankie pulled her phone out of her pocket and pressed the speed dial for Emma. She held her breath until she heard her friend's voice.

"Emma Sloane."

Thank God. "Emma, it's Frankie. We have a problem."

THREE HOURS LATER, after Frankie locked the door behind the last stragglers, she hurried to help Cal clean up. She'd been tense all afternoon, afraid someone had seen Ramon at FreeZone. And that the Vipers would retaliate.

After Frankie's quick conversation with Emma, Cal had driven Ramon to meet the social worker. She had a foster home on the far northwest side of the city, she'd said. It was temporary, but Ramon could go there until she found a more permanent placement.

Frankie hadn't taken a deep breath until Cal walked in an hour later and nodded at her. He slipped back into his role easily, familiar with their rhythm and routine.

He'd become a part of FreeZone. The kids relied on

him. She relied on him. They would all miss him when he left.

She most of all.

But he *was* leaving. His life was a million miles away from this seedy, sometimes-dangerous neighborhood.

"You ready to go?" Cal called.

"Absolutely." She grabbed her bag and pulled out her keys. He slung an arm over her shoulder.

"I was thinking Chinese," he said. "Anyplace good around here?"

At his casual assumption that they'd be eating together, the tight band around her heart loosened slightly. Maybe she hadn't completely screwed things up last night.

"Right around the corner from my place."

"Let's go. I'm starving."

As soon as they were in her apartment, he dropped the paper bag of takeout on the table and gathered her close. She clung to him, savoring the steady beat of his heart against hers, the strength of his arms around her. The stresses of the day melted away.

"Frankie," he murmured into her hair, "I'm sorry I didn't go with you the other night. To help your brothers at the restaurant. I kicked myself all the way home."

"It's…" *okay,* she started to say. But it wasn't. He'd hurt her with his eagerness to leave. And she'd retaliated last night.

"I wanted you to come," she said into his shirt. "I didn't want you to go like that."

"I wanted to be with you," he said quietly. "But I've never been a 'meet the family' kind of guy. It freaked me out."

"They're just brothers. No big deal." She'd gripped his shirt in her fist. Relaxing her hand, she smoothed out the wrinkles. "I shouldn't have asked."

"If you want something, you should always ask."

Not when I know it's something you aren't willing to give. "I wanted you to stay last night, too. I'm sorry I kicked you out."

"Making me do the walk of shame. I felt so cheap." He leaned back and grinned down at her. "I don't know how you'll make it up to me."

The serious conversation was over. So instead of getting sloppy and emotional, she began to unbutton his shirt. "You have any suggestions?"

"Oh, honey, I have a ton of them." With his shirt hanging open, he pulled her T-shirt over her head. His grin faded when he saw the bright pink bra with the ribbons at the front clasp. "That's a good start."

She took his hand and led him toward her bedroom. "It gets better."

CHAPTER TWENTY

AFTER THEIR BREATHING SLOWED, Cal gathered her close on the rumpled bed. As he stroked her back, they talked about the bakery, the kids at the center, his rehab session that morning.

Like a real couple, Frankie thought uneasily. But they weren't. The intimacy was a facade. She had less than three weeks left with him.

He pressed a kiss to her hair and sat up, leaning back against the pillows. She snuggled in and rested her head on his chest. "Tell me about your brothers," he murmured.

"You want to talk about my family?" She twisted to look at his face. "Really?"

"They're important to you. So I want to know about them."

Her throat swelled at the same time as she warned herself not to give his question too much weight. He was sorry he hadn't gone to help her family. He was making up for it by asking about them now.

"There's three of them, right?" he prompted.

"Nathan, Patrick and Marco. Patrick is an FBI agent in Detroit. Nathan and Marco run the restaurant, Mama's Place. It's in the northwest corner of the city, in the Wildwood neighborhood."

"Is that where you learned to bake?"

"Mostly." Memories flooded back. Of her mother patiently showing her twelve-year-old daughter how to make a pie, knead bread, bake a cake. Frankie had loved those afternoons in the kitchen with her mom. The cooks would be chopping, shouting at each other. Her father, supervising them, shouting right back. She and her mom had been a little island in the middle of the madness. "My mother taught me a lot. I picked up more by working in bakeries and restaurants."

"Did your parents work in the restaurant, too?"

"Yes." She tugged the sheet up to cover her breasts. "After they were killed, Nathan dropped out of college to raise us. He kept the restaurant going."

"That's tough." Cal twined his fingers with hers. "I'm sorry."

She swallowed the lump in her throat and tried to smile. "It was a long time ago. It's easier now to focus on the good memories. To remember how it was when they were alive."

"Sounds like a great family," he said, and his tone was wistful.

"What about your family?"

"Later," he said, peeling the sheet away. "Dinner was ages ago. I want dessert." He kissed her until she gave in and wrapped her arms around him.

"Me, too," she whispered.

MUCH LATER, Cal scooped her off the bed and carried her into the bathroom. It reminded him of the one in his father's house—the same white bathtub surrounded by the same green tiles, the same dull silver fixtures. But Frankie's bathroom was bright and quirky, from the shower curtain that was a colored map of the world, to the seashells in glass jars on the vanity and the back of the toilet.

His father's bathroom had been nothing but a place for

necessities. The shower curtain had been dull brown and mildewed along the seams. The mirror on the medicine cabinet had a long, diagonal crack, and the only decoration was a box of tissues.

Cal turned on the water, waited for it to warm, then stepped into the small tub with Frankie. He'd never showered with the women he slept with. But he was doing a lot of things with Frankie he'd never done before.

She turned to face him and smiled, making his chest tighten. She looked like a water goddess. Rivulets ran down her shoulders, her chest, her legs, plastered her hair against her head. "This is cozy."

The tub was too small for both of them. But he didn't care. "I like cozy."

She relaxed against him. "Me, too," she murmured.

She leaned around him, grabbed a bar of soap and lathered it over his chest. It bubbled and foamed and slid down his body.

"I should be washing you," he said, taking the soap away from her. "You're going to make me smell girlie."

She smiled again. "I think you're man enough to carry off a little cucumber-scented soap."

"The bathroom in the house where I grew up looked just like this. Didn't have any fancy soap, though. Or fancy decorations."

"Yeah?" She took the bar and turned him to scrub his back. "Tell me more."

He should have kept his mouth shut. The water, the warmth, the cocoon of the tiny tub had loosened his tongue. He wished he could toss off a joke and change the subject.

He never talked about his father. Cal's memories were buried in a deep pit, and he wanted to keep them there. He searched for a quick line about his old man, something easy and funny, until he could distract her. With some shower sex, if he was lucky.

But she'd shared something private about her family. Her pain at her parents' deaths. If he wanted the intimacy he'd thrown away, he needed to reciprocate.

He placed his palms against the slippery tile and focused on her hands, which were drawing circles on his back. "My mom died when I was a baby. It was just my father and me." He cleared his throat. "He signed me up for peewee-league football when I was six or seven, and as soon as he saw that I was pretty good, football was it. All he ever talked about."

"Is that what you wanted?"

A question his father had never asked him. "Who knows? A kid wants to make his dad happy. Make him proud. And having a football star for a son was everything to my old man."

Frankie turned him to face her. "I'm so sorry, Cal."

"Hey, I love being a football player. And I make a good living at it."

"Sounds as if you didn't get a chance to figure out anything else you'd like to do. Anything else you were good at."

"I told my father once that I wanted to teach math. But I was just a kid." His dad had made fun of him for weeks. What kind of idiot wanted to teach losers how to add and subtract when he could be playing football?

Cal had been careful not to make that mistake again.

"But hey, I had all the glory. I was the quarterback on my high-school team. All the girls chasing me. Every guy's wet dream."

Frankie held his face in her hands. "Cal, you know that's not what families are really like, don't you?" She searched his eyes, as though she felt sorry for him. *Jeez.*

"It worked out fine. I don't have strings and I like it that way." Frankie was tangled in strings. Every kid who walked into FreeZone became woven into her life.

Maybe part of him wanted that, too—to come home from practice, tell Frankie what the coach had said, the stupid things the guys had done, how his knee felt.

But it wasn't going to happen. His time at FreeZone was almost finished. Once camp started, he and Frankie were finished, too.

He needed to focus all his energy on making the team. It was going to be tough enough without any distractions.

And Frankie was a huge one.

She said softly, "Alone is a sad way to go through life. My brothers drive me crazy, but I know they always have my back."

Cal wouldn't be alone. He had the team. They were all the family he needed. "That's why I like football. If you're pissed off or upset about something, you work it out on the field. You hit a guy a few times, take a few hits yourself. Clears your head."

She leaned against the wall, steam billowing around her. "You don't need football for that," she said. "There are other ways to clear your head."

She was talking about relationships again. About exposing your soul to someone else.

Enough of this. He grabbed the soap and rubbed it over her chest, leaving suds behind. "You're right, Francesca. There are many better ways. Let me show you one of my favorites."

Frankie's eyes reflected the internal debate he knew she was having—continue the conversation or let it go. Allow him to retreat and regroup.

Finally, she smiled, but there was a hint of sadness in

it. "I love to learn new things," she said as she pressed her soapy body against his.

"I ADMIRE YOU FOR BEING willing to tell your story, Ms. Devereux." The reporter turned off her tape recorder and studied Frankie's office at FreeZone. Lisa Halliday was a serious-looking woman, with dark hair pulled into a low ponytail. She was casually dressed in a pair of jeans and a sweater.

It had taken a week for Frankie to connect with her and set up an interview.

"I should have told it a long time ago." Frankie's hands were still shaking and she shoved them between her thighs. Telling Lisa what had happened, even without the graphic details, brought it all back. "But I wanted to forget about it. And I almost had until I saw the article in the paper."

Lisa touched her arm. "You'd be surprised how often that happens—that someone's able to suppress their memories until an unexpected reminder jolts them loose."

"So what's our next step?" Frankie asked.

"I'm going to do some research. Talk to some people. Ideally, I'll find someone else with a similar story. But even if I can't, I'm going to write the article. You deserve to have your story told. And maybe it will help another victim come forward."

"Will you, um, use my name?" Maybe she could escape without Bascombe knowing for sure she was the one who'd outed him.

Maybe that was the coward's way.

"That depends. I will if you're comfortable with that and if you give me permission. If not, I can just identify you as a woman who runs a center for at-risk kids."

"Thanks, Lisa." Frankie stood and held out her hand. "Keep me posted."

She walked the reporter out, then picked up her cell phone. She pushed a button, and a few minutes later, Patrick said, "Hey, Frankie. What's going on?"

She heard voices in the background. "Have you found anything?"

A door closed, cutting off the noise. "Not yet, but I'm still working on it. I'm going to ask another agent to help me. He's done a lot of work on pedophiles."

"I just talked to the investigative reporter. She'd like to find someone else who had a similar experience."

"Yeah, that would be good. I'll do my best. Okay, Bunny?"

"Thanks, Paddy. Love you." She snapped her phone closed.

That night, as she and Cal walked into her apartment, she forced all thoughts of Bascombe from her head. She'd taken the next step. It was okay to let it drop for now. Okay to concentrate on Cal and their remaining time together.

Although they'd never discussed it, they'd fallen into a routine. After FreeZone closed, they picked up food, went to her place and fell into bed. She knew the routine wouldn't last. Knew she had less than two weeks. She was determined to savor every minute.

Tonight, though, she didn't want to fall into bed. She was still edgy from her interview with the reporter. Telling Lisa what had happened years ago had left her shaky. Frankie set the pizza on the table and pulled a beer and an iced tea out of the fridge. "Eat first?"

"SURE." Cal settled into a kitchen chair and opened the beer. "What's up?"

"Just hungry. I didn't have lunch today."

She twirled her iced-tea bottle on the table and flipped up the lid of the pizza box. But instead of taking a piece, she picked at the crust. "How's the rehab going?"

"The knee is improving." It still hurt, but he didn't mention that. It would lead to talking about training camp. And he didn't want to think about that right now.

"That's good."

She tried to smile, but her expression was almost sad. As if she suspected that he was lying, but wouldn't dig any deeper. That she didn't want to talk about training camp, either. That she wanted to live in the moment. Store up memories.

He needed to store them up, too. They had less than two weeks left. Ten days before he finished his community service and reported to training camp.

Too little time before he said goodbye to Frankie.

Thank God he'd set up that benefit. It was in a week and a half, and it was his parting gift to her. She'd see how important she'd been to him.

He was keeping it a secret because he wanted to surprise her. But he wasn't sure how to get her to the hotel.

"We're doing this backward," he blurted.

"Doing *what* backward?" She gave him a puzzled look.

"This whole dating thing."

"We're dating? Really?" She picked up a piece of pizza and nibbled on it.

"See, that's what I mean. Usually, a guy gets to know a woman before they sleep together. They meet for coffee. Go out for dinner a few times. Exchange long, soulful looks into each other's eyes."

"I think we've got the soulful looks down pat." She finally smiled as she fluttered her eyelashes at him.

No wonder he couldn't keep his hands off her. That siren's smile of hers turned his heart inside out. He couldn't concentrate when she looked at him as if he were the only thing in her universe.

"And I know you pretty well," she added.

A shadow of sadness crossed her face. It was gone so quickly that Cal told himself he'd imagined it. "I mean it, Frankie. I want to go on a date with you."

She frowned in puzzlement. "You do?"

"Of course I do. Why wouldn't I?"

She crossed her arms over her chest, but he didn't think she realized it. "Because I'm not the kind of woman you normally date," she said quietly.

"That's bull," he said, but uneasiness slithered through him. Frankie *wasn't* his usual type. And he felt things for her that he'd never felt for another woman.

"I'm not a supermodel or an actress. I'm not famous. Or rich."

"You're so much more than any of those other women." She was real. Genuine. Passionate about everything. Not afraid to say what she thought. None of the women he'd dated had ever treated him the way Frankie did—like a normal, everyday guy.

She snorted, killing the moment.

"That's it. I'm taking you someplace nice. Someplace fancy, where everyone can see you and be jealous of me."

"You don't have to do that, Cal." She set her pizza down. "We can call this a date. See? We're talking and eating. Our food isn't even cold."

"We'll go to a restaurant," he insisted. "We'll work our way up to the big show."

"There doesn't have to be a big show."

"Oh, yes, there does. Ten days. I'll be done with my community service, and we'll go someplace fancy. A night on the town. See and be seen."

"'See and be seen'?" She shook her head. "I'm not in-terested in that, Cal. I just want to spend time with you."

She left the words *before we're done* unsaid, but he heard them, anyway. He didn't want to be done with Frankie, either, but he didn't have a choice.

"Well, you can spend time with me at a fancy place." The team had booked the Palmer House for the benefit. "Maybe at one of those big-deal downtown hotels."

"Can I say no?"

"You can try." He reached across the table for her hand. Kissed it. "But I know how to make you say yes."

THAT WEEKEND, Frankie had just pulled up to Annie's house when the door opened and Martha ran down the stairs. The teen barely resembled the young woman they'd dropped off here almost a month ago. Frankie and Cal had been here to see her several times, and the transfor-mation had been gradual, but her appearance today was still a surprise.

Her shiny blond hair fell in soft curls down her back. She'd gained a little weight and lost the gaunt, haunted expression. She was even smiling.

"Hey, Frankie," she said as she got into the car.

"Are you sure you want to do this, Martha?" The car sputtered at the curb as Frankie waited, certain Martha would change her mind.

"I love to go shopping," the girl said happily. "Even if it's not for me."

"You're a freak," Frankie muttered.

Martha grinned. "I'm not changing my mind. Because if I did, you wouldn't get a dress. You'd go on your fancy date in those cargo pants and a ratty tank top. And that would make *you* the freak."

"I had no idea you were such a smart-ass," Frankie

said as she put the car in gear. "Annie's a bad influence on you."

The girl's smile softened. "Annie saved my life. I adore her."

"Annie certainly helped. But you saved yourself, Martha. You survived on the street and you looked for help." Martha still had problems to solve. But right now, she was just a normal kid, happy to go shopping.

When they pulled up in front of the Second Time Around consignment shop, Martha frowned. "What are we doing here? I thought we were going to a mall."

Frankie shuddered. "I always buy my clothes at places like these. It's like a treasure hunt. And the clothes are a lot cheaper."

"There's a reason they're cheaper, Frankie." Martha shook her head. "You think Cal is going to want to see you in a secondhand dress?"

"Who says I'm going out with Cal? I know lots of guys who would take me out for a fancy dinner."

Martha rolled her eyes like a typical teen. "Duh, Frankie. I've seen the way he looks at you. And you look back."

She'd be more careful, Frankie vowed. She didn't want the kids to figure out that she and Cal were…together. It would only bring up painful questions after he left.

"This store has a section for designer clothes," she said. "It's usually out of my price range. But I'm splurging today."

"See, I knew it," Martha said as she slammed the door. "You wouldn't splurge unless you were going out with someone special. It's Cal."

An hour later, the pile of rejects was enormous. Martha shook her head at Frankie's latest choice and pushed her into the dressing room. "The stuff you're picking is totally lame. You stay here. I'll find something."

Under normal circumstances, Frankie would have argued. But Martha was having fun. Frankie had let the girl feel she was helping.

A few minutes later, Martha was back. "I found it," she said with a huge smile. "This one."

It was an electric-blue satin dress with a plunging neckline and a low back. And a short skirt. "That's not exactly my style, Martha."

"You will look amazing in this." She thrust it toward Frankie. "Trust me. I know what I'm talking about."

"I don't know." Frankie studied the delicate, feminine dress that wasn't even close to her style.

"Just try it," the girl pleaded. "Give it a chance."

"Fine." Frankie closed the door and shimmied into the dress. It fell in soft waves down her body, clinging to her hips and stopping just above her knees. The V-neck accentuated her breasts, and the color...the color was gorgeous.

She walked out and Martha gasped. "It's even better than I thought it would be," she squealed. "Turn around."

The skirt floated around her legs as Frankie did so, and when she faced Martha again, the girl was grinning. "I will personally kill you if you don't buy that dress. It fits you perfectly and makes your eyes *soooo* blue."

Frankie pulled her into the dressing room and wrapped her arm around the girl's shoulders. They both stared in the mirror, blond head taller than black one, Frankie's frame skinny next to Martha with her swollen abdomen. Frankie fingered the dress as she watched herself and Martha in the mirror. The woman with the huge, bright blue eyes and the creamy skin wasn't Frankie. It was Francesca. "You think so? Really?"

"Jeez! Didn't your mother ever take you shopping?"

"No." She let Martha go and smoothed the dress down her thighs. "She died when I was pretty young."

"That sucks," the girl said softly.

"Yeah." Frankie struggled to smile, to make Martha comfortable again. "But now I have you to help me."

"Cal will *die* when he sees you in that dress."

Frankie adjusted the bodice. "I shouldn't get it, then. I'd like him to live through this date."

"Yeah," Martha crowed. "I *knew* it was Cal. You have to buy it. That dress will kick his ass."

"I guess this means I'll have to buy shoes, too," she replied. "Or do you think I can get away with my Doc Martens?"

Martha looked so horrified that Frankie hooted with laughter. "Gotcha."

The girl crossed her arms over her baby bump. "Ha-ha. You're so funny."

"Let's go pay, then have lunch," Frankie said, still grinning.

The sandwich shop was noisy and crowded. Martha held her sandwich in one hand, using the other to gesture as she talked about living at Annie's house and going to school in a program for pregnant girls.

As she took another bite, she rubbed her belly absently, then pressed on the left side. "Baby kicking?" Frankie asked casually.

Martha's hand dropped away. "Yeah. It does that a lot lately."

"It must be amazing to feel your baby moving."

The girl raised one shoulder. "It's weird."

"Do you know what you're going to do once the baby's born?" Frankie held her breath. Martha refused to discuss her plans with anyone. Including the doctor.

She pushed the rest of her sandwich away. "I'm giving it up for adoption."

"That's a tough decision."

"Not really." Martha twisted a lock of hair around her finger and didn't meet Frankie's gaze. "I don't want any reminders about the father."

Oh, God. Frankie reached across the table and took her hand. "Honey, were you raped?"

"No. It wasn't exactly rape." She kept her head down.

Not exactly? "But it was ugly," Frankie said gently.

Martha nodded, still staring at the bulge of her belly. "Yeah. Ugly."

"Did someone coerce you?"

"I don't want to talk about it," the girl said. She slid out of the booth. "I should get back to Annie's. She'll wonder where I am."

"Okay. But you can call me anytime if you want to talk. I know a good social worker, too." Frankie pulled a business card out of her bag. "If you'd rather talk to a stranger, you can call Emma."

Martha shoved the card into her pocket without looking at it. "Sure."

Neither of them said much on the way back to Annie's house. But as Martha got out of the car, she bent down and said, "Will you and Cal come to see me before you go on your date?" She smiled, and the sadness was gone from her eyes. "I don't trust you to get everything right."

"Hey! I know how to do girlie things."

"You're a girlie loser." Martha leaned into the car and hugged her. "But you're still pretty cool. Thanks, Frankie."

The teen ran into the house, and Frankie waited until she was safely inside before driving away.

CHAPTER TWENTY-ONE

AT THE SOUND OF THE DOORBELL, Frankie wiped her hands on the towel and took one last look in the mirror. Showtime.

She buzzed the lock downstairs, then stuck her head out into the hallway. Her heart raced as Cal climbed the stairs.

The tailored jacket of his suit clung to impossibly wide shoulders, and his dress pants broke perfectly over gleaming shoes. He wore the suit with the confidence of someone comfortable with his power.

She'd never seen Cal dressed up. Okay, maybe she'd seen an internet photo of him in a tuxedo. But never in person. Watching him come toward her in the dark suit, light blue dress shirt and striped tie took her breath away. He was the sexiest man she'd ever seen.

"Wow," she said as he got closer. "Wow."

As he neared the top of the stairs, he said, "Martha warned me you were going to try to wear those boots of yours. Is that why you're hiding behind the door?"

She stepped back to let him come in. This was just a date. With a man she already knew well. She wasn't trying to impress him. But her hands were suddenly sweaty again.

"No boots, thank God," he said as he glanced at her feet. Stared at the hideously uncomfortable, strappy black stilettos. "You buy those to drive me crazy?"

"I might have."

A familiar gleam filled his eyes. Her heart raced and heat sizzled through her as his gaze crawled up her legs to her dress, then her face. Then dropped to her dress again.

"Oh, my God," he finally said. "Frankie. Wow. Wow right back atcha."

He reached for her hands and kissed one, then the other as he continued to stare. "I've changed my mind. We're not going anywhere but your bedroom. No way am I letting anyone see you looking like that."

"You approve of the dress."

"Oh, yeah." He drew one finger down the deep V-neck, then smoothed both hands over her bare shoulders. "*Approve* doesn't even come close."

He lowered his head to kiss her, and she melted against him. But instead of pulling her close, he reluctantly eased away from her.

"We should, uh, get going. If I kiss you again, we'll never make it to dinner."

"That's okay with me," she murmured, running her hands down his lapels. "It's just food. We can eat later."

"I promised you a real date and that's what you're getting. Besides, you got those sexy shoes for me. That beautiful dress. I'm not going to waste them."

"I don't think they were wasted." The memory of Cal's response would warm her for a long time after he was gone.

"No." He glanced at his watch. "We should get going. So we can hurry back."

"Okay." She gathered up her purse and keys. "But you know we don't have to do this."

"Yeah, we do." He ran a palm over his hair. "I would get into so much trouble if I broke this reservation."

"Really? Cal Stewart is afraid of a maître d'?"

"You don't know who I'm dealing with," he muttered.

"Okay, now I can't wait to go." She turned the dead bolt and dropped the key in her tiny purse. She headed for the stairs, but he stopped her with a hand on her arm.

"You know I don't just want to have sex with you, Frankie," he said, tucking a strand of hair behind her ear. "Don't you? I want to take you out. Show you off. Spend time with you."

She gripped the thin chain of her purse until the links pressed into her palms. "I want to spend time with you, too, Cal."

She wanted so much more than that. But fantasizing about happily-ever-after scenarios was a sure path to a broken heart.

He twined his fingers with hers as they descended the stairs from her apartment. He hesitated as they entered the alley. "I parked behind your car because there wasn't anything on the street, and I didn't want to make you walk. Maybe it wasn't my best idea ever. I should have double-parked out front so you wouldn't have to deal with the smelly alley."

"It's just an alley," she said, tugging him along. "No big deal."

Weeds grew up from cracks in the concrete, and garbage cans stood at attention down the length of the alley. Dumpsters lined the courtyard where she parked, and a rat scurried beneath one as they got closer. If she needed a visual reminder about the gulf between her life and Cal's, this was it.

"I hate that you have to live in this dump."

"I like my apartment. The rats are part of its ambience."

His hand tightened on hers. "Do you have any idea how special you are?"

His gaze searched her face, and her heart began to

pound. She went on her tiptoes and pressed a kiss to his mouth. "You make me feel special, Cal."

He cupped her face in his hands. "I've never known anyone like you." He stared down at her, but she couldn't read his expression. Finally, he kissed her, murmuring, "I'm crazy about you, Francesca."

Wishing things could be different, that they could go from "crazy about you" to something more serious, Frankie let her lips cling to his for a moment. Then she drew away. "I like you a little bit, too, Caleb."

Grinning, he wrapped an arm around her waist as they approached his car. "Let's go see Martha. She gives me that complete adoration I don't get from other people."

"You TOTALLY ROCK, Frankie," Martha said, fussing with the drape of the dress. "Told you so." She turned to Cal. "What do you think?"

Cal kissed her hand. "You are a genius for finding that dress. Do me a solid? Go with Frankie every time she shops for clothes."

Martha's eyes lit up. "That would be awesome."

"So, how do *I* look?" he said, lifting his palms. "Aren't you going to tell me I rock, too?"

"You always rock, Cal," Martha exclaimed, and her face turned bright red. "But you look sick in your suit."

"Sick?" He turned to Frankie. "I was hoping for amazing. Maybe even stupendous."

The girl collapsed into giggles, and Frankie laughed. "Time to move on, Cal. I don't want all the praise to go to your head."

Martha positioned them next to each other, insisting they wrap their arms around each other's waist, then grabbed Annie's camera to take a picture. Frankie loved that the girl was behaving like a typical teen rather than a frightened runaway.

When they said goodbye, she hugged Martha tightly. "I'll save this dress for you," Frankie whispered. "You can wear it for a special guy someday."

Martha's smile filled her face as she waved from the porch.

"She looks great," Cal said as they drove away from Hope House. "Happier."

"Of course she was happy." Frankie smiled. "Her crush came to see her."

"Poor kid. She should be mooning over some nerdy high-school boy."

"She will eventually. But right how, you're safe. She needs someone to tease her and treat her like a normal kid." Frankie put her hand on his arm. "You're good for her, Cal."

His jaw clenched. "I'd like to be good for the guy who knocked her up. I could be real good for him."

"That's my Cal. Always with the ass-kicking."

He glanced over at her. "I like that."

"I know you do."

"Not the ass-kicking part. The 'that's my Cal' part."

Frankie curled her fingers around her purse. "It was just an expression. That's all. You know, the kind of thing you'd say to your dog. Or your friend." Oh, God. She was babbling. She never babbled.

"Give it up, Frankie," he said, his mouth twitching. "You are so busted."

"Moving on. Where exactly are we going?"

He stopped at a light and smiled. "It's a surprise."

SIX HOURS LATER, Cal felt Frankie lean against him as they stood on the sidewalk in front of the Palmer House, waiting for the valet to bring his truck. She'd spent the evening charming the socks off everyone from his teammates to the movers and shakers of Chicago. She'd tucked a lot of checks into that tiny purse of hers.

He hoped she was sticking close because she needed to touch him. He suspected it was because she was too tired to keep herself upright. He dropped a kiss on her hair. He'd take her any way he could get her.

He froze. That wasn't part of the plan. Training camp started in a few days, and he had to be there. His time with Frankie would be over.

So he'd make the most of this evening. Their last one together.

He peered down the street, relieved to see his truck approaching. He'd planned on taking Frankie to his condo tonight. He was looking forward to showing her his home, seeing her reaction. Making love with her on his king-size bed. Taking a shower together.

She would be the first woman he'd ever taken to his condo. He liked to go to the woman's place. That way, he could escape.

But he didn't need to worry about escaping Frankie. They both knew this was ending.

After they were on the road and he was maneuvering beneath the elevated tracks on Wabash, Cal cleared his throat. "I was hoping you might want to stay at my place tonight. Is that all right?"

She'd leaned down to take off her shoes, and smiled as she straightened. "I'd love to see where you live, Cal." She wriggled her toes, and the bright red polish on her nails gleamed in the dim light. "Since you admired my shoes so much, you can massage away the pain they caused."

"I can do that." He let out his breath. This was the Frankie he was used to—the one who joked and teased, who kept everything light. She would understand that this was his way of saying goodbye.

By the time he slid his key into the lock of his condo, though, his mind was racing. Would she think he was sending a signal by bringing her here? The "I'm serious about you" vibe?

Or would she understand that he appreciated all she'd done for him and was trying to thank her for giving him back his focus and his energy? For making him see how important family was.

He'd realized she was right. And the team was his family.

Frankie stepped through the door, then stopped dead. Her sexy shoes dangled from one hand as she stared out the living-room window. Lake Michigan was a dark, rippling presence. The lights from a few scattered boats twinkled on the black surface. The moon had risen now, too, a gold crescent reflected in the choppy water.

"What an amazing view," she said softly.

"I hardly notice it anymore," he said as he closed the door behind them.

"I could spend hours watching the lake."

"It's amazing," he said, watching her. He'd wondered all evening what she was wearing beneath that dress.

It was driving him crazy.

She turned and slid her arms around his neck. "I think there was talk of a foot rub."

He settled his hands on her waist, feeling her warmth beneath the sleek material, loving the way it slid over her skin. "Don't you want the grand tour? There are great views from the other windows."

She tilted her head up to look at him, but her face was in shadow. "I've already seen the view. Now I only want one thing, and I'm looking at him."

God. He pulled her closer, gripping her tightly, as if she would vanish if he didn't hold on. "Right back at you, Francesca."

Cal stroked his hand over her back, lingering on the skin her dress revealed. She was silky smooth. Warm. And she trembled when he touched her.

"I love this dress," he whispered. "I couldn't take my eyes off you tonight. When you were talking to all those people, I wanted to snatch you away. Bring you back here and have you for myself."

She sucked lightly beneath his ear, and he shuddered. "I wanted that, too." Her breath tickled him, made him ache. "I love what you did for me, Cal. You convinced a lot of people to give me money, but you're the only one I saw."

He swept her up in his arms and carried her to his bedroom. Frankie barely glanced at the wall of windows. She held his gaze and kissed him.

He slid her down his body, savoring every inch of her. Ran his hands up and down her arms, relishing the contrast between soft flesh and toned muscle. "What are you wearing beneath that magical dress, Francesca?"

She smiled at him, that siren's smile that made him instantly hard. Then she reached for the side of the dress and slowly lowered a zipper.

The dress fell off one shoulder and caught at her elbow. He could see her nipples harden through the fabric. When he reached for her, she lowered her other shoulder and let the dress slide to her waist.

She wasn't wearing a bra. He groaned.

She smiled again. "I was going to tell you over dinner," she said. "So I could watch your reaction."

"You're a dangerous woman, Francesca."

Her smile faded. "Only with you, Cal. You're the only one who sees Francesca."

"Everyone else is blind." He gathered her into his arms, and the blue dress fluttered against his legs. Even through his pants, his skin burned.

"Are you Frankie tonight?" He nuzzled her hair, drinking in the scent of grapefruit. "Or are you Francesca?"

"Love me and find out," she whispered, sucking lightly at his neck.

He froze at the *L* word, then bent to kiss her. She wasn't talking about *love* love—happily ever after, two-point-three kids, a dog. She was talking about sex. He was good at sex. He was especially good at it with Frankie.

So he broke the kiss and tugged the dress over her hips, while she gripped his arms, the edges of her nails sharp against his skin.

The dress puddled on the floor, and she stood in front of him wearing a suggestion of black lace. His hands shook as he caressed her ribs, her waist, her hips. *I need you, Francesca.* He cleared his throat. "I want you, Frankie."

"I want you, too, Cal." She tugged his shirt out of his waistband and undid the cuff links, which clinked when she dropped them on his night table.

Unbuttoning his shirt took hours. She stopped after every button, kissing his chest, caressing his back. By the time she dropped the shirt on the floor, he was shaking.

She undid his belt and slid her fingers along his waist. He closed his eyes, trying to maintain control. He wanted to beg her to hurry, to plead with her to touch him. But she worshipped him with her hands and her mouth. Her chest rose and fell; her breath puffed against his skin. She wanted him as badly as he wanted her.

But she took her time. It was as if she was memorizing every inch of him. The way he tasted. The way he felt. The way he reacted to her touch.

Finally, when she pushed his pants to the floor, he toed

off his shoes and lifted her onto the bed. He was on fire, and he wanted her to burn, too. "Are you finished torment-ing me?" he murmured into her ear.

"Mmm." She wound one leg around his, drawing him closer. "I'm just getting started."

"It's my turn now." He did his best to ignore her hands as they glided over his back and down to his hips, but he trembled above her as he brushed his mouth over her nipple. She sucked in a breath, and he smiled in satisfac-tion.

He moved his attention to her other breast, swirling his tongue until she arched off the bed. When she sobbed his name, he slid down even farther. One taste and she shat-tered. He waited until her breathing evened, until her trem-ors slowed, then he came back up to start again.

"Cal." She lifted his head away from her breast. "I need you. Please. I'm begging you."

He needed her, too. He eased into her, and she reached for his hands. Palm to palm, fingers twined, watching each other, they moved together. Rose together. Came together.

Then held each other tightly, as if they would never let go.

THE NEXT MORNING, the sun was just rising when Cal woke up, legs tangled with Frankie's, his arms wrapped around her. He hated like hell to leave her like this. But he had no choice.

He drew his arms and legs away from her slowly, not wanting to wake her. When she made a tiny noise in her throat and stirred, he swung his legs to the side and stood.

His knee ached like a son of a bitch. That was what happened when he stood for hours at a time. He flexed the joint, gritting his teeth against the pain, then hobbled into the bathroom.

Fifteen minutes later, he stood next to the bed, watching Frankie sleep. The morning sun bathed her skin in a golden light, and he didn't want to leave. He wanted to crawl back in there with her.

He couldn't. He had to go. He planted a kiss on her hair. But there would never be anyone else in this bed but Frankie. After last night, he couldn't bring another woman here. It would be a betrayal of what he and Frankie had shared.

Grabbing a piece of paper from his dresser, he scribbled a note and set it carefully on the mattress next to her. Then he kissed her hair one more time and walked out of the room.

FRANKIE OPENED HER EYES, then quickly shut them. White light poured into the room, blinding her.

She was in Cal's bedroom. He'd made love to her last night. Just as she'd made love to him. When she got up, everything would be back to normal. He'd tease her, and she'd tease back. Just like every other morning.

But for one night, he'd loved her.

And she'd loved him.

She knew this wouldn't last. Training camp was starting in a few days, and that would be it. Cal had been clear.

Last night, he'd used his power to put FreeZone solidly in the black. He'd taken away her money worries and made FreeZone safe for her.

She loved him for giving her the freedom to concentrate on the kids.

No. She loved Cal. She'd been dancing around that knowledge for a while, but didn't want to pretend anymore. They wouldn't have forever, but she loved him, anyway. The benefit he'd put together for her was a very small part of it.

She loved the man he was. Loved the woman he made her. She'd lost Francesca a long time ago, and Cal had found her again.

She opened her eyes and reached for him, but he wasn't there. Sitting up, she held the sheet to her chest. No one could see in that window—they were too high in the air—but even so, she felt exposed.

"Cal?"

No answer. The apartment was silent.

She swung her legs over the side of the bed and saw the piece of paper on the sheet. "Don't worry about bakery—cleared day off with your boss. Went to rehab. Coffee in the kitchen. Last night was wonderful. I had a great time at FreeZone. With you. I'll miss you."

Frankie's heart ached as she read the note again, then set it on the night table. She'd thought they'd have the rest of the week, since he didn't have to be at training camp until the weekend. But this sounded like goodbye.

She subscribed to the "pull the Band-Aid off quickly" school of thought. Apparently, Cal did, too.

She dropped the sheet and stood. Trying to ignore the pain in her chest, the ball of tears in her throat, she reminded herself that football was Cal's life. He'd made that clear many times. Now that his community service was over, he needed to focus on football.

His bathroom was as big as her entire bedroom. Four people would easily fit in the shower. He'd set out towels and a spare toothbrush for her. Practical.

She could be as sensible as Cal. Last night had been magical. So had the past weeks with him. But that was all over. Time to get back to reality.

The water from the rainfall showerhead washed away her tears. Once she regained control, she dried off and put her beautiful dress back on. It was a reminder of the night before. A reminder that the benefit had been Cal's last gift to her, an end, rather than a beginning.

She held a cold washcloth to her eyes for a long time, then folded it neatly on the sink, squared her shoulders and walked out of the bedroom.

As she headed toward the kitchen, she spotted her purse on the hall table. She'd dropped it on the floor when Cal lifted her into his arms. Grabbing it, she stepped into his kitchen and saw that it matched the rest of his condo. Viking stove. Sub-Zero refrigerator. Granite countertops. Cherry cabinets.

An espresso machine stood on one end of the counter, and Cal had written instructions on how to use it. She made herself a cup, then sat at the table and opened her purse.

Twenty minutes later, she was still staring at the pile of checks on the kitchen table.

More than thirty thousand dollars. More to come from the silent auction.

Frankie's hands began to shake. She had never had that much money at one time in her entire life.

Her cheeks burned as she stuffed the pile of checks back into her purse. Cal had given FreeZone a safety net that would last for months, if not years. She would think about him every time she bought something for her kids.

She looked around Cal's apartment to fix everything in her memory, slid her feet into the uncomfortable shoes and walked out the door.

CHAPTER TWENTY-TWO

As FRANKIE WALKED toward her apartment, she saw a newspaper in the window of a convenience store. "DCFS" caught her eye, and her heart thudded against her chest. Lisa had told her the article would be in the paper this week, but hadn't specified which day.

Frankie bought a copy and hurried home. Then sank onto her couch and read the article.

Ten minutes later, her stomach in a knot, she stood up and paced the room.

Lisa hadn't found any of Bascombe's other victims and had honored Frankie's request to stay anonymous. The reporter had made it clear she suspected there were lots more. She'd written about pedophiles and their traits. Written about Bascombe's rise in DCFS, and the fact that until very recently he still made trips to juvie. To the teen centers in the city. That he made it sound as if he wanted to be involved. To make sure the correctional facility and the homeless shelters were doing their job.

The article implied there was more to it than that, but Lisa was careful not to accuse.

No one else would make the connection, but Bascombe would know the unnamed source was Frankie. She had to figure out her strategy.

Before she could do anything, her phone rang. Nathan. "Was that article about you?" he said without preamble.

"Yeah, it was. Patrick couldn't find anyone else. Neither could Lisa."

"Marco and I are coming over. We don't want you to be alone."

Her throat swelled. "You'd leave Mama's for me?"

"Hell, yes. You need us. We're there."

So simple. And such a gift. "Stay there for now. Let me see what happens. There's no way anyone but Bascombe would identify me, so I'm probably okay for now."

There was a long pause. "You sure?"

"Yes. If I need you, I'll come to Mama's. Okay?"

Another long pause. "Okay, Bunny. We love you."

"Love you, too, Nate."

Her skin felt two sizes too small for her. The newspaper article was making her jumpy. The stack of checks in her purse didn't help. And every square inch of her apartment resonated with Cal's presence.

His disposable razor still sat on the edge of the sink, a fleck of dried shaving cream on the handle. One of his socks peeked out from beneath her bed. Tiny slips of paper from their fortune cookies still lay on the kitchen table. *You will find happiness with a tall, dark stranger.* Cal had teased her about that one. Asked her who was going to take his place when he went to training camp.

She snatched the fortunes off the table and stuffed them into the garbage.

She had to get out of here.

After changing her clothes, she deposited the checks at the bank and headed for FreeZone. She could work on thank-you notes. That would keep her from thinking about Cal. At least for a little while.

When she arrived, the door was open a crack and she could hear people moving around inside. She froze. A few battered computers were the only valuable things in there. And even those weren't worth much.

She cautiously stepped inside. "Who's here?"

Her landlord hurried out of the back room. "Frankie. I tried to call you."

She checked her cell phone. The missed-call icon was flashing. So was the text message one. She clicked on the text. It was from Martha. I need to talk to you.

Making a mental note to reply as soon as possible, she slipped the phone back in her bag. "What's up, Derek?"

The thin man with long, stringy hair and a narrow face rubbed his hands down the sides of his worn jeans. "There are some city inspectors here. Doing, uh, inspections."

Bascombe. "What are they looking for?" Frankie's voice was calm, but inside, she seethed.

"One guy is checking the electrical system. The other guy is the health inspector. He says if you have food here, he has to check for infestations."

"Of what?" she asked, although she knew.

Derek glanced toward the back room and smoothed his hair back. "You know. Rodents. Bugs."

"We don't have rodents here. No bugs, either."

He held up his hands. "I know, Frankie. They're not going to find anything. I spray the place regular. But they gotta look."

She stepped into the back room. One man was on a ladder. He'd taken apart the light fixture and was probing at the wires. He glanced at her. "You the tenant?"

"Yes. Is everything okay?"

"This wiring isn't up to code. Neither is the wiring in the office."

"I'm sure Derek will take care of it," she said.

He cleared his throat. "We can't let you operate with faulty wiring. Fire hazard."

"What does that mean?"

"It means we have to shut you down until this wiring is up to code. Your landlord needs to fix it, then we'll come back."

And then they'd find something else wrong. Frankie knew how this worked. Bascombe had told the guy to make sure FreeZone stayed closed.

She just couldn't prove it.

"It's not only the wiring." Another man stepped out of the shadows. "You've got signs of rodents. And roaches. You'll have to take care of that, too."

"I've never seen a rat or a mouse here. Roaches, either." Her face grew hot and she deliberately took a few deep breaths. *Stay calm.* Bascombe probably hoped she'd go off on these guys. Make them look even harder when they came back.

"I found droppings, lady," the inspector said, his eyes sliding away.

She stared at him, but he didn't meet her gaze. Finally she said, "I have kids coming in an hour. What am I supposed to do with them?"

The health inspector shrugged. "Send them home."

They can't go home, she wanted to scream. But she bit her tongue. *Calm.* "Are you finished?" she asked.

"Yeah." The building inspector climbed down from the ladder, folded it and picked up his tools. He left the fixture dangling by its wires. "When your landlord gets things taken care of, he can give us a call. We'll schedule a return visit."

And there would be scheduling problems. It would take ages for them to come back.

She stood aside as they spoke to Derek. As she watched, Cal walked in, his determined eyes finding her immediately. He was carrying a newspaper.

Stunned to see him, she watched as he strode over. Held up the paper. "This is you, isn't it? That bastard molested you."

His voice was flat. Cold.

Deadly.

"Cal, there's nothing you can do." His arm was hard as iron when she grabbed it. "Please. Calm down."

"Calm down?" His voice got even quieter, a sure sign of the rage he was just barely keeping in check. "I'm supposed to ignore what he did to you?"

"Yes! This isn't your fight. You'll only hurt yourself."

"Not my fight? When I find out a guy molested my..." He clenched his teeth. "Molested a kid? Someone I care about?" He stared down at her. "Yes, this is my fight."

"Not now," she whispered. "Please. Not in front of them." Derek and both the inspectors were watching intently.

He looked around and scowled. "Who are these guys?"

"My landlord. Health inspector. Building inspector. They're closing FreeZone."

He stepped around her and started toward them. "The hell they are."

"Stop." She grabbed his arm again. "You'll make things worse."

"This is that bastard's doing."

"I'm sure it is. But arguing with the inspectors won't help. The kids will be here soon. I have to figure out what to do."

"Goddamn it, Frankie. Just once, can you put yourself first?"

"So I'm supposed to turn them loose? Let them wander the streets until they can go home?"

"What about that church where you park your car? Do they have meeting space?"

"I have no idea. I just use the lot."

"You wait for the kids. I'll go talk to *them*." He stared at the inspectors, who looked away and cleared their throats. "I'll be right back."

THREE LONG HOURS LATER, after staggering out of the church basement, Cal put his hands on her shoulders. "Will you tell me about it?"

She nodded. "We should eat first."

They got Chinese takeout and went back to her apartment. Her stomach revolted at the thought of food, but she wanted to keep things as normal as possible for as long as she could.

She dragged a water chestnut around on her plate, smearing it through the dark soy sauce. Cal ate steadily, but he watched her. Waiting.

"Okay," she said, pushing her plate away when she couldn't stand it anymore. "You already know I was on the street when I was fifteen. I ran away. My parents had died a couple of years earlier, and I was angry. I resented Nathan because he wasn't paying enough attention to me, and he became the symbol of all the grief and fear I was trying to bury." She glanced at Cal, then away. "Which I figured out later. After a lot of therapy."

She focused on picking up a grain of rice with her chopsticks. "What I didn't realize was that Nate wasn't coping, either. He was terrified. He was only twenty-four and all of a sudden he had a restaurant to run and three younger siblings to raise. He didn't notice I was in trouble."

Cal reached across the table and took the chopsticks, then clasped her hands in his. "It's okay, Frankie. You can't tell me anything that will make me think less of you."

She inhaled a shaky breath and drew her hands away. He hadn't heard her story yet.

"On the street, I was always hungry, always scared. There were days when I didn't eat at all. After a couple of weeks, I wanted to call Nathan, but I was too stubborn." She bent her head, remembering the way her brother had cried when she had finally contacted him. "One night, a kid living in the same abandoned building suggested we get some money from a convenience store. Stupidly, I thought that meant he had an ATM card, and I remember being angry that he hadn't used it before this.

"He didn't have a card. He had a gun. And the next thing I knew, I was in the middle of an armed robbery. The cops caught us, of course, and they sent us both to juvie."

She jumped up and started pacing, wrapping her arms around her waist. "I sat in a locked room, by myself, for a couple of days. They charged me with armed robbery and told me they'd get me a public defender. Then Bascombe walked in. He told me his name was Dave, that he was a social worker and wanted to help me. I figured out later that he had probably arranged to keep me isolated. Made it easier to prey on me.

"Those two days…I was terrified. Frantic to get out." She stared through the window, but instead of the brick of the building across the alley, she saw Bascombe's face. Friendly. Sympathetic. "I wanted Nathan. Wanted my family back. I told Bascombe I'd do anything if I could call my brother. I knew Nathan would help me. Nathan would fix everything.

"Bascombe smiled." A shudder ripped through her. "Then he tugged on my belly-button ring and said he knew what kind of girl wore those. Before I could react, he grabbed me and covered my mouth. He bent me over the desk chair and stuck his other hand down the back of my pants." His hand had been rough. Hot and sweaty. His nails too long. For months afterward, she'd woken in the middle of the night, feeling the sting of his nails on her skin. She would stand in the shower until the water ran cold, washing herself. "When he...when he tried to put his fingers in my...in my..." She pressed her hands to her eyes.

"God, Frankie!"

Cal pushed away from the table and stood behind her. His hands hovered over her shoulders and she stiffened. *Please don't touch me. If you do, I'll fall apart completely.*

His hands dropped away.

"I started to kick. Squirm. When I bit him, he let me go, and I ran for the door." She wrapped her arms around herself again, trying to stop the shaking. "I pounded on the door, and he grabbed my hands to stop me. He told me he was disappointed. I'd said I would do anything, and since I'd changed my mind, I needed to keep my mouth shut. If I told anyone, he'd kill my brothers."

She stared out the window, pleased she'd managed to get through the story without breaking down completely. "That was the last time I heard of him until I saw an article in the paper that he'd been appointed head of DCFS."

Cal turned her around. He gently wiped tears from her cheeks. "Honey, you know he can't do anything to your brothers."

"I know that now. I didn't back then."

"Why didn't you tell me, that first time he came around?"

"You think I don't know what you would have done? I didn't want you to go to jail."

"So you went to a reporter?"

"I went to Bascombe first. Told him to resign, or I'd go public."

"That's how he knew the article was about you."

"Yes."

"What you did was really brave, Frankie. God knows how many other kids he assaulted and raped. You put yourself on the line to stop him." Cal folded her in his arms.

"I know. I have nothing to be afraid of, really. But every time I see him, I'm fifteen years old again and back in that room." She clung to Cal, wishing she could stay there forever, absorbing his strength. But after a few minutes, she stepped away.

Cal's mouth tightened. "The police better take care of this fast. Or I'm going to destroy that bastard."

"No, Cal! You can't go near him."

"You think I can listen to you describe what he did to you and do nothing? Not a chance."

"Let the police handle it. Promise me, Cal."

His jaw worked, then he nodded. "Fine. I'll take care of FreeZone, then. Since you seem to like that dump you're in, I'll buy it. I'll have it renovated and brought up to code. Then you won't have to wait on your landlord, or worry about the inspectors, either."

She grabbed him, horrified. "No! You're not buying that building for me."

"Why the hell not? I have more money than I need. Might as well use some of it to help you save FreeZone."

He was trying to rescue her again, the way he had with the benefit. She got that, but she couldn't accept it.

She laid her hands on his face. "That's very generous, and I appreciate it. But I don't want your money. I'm not going to be one more person who asks for *stuff* from you."

"You're not asking. I'm offering. I want to help you, Frankie," he said, holding her hands. "If you don't want money, what do you want?"

She swallowed. She'd taken the hardest step—she'd bared her past to Cal. Now she had to go the rest of the way. It was time to stop being that tough girl who kept her real self hidden. Time to become the woman she was meant to be. "I want *you,* Cal. The man who saw Francesca instead of Frankie. The man I love."

He paled. "Don't say that, Frankie! You know I care about you, but that's as far as it can go. The only thing I'm good at is football. I have to focus on that."

"Is that all you can have in your life?" Did he have any idea what it had cost her to say she loved him? "No other football players have relationships?"

"Some do. But *I* can't. Especially not now. If I don't give everything to football, I won't make the team. And I have to make the team. It's all I have."

"You could have so much more than that if you gave yourself a chance. I've never told anyone I loved them. Never felt it, either. I love you, Cal. Not your money or your influence or your fame. I love the guy who helps gangbangers he doesn't even like. The man who saw *me,* even when I was hiding.

"You're a lot more than just a football player, Cal. You're not just that guy who kicks butt on Sunday afternoon."

He stared at her and swallowed. The terror in his eyes made her throat burn. "That's *exactly* who I am, Frankie. A jock. A guy who does one thing, but does it really well. That guy has training camp in two days, and I have to focus on that. I have to concentrate on making the team. Football is my life. You understand, don't you?"

She closed her eyes, unable to bear the desperation in his eyes. "I used to think FreeZone was my life. Now I know better. You'd know better, too, if you really looked at yourself. If you gave us a chance."

"I'll give you anything you want, Frankie. Anything but that." He swallowed.

"You're walking away? I stripped myself bare for you, and that's all you can say? That you can give me money, but nothing more?" Her knees trembling, she reached for the counter behind her.

"You're asking for something I can't give you, Frankie." He shoved his hand through his hair. "The season will be over in January. Maybe we can hook up again then."

"'Hook up'?" She shook her head. "Francesca deserves more than hooking up with the man she loves." Her heart breaking, she said, "I hope football can give you what you're looking for."

He turned and walked slowly toward the back door. He paused in the doorway, but didn't look back. Finally, he left without saying goodbye.

When Frankie heard his car drive down the alley, she picked up her plate of Kung Pao chicken and scraped it into the garbage. Then she crumpled in on herself and let the tears fall.

CHAPTER TWENTY-THREE

CAL STOOD ON THE PORCH outside Frankie's kitchen, willing himself to go back in, gather her close. Tell her he wanted to stay.

He couldn't do it. It killed him to walk away, but he didn't have a choice. When he was with Frankie, he couldn't think about anything else. Football was a million miles away.

It would take everything he had to make the team this year. He had to be focused on that. He couldn't afford any distractions.

His hand tightened on the doorknob, then he unclenched his fingers, one by one. Let his hand drop. Walked away.

Each step felt as if he were walking in quicksand.

He finally reached the parking lot. Stared up at her window for a long time. One glimpse of her and he might have run to her. But she didn't look out. Didn't expect him to return.

He'd told her often enough that football was everything to him, so he shouldn't be surprised that she believed him.

He threw the car into Reverse and backed into the alley. The brick walls closed in on him but he didn't stop. When he reached the street, he drove blindly to Halsted, then headed toward Lake Shore Drive. There were whitecaps on the lake today, crashing onto the rocks. Breaking into tiny droplets that flew in every direction, then vanished.

He kept his gaze fixed on the traffic in front of him,

but all he saw was Frankie, tears trickling down her face, telling him what Bascombe had done.

Cal had always prided himself on being a guy who manned up.

Not today. He'd hurt Frankie. Let her down. Walked out the door.

But she'd asked too much of him. He wasn't a relationship guy. And she'd known that going in.

It wasn't fair to change the rules this late in the game.

His tires squealed as he pulled into his parking garage, then swung into his space. He trotted to the elevator, eager to get home. To let his own familiar environment calm him. Assure him he'd done the right thing.

But the minute he walked in the door, Frankie was there. She'd left a note on the table in the foyer. "Thank you for the benefit. And what came after. It was a magical evening."

He crumpled the note and tossed it into the trash, then dug it out and smoothed out the wrinkles. Stared at it for a long time before shoving it into a drawer.

His bed was still rumpled and smelled like Frankie. So did the towel she'd used after her shower. He tortured himself with her scent for a moment, then tossed the towel into the hamper.

In the kitchen, she'd added "thank you" to his note with the espresso instructions.

God, she was everywhere. He grabbed the phone and dialed his cleaning service. "This is Cal Stewart," he said when a woman answered. "I need someone to clean my place tomorrow."

He listened impatiently, then interrupted. "I know I'm not scheduled. I don't care what it costs. I need my place cleaned. Tomorrow. Unless you can make it today."

He heard pages turning, then the receptionist put a hand over the mouthpiece. Finally she came back on the line.

"It will be double the regular cost, Mr. Stewart."

"Great. I'll leave a check. Thank you."

He threw himself on the couch, the only place in the apartment where he couldn't feel Frankie's presence. He had to figure out a way to get through the rest of the day. To distract himself until he could go back to rehab tomorrow. Training camp the next day.

Well done, son. His father's voice in his head was satisfied. Happy. *You did the smart thing. Football is what's important. Nothing else.*

Cal picked up a red-and-yellow vase and flung it at the wall. It shattered into a thousand pieces that glittered like diamonds in the sun.

He still felt like crap.

Something crinkled in his back pocket, and he pulled out a piece of paper torn from a notebook. Sean's email address and Facebook name. Below them, Sean had scrawled, "Good luck at training camp."

FRANKIE DIDN'T REMEMBER the text message from Martha until the next morning, but managed to get her on the phone before she left for school.

"Hey, Martha, I got your text. What's up?"

"Frankie." The teen's voice was low, as if she was trying not to be overheard. "There was an article in the paper yesterday. About the head of DCFS."

Frankie's stomach began to churn. *Please, God. No.* "I saw it," she said carefully.

She heard Martha breathing, and waited. Finally, the girl whispered, "Was that woman you, Frankie? I thought maybe it was, because you understood about the teen center."

Oh, Martha. Frankie's eyes welled up. "Yes, sweetie, it was."

The girl began to sob. "I need you, Frankie."

"I'll be right there."

THE SECOND DAY of training camp was hellishly hot. Cal needed some water, but that would have to wait. One more play before they took a break.

He lined up, watched the play develop and charged toward the receiver he was covering.

Three guys got there at the same time and collided, and he ended up on the bottom of the pile. Someone pushed on his knee as they stood, and he almost screamed.

No one had twisted it or kicked it. It had just been two hundred and fifty pounds of linebacker pressing down, sending agony through Cal's whole body.

The guys on top of him rolled to their feet one by one. When it was his turn, he managed to stand by himself. Only desperation and his will kept him from limping as he walked off the field.

He stood in the shade and grabbed his water bottle, waiting for the pain to recede to the usual dull ache. As he waited, sweat pouring down his back, the coach barked for the rookies to get back on the field.

Some of them were damned good, including Tommy Grover. Cal tossed the empty bottle into a recycling bin, shifted the weight off his knee and reached for another drink. With help and a little time, Tommy would be great.

He flexed his knee and winced. Son-of-a-bitch knee. He flexed it again, barely managing to conceal his grimace.

They'd done sprints to open the camp yesterday. He'd been slower than normal, but he didn't think the coaches had noticed. They were paying more attention to the rookies and the guys they'd signed in the off-season.

It wouldn't take many more plays like the last one, though, before everyone would know he'd lost his edge. Experience might outplay young and motivated for a while, but eventually, the coaches would catch on.

Maybe after a few more days of practice, the damn joint would loosen up.

Son-of-a-bitch knee.

He'd managed to pass his physical that morning, but the doctor had hesitated at the end. "You sure you want to do this, Stewart?"

"Why wouldn't I? My knee's great." He'd done some high steps, some side-to-sides. "Never better."

The doctor had shaken his head. "You guys are all the same." He'd signed the form, and Cal had hurried out the door.

He'd reached for his cell phone, almost pressed Frankie's speed dial. But he caught himself in time and shoved the phone into his pocket.

He wanted to tell her about the exam. Camp. The guys. He wanted to confess his fears to her, for God's sake. He wanted her to look him in the eye and tell him he could do anything he wanted to do. That he'd make the right decision. That he was smart enough to figure this out.

But he'd lost his right to call her when he'd walked out on her.

Didn't stop him from wishing it was different. That *he* was different.

Now, in the afternoon heat, his position coach appeared next to him. "How's it hanging, Stewart?"

"Good, Coach." He swigged some more water and tossed the bottle. "Frigging hot out here."

Kelleher nodded, watching the guys on the field. "We'll run 'em awhile longer. See what they're made of." He glanced at Cal. "What do you think of Grover?"

"I'm impressed. Give him a couple years of seasoning and he'll be a keeper."

Kelleher grunted. "Thinking he's got the makings of a starter."

Grover played his position. "Might. Might not."

Kelleher slapped him on the back. "We'll see, won't we?"

Cal watched him walk away. Son of a bitch.

EVERYTHING HAD MOVED FAST. Two days after the article was published, the day after Martha told her how she'd gotten pregnant, Frankie stood with her offstage, waiting for their turn at the press conference. "You don't have to do this, Martha." She put her arm around the girl's shoulder. "It was incredibly brave of you to go to the police. You don't have to be publicly involved."

She hugged Martha close, ignoring the voice of the police chief speaking to the press. Frankie glanced at Nathan and Marco, standing close by. "Tell her, guys."

"She's right, Martha," Marco said. "Let Frankie do it herself."

"No!" Martha said fiercely. "I want to be involved. Everyone's taken his side. He's spreading lies about you, and people believe him. He has to pay for what he's done."

Bascombe had taken the offensive and talked about Frankie's troubled past.

"He'll pay," she assured her, nodding at Martha's belly. "You gave the police the evidence they need. If you do this, sweetheart, you can't take it back. Once you go out there, the whole world will know what happened to you."

"I don't care." The teen straightened her shoulders. "It wasn't my fault. I have nothing to be ashamed of."

"Of course you don't." But Martha had no idea what

it was like to have people watching her. Pointing fingers. Whispering as she walked by.

The police chief glanced at them. It was the signal for her and Martha to join him onstage. "Last chance, Martha. Are you sure?"

"I am." She straightened the maternity blouse, looking far too young to be a mother. "Let's do this."

As they walked onto the stage, camera flashes exploded in front of them. Martha faltered for a moment, then reached for Frankie's hand. Linked together, they walked to the podium.

The police chief nodded at them, then raised his hand for silence. When the crowd quieted, he said, "I want to make it clear that neither I nor Ms. Devereux pressured this young lady to come here today. We would have acted on her information regardless. But she wanted the public to hear her story."

Frankie's palms were slippery and her face hot from the lights. She glanced toward the side of the stage, and Nathan nodded at her. Marco gave her a thumbs-up and a proud smile. She blinked twice, took a deep breath, squeezed Martha's hand and stepped to the microphone.

"My name is Francesca Devereux. Douglas Bascombe has been talking about me, and he's right—I'm the unnamed woman in Lisa Halliday's article about Bascombe and DCFS." She swallowed as a bead of sweat trailed down her back. "I wanted to speak publicly because it's important to keep predators away from our children. We need to look more carefully at the people who have power over the most vulnerable members of society."

The room was quiet now, but Martha still clung to her hand. "I met Doug Bascombe more than ten years ago, when I was an inmate at the juvenile detention center."

She told her story calmly, leaving out the graphic details, but not shying away from the fact that she'd been assaulted. She glanced at her brothers several times, and they smiled at her each time. Encouraged her.

"There's no evidence of what Doug Bascombe did to me," she finished. "He's right—it's his word against mine. And the statute of limitations expired long ago. But this brave young woman insisted on sharing her story with you."

Martha gripped Frankie's hand more tightly. She looked around the room, then nodded and stepped to the mic.

"My name is Martha Warren," she said in a small voice. "I'm sixteen years old, and I live in Deerfield. Eight months ago, I was arrested for underage drinking at a party." Martha's voice grew stronger and she stood straighter. "Because my parents wanted to teach me a lesson, I spent five days in juvie. While I was there, Douglas Bascombe approached me. He told me he could get me out of jail if I'd have sex with him." She stepped from behind the podium. "He raped me, and I'm pregnant with his baby."

The audience gasped, and the flashes went off again. Frankie wrapped her arm around Martha's shoulders. She wanted to step in front of the girl. Protect her from the storm that was breaking over her.

But Martha was stronger than Frankie had been at that age. The girl lifted her chin, stepped back to the microphone and said, "He's still molesting girls. I saw him less than two months ago talking to a girl at one of the teen homeless shelters. Frankie is telling the truth about Bascombe." She rubbed her hand over her belly. "This is the proof."

The reporters shouted questions until their voices blended into a huge wave of sound. Frankie tightened her arm around Martha's shoulders, and when the police chief nodded, she led the teen off the stage.

Nathan enveloped both of them in a hug, holding them close for a long moment. Then the police chief spoke again.

"At this moment, Douglas Bascombe is under arrest for criminal sexual assault and sexual assault of a minor. I expect to add other charges in the next several days. I want to urge anyone who's had similar experiences with Mr. Bascombe to talk to us. Finally, I want to thank Martha, and Ms. Devereux, for having the courage to ignore threats and come forward."

Nathan finally released them. "Let's go home," he said quietly.

CHAPTER TWENTY-FOUR

JUST LIKE THE OTHER EVENINGS at camp, Cal parked himself in the dormitory lounge and pretended to watch television. Tonight, it might have been a mistake. He'd taken another hit to his knee today and was afraid he wouldn't be able to make it to his room without limping.

Living in the dorm was supposed to foster team unity, but it was a pain in the ass. It was impossible to hide any-thing when you lived with eighty other guys. Have a sore knee? Everyone knew about it. Calling your wife or girl-friend? Everyone knew about that, too.

Tonight, apparently, all his teammates had a woman to call. They wandered around after dinner, phones to their ears, smiling and happy. Cal stared at the television. If he hadn't been such an ass, he'd be calling Frankie. Instead, he was stuck in this room, exhausted and lonely, until ev-eryone else left.

Chet Sorkowski plopped down on the couch next to him, phone stuck to his ear. From the silly grin on his face, he had to be talking to one of his kids.

"I want to be home with you, too, Chrissy. But I bet your brother will play horsey with you."

Cal tried not to listen, but Chet had a loud voice.

The big redhead laughed. "Yeah, he's not as strong as me. But I'll be home soon. Then I'll play horsey all you want." He made a snorting noise that was the lamest horse sound Cal had ever heard, but apparently his kid liked it. He could hear her giggling.

"I love you, too, honeybun," Chet said. "Can you put your mom on the phone?"

After a moment, Chet said something in a low murmur that sounded like "I miss you, baby." He glanced at Cal and stood up, heading down the hall to his room.

Cal flexed his knee. The ice bag he'd had on it had dulled the pain, but it still felt as if someone had stuck a knife in the joint.

Envy and sadness swept over Cal. Would he ever be able to get on his hands and knees and play horsey with his kids?

If he had kids. Football was his life, right? No room for a wife or family.

No other football players have relationships?

A lot of the guys seemed to manage it.

Restless, he rearranged the ice bag and settled in to wait. A lot of his teammates iced in the evening, so he didn't stick out. But limping to his room? They would notice that. So he'd watch television until he was the last one here.

When the ten-o'clock news came on, he was still staring at the television, missing Frankie, cursing his knee. Two other guys were here, too, rookies he'd met a couple times. He was barely paying attention when he saw Frankie on the screen in front of him. Cal sat up, sending the ice bag to the floor with a thud.

"In a late-afternoon press conference, two women claimed to have been assaulted by Douglas Bascombe, the head of the Division of Child and Family Services." The camera panned over Frankie and Martha, standing at the podium. The teen gripped Frankie's hand as her gaze darted around the room. Flashes went off and people shouted.

The camera zoomed in on Frankie. She wore a red blouse and a black suit jacket—completely un-Frankie-like. But she didn't look nervous or uncomfortable. She was composed. Confident. Calm under pressure.

That was his Frankie.

Not anymore, she isn't.

She stepped forward and began to speak, but the volume was too low for him to hear. When he finally got the remote, she'd stepped away and Martha was trembling at the microphone.

He didn't have to hear, though, to know the reaction when she stepped away from the podium to reveal her belly.

Was Bascombe the bastard who'd gotten her pregnant?

As anger coiled inside Cal, a sober-looking blonde woman appeared on the screen. "Charges were filed against Douglas Bascombe late this afternoon."

They showed the press conference again, and Martha and Frankie standing side by side. His teammates snickered and elbowed each other.

"Whatever else he is, the dude has good taste," one of them said.

"That dark-haired one is a little skinny, but she looks hot," the other replied.

Cal surged off the couch, ignoring the pain in his knee, and grabbed the second kid by his shirt. "What kind of an asshole are you?" He shook him until his long blond hair flew around his face. "Those two women were assaulted. God!" He threw the kid to the floor, where he stared up at Cal, dazed.

Cal looked at the other rookie, who shrank away from him. "You want to say anything else, hotshot?"

"Uh, no. No. We didn't mean anything."

Cal looked from one to the other, then turned away. *I gave up Frankie so I could spend my time with guys like you? What kind of stupid shit am I?*

He switched off the television, lost in thought. It had taken a lot of courage for Frankie to stand in front of the cameras and talk about what had happened to her.

She was so strong. So brave. He was proud of her determination to stop a predator.

He should have been with her. He should have gone with her to the police, held her hand while she told them what Bascombe had done.

He should have been at the press conference.

Cal was supposed to be tough. Strong. Fearless.

He was none of those things. Frankie, a woman half his size, had him beat in all categories.

And he'd given her up for football. Given up everything they had together so he could be the hero on Sunday.

He grabbed the bag of ice from the floor and limped to his room. Frankie was taking chances, putting herself out there, doing the right thing.

He had his head up his ass.

He also had a lot of thinking to do.

THE EVENING AFTER the press conference, Frankie was curled up on the couch, reading a thriller, when her buzzer sounded. She ignored it. The press had been relentless. She'd turned her phone off, as well.

But it buzzed again. Longer this time. So she unfolded herself from the couch and peered out the window.

Her heart stuttered. Cal.

What was he doing here? Pain, anger and grief roiled inside her as she put her hand on the buzzer. Hesitated. Eventually, she pushed it.

By the time he reached the top of the stairs, she was shaking. She opened the door before he could knock. "Cal."

"Hello, Frankie."

She let herself study him. His face was tanned. Probably from being outside at training camp. He looked thinner, too. "What are you doing here?"

"Will you let me in?"

She shrugged and stepped back. When he came inside, the memories hit her squarely in the chest, stealing her breath.

She settled into a chair and drew her knees up, clasping her arms around them. He paced the room, looking at the pictures, the books, the view from the window.

"Why are you here?" she asked, tired of his stalling.

Finally he faced her. There were dark smudges below his eyes and new lines bracketing his mouth. His eyes, which used to twinkle, were deep pools of misery. "To apologize for walking out on you."

He sat on the couch directly across from her and leaned forward. "I can never make up for that. I saw your press conference yesterday. Read the papers today. I should have been with you."

"I managed on my own."

"Of course you did. You don't need anyone."

She'd needed him. And he'd left her. "What's your point?"

"I'm sorry, Frankie. Sorry I ran. Sorry I didn't have the courage to accept what you were offering. Sorry I hurt you."

His words were blows, and they landed squarely. She sucked in a painful breath. "Do you expect me to kick your ass, then say it's okay? Say, 'Let's go back to the way we were'? Not going to happen, Cal."

His mouth tightened. "Because you don't care anymore?"

"Because I care too much." She jumped up and stared out the window, remembering the sight of Cal walking out the door. "I've never let anyone get as close as I let you. Do you have any idea how hard it was to tell you what Bascombe had done? To tell you I loved you?" Her eyes burned, and she clenched her teeth. She refused to cry in front of him. "I'm not sure I can take that risk again."

He stood, but he didn't try to touch her. "I know," he said quietly. "I know what I did to you. I wouldn't blame you if you never wanted to see me again, but I hope you'll give me a chance." He shoved trembling hands into his pockets. "The first day I was at FreeZone, you told me everyone deserves a second chance."

She shouldn't have buzzed him in, let him argue his case. She should have ignored him.

But she was tired of righteous anger. Tired of being alone. Tired of longing for him, every minute of every day. "Give you a chance for what?"

He moved so he was facing her. "To prove that I love you, Frankie. Because I do. I think I fell in love with you the day I met you. You stood up to those two gangbangers, then you stood up to me. You were so fierce. So protective of the kids. I wanted that caring, that love, for myself. I was just too scared to take it when you offered."

"Words, Cal. Words." He was saying everything she'd wanted to hear, but it wasn't nearly enough. She forced herself to ignore the vulnerability in his face, the yearning in her heart, and took a breath. "You walked out on me. Walked out the door after I relived the most painful episode of my life for you. How can I trust you again?"

"I don't know. But you think the best of everyone. You always see the potential, not the reality. My reality was screwed up. But maybe you can look beyond it and see a little potential." He flexed his hands, kept his gaze on her. "I've learned a lot about myself this week. Most of it not very flattering. But I did figure out one thing I'm absolutely positive about."

"What's that?" she asked, a tiny sliver of hope cutting through her distrust.

"I learned that I love you, Frankie. That I'm yours. Forever. I want to marry you. Have kids with you. Spend the rest of my life with you."

The lump in her throat grew and grew. She swallowed hard, trying to dislodge it. "Is that supposed to make me fall at your feet, Cal? Make me say that everything is forgotten and let's live happily ever after?"

"Of course not. I know you better than that." He watched her steadily, and the regret in his eyes made her chest burn. "I know those are just words. I know I have to prove myself. I just want a chance to do that."

"When, Cal? After the football season is over? When you have time for me again?"

"Starting today." He shoved his hands into his pockets again and jiggled his foot. "I quit the team. I'll help coach the rookies at camp, but then I'm through."

"What?" She took a step toward him. Stopped. "Football is your life. You told me over and over it was all that mattered to you."

"I thought it was. Since I was a kid, I've been programmed to be a football player. A star. My coaches, my father, all pounded it into me—you have to focus on football. No distractions. No other interests.

"You were a huge distraction. When I was with you, I couldn't focus on anything but you. Couldn't think about anything but you. Didn't want anything but you."

"So you left me."

"I was scared, Frankie. Without football, I didn't know who I was. What I could do."

"So what changed?" She crossed her arms over her chest to keep from touching him.

"I'm one of the stars on the team. The rookies came to me for advice. The coaches asked for my opinions. I was Somebody."

He reached for her, then let his hand drop. "But it was nothing without you. Empty. Lonely. I realized I don't need the cheers from the crowd, the rush of making a good play, to be happy.

"I need you, Frankie. I want to be *your* somebody. I don't want a one-dimensional life. I want all we can have together. I don't want to be the star. I want to be the man *you* saw, not the guy the fans see."

She glanced at his knee, covered by his jeans. "Did you quit because you hurt yourself again?"

"Ouch." He rubbed his knee and looked away. "That's a fair question, I guess, but my knee has nothing to do with it. I would have made the team. I would have played." He took a step toward her. "But you shamed me. I saw your press conference with Martha. I was so damn proud of you. You had so much courage. So did she.

"More than I had. I couldn't bear to face the truth— that my life was shallow. Not what I really wanted. You showed me what a coward I was."

He took another step. "I want to play with my kids, Frankie. *Our* kids. I liked working at FreeZone. I liked knowing I was making a difference in a kid's life. *That's* the person I want to be. I want a life with you. I want to spend every day and every night proving how much I love you."

The vise that had squeezed her heart for the past several days eased a little. Not completely, though. She wasn't ready to jump into his arms. She was too afraid to take that chance.

"So you just gave it all up? Really?"

"Nothing about football is important. Not like you are. You give everything you have, and I want that. I want you to teach me how to be that kind of person."

"How do I know you're not going to wake up tomorrow and say, 'Oops, I made a mistake'?"

He smiled. "I'm officially retired. Signed the papers this afternoon. I'm going back to school to get my teaching certificate, then I'll teach high-school math and maybe coach the football team." His smile faded. "You made me figure out what I really wanted. I want you, Frankie."

The old Frankie would have walked away. She would have protected herself, made sure she wasn't hurt again. But she loved Cal. Knew she always would. Slowly, she held out her hand. He lifted it to his mouth, kissed her palm. Then he twined his fingers with hers.

"I'm scared, Cal," she whispered. "I think I used up all my courage. I can't make myself take the next step."

"Take as long as you need. I'm not going anywhere."

He cupped her face in his hands and kissed her. She held herself rigid, knowing that if she yielded to him, she'd always wonder if she was letting sex muddle her brain.

To her surprise, he broke the kiss. "I'll see you tomorrow at FreeZone." He smiled once and left. She moved to the window to watch him climb into his truck and drive away.

She stood there for a long time, but he didn't come back. Finally, she dropped into bed. This time, when she smelled Cal on the pillowcase, she didn't cry herself to sleep. She wrapped her arms around the pillow instead.

HE SHOWED UP THE NEXT DAY at the church that was their temporary FreeZone. When the boys asked him why he wasn't at training camp, he told them he'd quit the team, that it was time to move on. Time to live a real life.

He laughed and joked with the kids, traded fist bumps, teased them. He wasn't doing all that to impress her. He genuinely liked them. Enjoyed spending time with them.

Cal was going to be a great teacher.

When the kids left, he said goodbye to her and followed them out the door.

He showed up every day after that, and it was as if he'd never been gone. When Julio told him he'd decided on a college, one that encouraged its student athletes to graduate, Cal retorted that it was about time. Then he hugged him, pounding his back the way men did.

Another kid saved. Not with preaching or earnestness, just a simple nudge. And advice from someone the kid respected.

The day they moved into the renovated FreeZone, Cal came early to move boxes and stayed late to finish setting up. He never asked if she'd made a decision. He was careful not to touch her. He was giving her what she'd said she needed—space and time.

After more than a week, she'd had enough of both. She loved Cal. He'd said he loved her and wanted to make a life with her. It was time to take a chance, to trust that he meant what he said.

What if she was wrong?

If she was, he'd break her heart. But she had to be willing to risk that to have a future with Cal.

On the last day of summer school, she waited until everyone had arrived. The kids were celebrating summer break, and Cal was in the middle of a noisy game of basketball. She put her fingers to her lips to whistle, then dropped her trembling hand.

She could wait. She could do this when they were alone

and not expose herself publicly again. But that would be the coward's way.

She wanted Cal to understand she was all in. No reservations. So she closed her eyes, took a deep breath and let out a piercing whistle, the one that meant *Quiet. Now.*

Everyone in the room froze, staring at her.

She cleared her throat. "I have something I need to say."

She wove her way around clumps of kids, skirted the new foosball table and reached Cal. She wiped her sweaty palms on her thighs and took his hand. His fingers curled around hers, and she knew she'd come home. Found the place she wanted to be.

With a tug, she drew him to the center of the room. The kids gathered around in a circle, just as they had the day he'd arrived, when he'd confronted Speedball and T-Man.

With her hands shaking, her heart battering against her ribs, she dropped his hand and got down on one knee. The kids' voices rose in a questioning murmur, and Cal reached for her.

"No, Frankie. This isn't necessary," he whispered.

"Yes, it is." She cleared her throat once more. "I love you, Caleb Stewart. Will you marry me?"

The kids gasped, then shouted and clapped. Cal drew her to her feet, holding her hands tightly, and glanced around the room. "Can we have a little dignity here? A guy doesn't get a marriage proposal every day."

"What are you going to say?" Julio yelled.

"Say yes, man," Sean urged.

"This is the most romantic thing *ever*." Harley sighed.

Frankie's face burned as the kids hooted and cheered and shouted encouragement. Then Cal smiled, and the noise faded away. The two of them were the only people in the universe.

"I love you, too, Francesca Devereux. Yes, I'll marry

you." He held her face and bent to kiss her, and she wrapped her arms around him.

Desire, love, need washed over her in a wave. Cal slid his arms around her, and she pressed closer. When she forgot where they were, who they were with, he eased away from her. "If we're not careful, we'll go R in front of a PG audience," he murmured, nuzzling her neck. "But I can guarantee the sequel will be worth the wait."

EPILOGUE

One month later

"HEY." CAL TUGGED HER to a stop. "Look at what your brothers did." He nodded at a new photo in the entryway at Mama's Place.

It was one of Cal's old publicity photos, signed, "To Nathan and Marco."

"What did you think they were going to do with it?" Frankie asked, grinning. "Use it for target practice?"

"Maybe," he muttered. He touched the frame with one finger. "I'm still not sure they've forgiven me."

"They're throwing us an engagement party. Trust me, they've forgiven you."

She pulled him into the restaurant itself, then stopped in surprise. A huge banner ran from one side of the restaurant to the other: Congratulations, Frankie and Cal!

Her heart swelled as she saw all the people smiling and clapping. Then she spotted someone she hadn't expected. "Patrick!" She tightened her grip on Cal's hand and towed him in her wake. "I don't believe it."

"Paddy!" She threw herself at her brother, holding him tight. "I didn't know you were going to be here."

"My baby sister gets engaged, and you don't think I'll show up for the party?" He squeezed her so tightly she could barely breathe. "Besides, I have to make sure this guy has FBI clearance before I let him marry you."

Cal stuck out his hand. "Why am I not surprised by that? Good to meet you, Patrick."

"Same here." He smiled. "Saw the Cougars' first game. Looks like they miss you already."

"That's it? No interrogation?"

"I'm guessing Nathan has that covered. I don't want to scare you away."

"Not possible," Cal said, taking Frankie's hand.

"Right answer." He glanced toward the kitchen. "Let me drag Nate and Marco out here."

He headed toward the kitchen, stepping to one side when a waitress pushed through the door with a tray of appetizers. Darcy's short auburn hair gleamed in the lights as she hurried past Patrick. She didn't glance at him, but Patrick watched her cross the room and deposit her tray on the buffet table. He waited while she arranged the appetizers, then followed her back into the kitchen.

The FreeZone kids gathered around, all talking at the same time. Ramon stood behind them, his arm around his mother. Yolanda had completed her rehab and was working at a fast-food restaurant in the western suburbs. Ramon was thriving at the local high school. Both of them looked relaxed and happy.

Martha and Annie stood off to one side, smiling. Annie reported Martha had been talking to her parents. Going to Lamaze classes. Finalizing her adoption decision.

"Thank God you always see the potential, Francesca." Cal pressed a kiss to her head. "In everyone. Including me."

"I didn't have to look very hard," she said, turning to kiss him.

"Hey, Frankie. Cal," Nathan said. "You're here." He hugged her, then Cal, who looked shocked. Her brother laughed. "You're family now, dude. Better get used to it."

"Does that mean you'll tell me how Frankie got the nickname Bunny?"

"Don't you dare, Nathan Devereux," she muttered.

"No more secrets in this family, right?" Her brother smiled, although it looked forced. "Either he's family or he's not."

"Fine," she said. She narrowed her gaze at Cal. "One smile, one smirk, and you will regret it."

"She had this rabbit Halloween costume when she was three or four," Nathan began, smiling again. "She loved that costume. Wore it every day for months. Finally, it fell apart. But by then, everyone was calling her Bunny."

"That's a great story," Cal said, tightening his hold on her. She knew he was picturing a time when they might have their own little girl in a bunny costume.

As they ate and mingled, Frankie watched Cal joking with her brothers, talking to the kids, greeting a few of his ex-teammates who showed up. He looked comfortable. Relaxed. Happy with his decision about football.

Finally, as the party was winding down, he drew her to the side and pulled a crumpled envelope out of his pocket. "I have an engagement present for you."

"I didn't know we were doing presents."

"You do now." He handed her the envelope. "I wanted to do this in public so you couldn't throw it at me."

"That sounds ominous."

Cal shoved his hands in his back pockets. "Open it, Frankie."

The envelope was thin. Insubstantial. She tore the flap and slid out a single piece of paper. Notarized.

Finally, she looked up at him, her eyes swimming in tears. "It's the deed to FreeZone."

"I bought it from Derek. Now you don't have to worry about where FreeZone will be."

She stared down at the paper, the words blurring. "Cal, this is… You are…" She flung herself at him and wrapped her arms around him. "I love you," she said into his chest. "I love that you did this for me."

"I wanted to make all your dreams come true."

"Oh, Cal." She kissed him with all the love and emotion she felt. "You did that a long time ago."

* * * * *

HEART & HOME

Heartwarming romances where love can
happen right when you least expect it.

COMING NEXT MONTH
AVAILABLE MARCH 27, 2012

#2179 A COLD CREEK REUNION
The Cowboys of Cold Creek
RaeAnne Thayne

#2180 THE PRINCE'S SECRET BABY
The Bravo Royales
Christine Rimmer

#2181 FORTUNE'S HERO
The Fortunes of Texas: Whirlwind Romance
Susan Crosby

#2182 HAVING ADAM'S BABY
Welcome to Destiny
Christyne Butler

#2183 HUSBAND FOR A WEEKEND
Gina Wilkins

**#2184 THE DOCTOR'S NOT-SO-LITTLE
SECRET**
Rx for Love
Cindy Kirk

You can find more information on upcoming Harlequin® titles,
free excerpts and more at www.HarlequinInsideRomance.com.

REQUEST YOUR FREE BOOKS!
2 FREE NOVELS PLUS 2 FREE GIFTS!

Harlequin®

Super Romance®

Exciting, emotional, unexpected!

YES! Please send me 2 FREE Harlequin® Superromance® novels and my 2 FREE gifts (gifts are worth about $10). After receiving them, if I don't wish to receive any more books, I can return the shipping statement marked "cancel." If I don't cancel, I will receive 6 brand-new novels every month and be billed just $4.69 per book in the U.S. or $5.24 per book in Canada. That's a saving of at least 15% off the cover price! It's quite a bargain! Shipping and handling is just 50¢ per book in the U.S. and 75¢ per book in Canada.* I understand that accepting the 2 free books and gifts places me under no obligation to buy anything. I can always return a shipment and cancel at any time. Even if I never buy another book, the two free books and gifts are mine to keep forever.

135/336 HDN FC6T

Name	(PLEASE PRINT)	
Address		Apt. #
City	State/Prov.	Zip/Postal Code

Signature (if under 18, a parent or guardian must sign)

Mail to the **Reader Service**:
IN U.S.A.: P.O. Box 1867, Buffalo, NY 14240-1867
IN CANADA: P.O. Box 609, Fort Erie, Ontario L2A 5X3

Not valid for current subscribers to Harlequin Superromance books.

**Are you a current subscriber to Harlequin Superromance books
and want to receive the larger-print edition?
Call 1-800-873-8635 or visit www.ReaderService.com.**

* Terms and prices subject to change without notice. Prices do not include applicable taxes. Sales tax applicable in N.Y. Canadian residents will be charged applicable taxes. Offer not valid in Quebec. This offer is limited to one order per household. All orders subject to credit approval. Credit or debit balances in a customer's account(s) may be offset by any other outstanding balance owed by or to the customer. Please allow 4 to 6 weeks for delivery. Offer available while quantities last.

Your Privacy—The Reader Service is committed to protecting your privacy. Our Privacy Policy is available online at www.ReaderService.com or upon request from the Reader Service.

We make a portion of our mailing list available to reputable third parties that offer products we believe may interest you. If you prefer that we not exchange your name with third parties, or if you wish to clarify or modify your communication preferences, please visit us at www.ReaderService.com/consumerschoice or write to us at Reader Service Preference Service, P.O. Box 9062, Buffalo, NY 14269. Include your complete name and address.

HSR11

*Taft Bowman knew he'd ruined any chance he'd had
for happiness with Laura Pendleton when he drove her
away years ago...and into the arms of another man,
thousands of miles away. Now she was back, a widow
with two small children...and despite himself, he was
starting to believe in second chances.*

*Harlequin Special® Edition® presents a new installment
in USA TODAY bestselling author
RaeAnne Thayne's miniseries,
THE COWBOYS OF COLD CREEK.*

*Enjoy a sneak peek of
A COLD CREEK REUNION*

Available April 2012 from Harlequin® Special Edition®

A younger woman stood there, and from this distance he
had only a strange impression, as though she was somehow standing on an island of calm amid the chaos of the
scene, the flashing lights of the emergency vehicles, shouts
between his crew members, the excited buzz of the crowd.

And then the woman turned and he just about tripped
over a snaking fire hose somebody shouldn't have left
there.

Laura.

He froze, and for the first time in fifteen years as a fire-
fighter, he forgot about the incident, his mission, just what
the hell he was doing here.

Laura.

Ten years. He hadn't seen her in all that time, since
the week before their wedding when she had given him
back his ring and left town. Not just town. She had left the
whole damn country, as if she couldn't run far enough to

get away from him.

Some part of him desperately wanted to think he had made some kind of mistake. It couldn't be her. That was just some other slender woman with a long sweep of honey-blond hair and big, blue, unforgettable eyes. But no. It was definitely Laura. Sweet and lovely.

Not his.

He was going to have to go over there and talk to her. He didn't want to. He wanted to stand there and pretend he hadn't seen her. But he was the fire chief. He couldn't hide out just because he had a painful history with the daughter of the property owner.

Sometimes he hated his job.

Will Taft and Laura be able to make the years recede…or is the gulf between them too broad to ever cross?

Find out in
A COLD CREEK REUNION
Available April 2012 from Harlequin® Special Edition®
wherever books are sold.

Celebrate the 30th anniversary
of Harlequin® Special Edition® with a bonus story
included in each Special Edition® book in April!